DENIZEN
— of the —
DEAD

DENIZEN
— of the —
DEAD

THE HORRORS OF
CLARENDON COURT

edited by
Stewart Home

CRIPPLEGATE BOOKS
MMXX

Published by
CRIPPLEGATE BOOKS
London

ISBN: 9781527261549

August 2020

Front cover features a still of Siu Lan Ko's live art piece *49* performed as part of *Infraction* (Sete, France, 2008), photograph by Abel Segretin.

The image on page two is a video grab from participant film footage of the 2017 Hex In The Park protest against overdevelopment in London's EC1 area, with the Clarendon Court site in the background.

Spell Series created by the w.o.n.d.e.r. coven.

Twelve symbols plus one interjected throughout the book. Each individual symbol of this living spell was contributed by one member of the coven. Combined in the correct order they are the lock and key of one complete spell designated to transform the neoliberal project and overdevelopment as represented by Clarendon Court.

CONTENTS

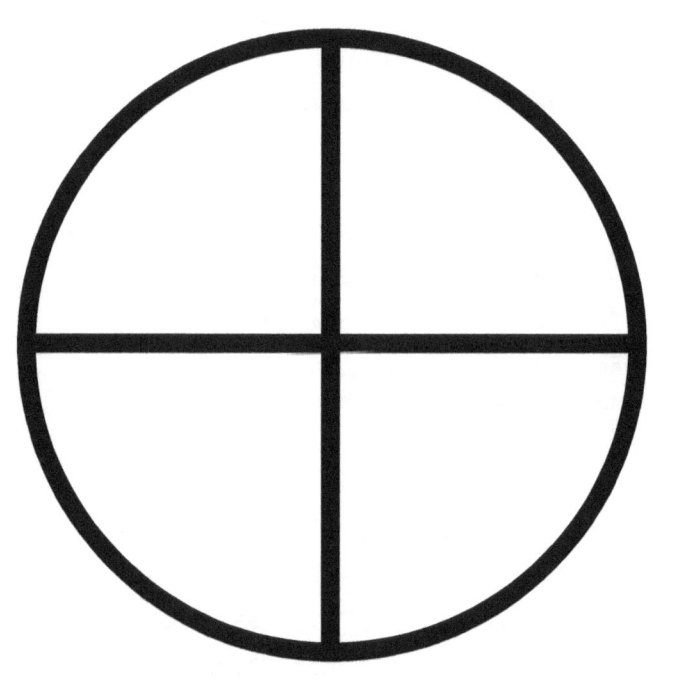

INTRODUCTION

STEWART HOME

This anthology of horror stories set in and around 43 Golden Lane in central London is a continuation of a series of protests against a luxury apartment development. Taylor Wimpey's new building at this address replaces 110 social housing units for key workers with 99 much bigger investment flats. The new apartment block is considerably larger than the one that was demolished to make way for it and now overshadows local social housing, a park and schools. Some council flats have lost 70% of the light in their living rooms and afternoon sunshine is blocked from the heavily used Fortune Street Park. While impoverished local councils often roll over for developers, the City of London which is home to this luxury development is the richest and most undemocratic council in the UK, and one which very proactively represents and lobbies for corporate interests.

The feudal local politics and potential conflict of interests that led to planning permission being granted for this development will be addressed at the end of the book. However, it is important to understand that Golden Lane is one of a number of streets that marks a boundary between the City of London and Islington. Although it was constructed in the City of London, the park and schools this development overshadows are in Islington's Bunhill ward. The apartments in The Denizen AKA Clarendon Court AKA The Turd are ghost homes that even before they were built were being pre-sold off-plan to property speculators, with marketing targeting in particular the nouveau riche in South East Asia, hence a sales promotion push in places like Hong Kong. This Taylor Wimpey development is on the corner of Fann Street, at the other end of which Blake Tower was recently converted from student accommodation to luxury flats also aimed at property investors. Nearby in Moor Lane there is a luxury block known as both The Heron and Milton Court, which unlike much of the luxury property in what developers and estate agents call the City Fringe, was marketed mostly to Russian nationals rather than the new rich in China.

The names of these luxury developments are sometimes changed upon their completion because they have become infamous symbols of planning and housing policy failure. A few minutes' walk north of Golden Lane on Central Street there is a recent construction now called Dance Square, it gained notoriety under its original name of Central Square around the time construction was completed due to the extortionately high prices of the "affordable" housing the development contained alongside its regular luxury stock. In the UK providing affordable housing simply means properties are sold at eighty percent of market value, which in a London luxury block means it is way too expensive for the people it is supposed to benefit to actually purchase. In 2012, *The Guardian* described the portions of Dance Square supposedly built to address local housing needs as follows: "It is, probably, the most expensive ever new-build offered by a housing association, yet it still meets the official criteria used to describe "affordable" — and qualify for taxpayer support. Part-buyers of a 25% share in a flat will have to stump up £2,322 a month to cover the rent and mortgage. The housing association says buyers will need an income of £59,000 to qualify, but in reality even that income, nearly double the London average of £33,850, will leave them with little left over after paying the bills."*

Due to the way it overshadows the surrounding area and the questionable manner in which planning permission was granted, Taylor Wimpey's The Denizen has also achieved a level of notoriety that means its name will be changed im-

---

* *The £705,000 'affordable' home. Some housing associations are stretching the meaning of 'affordable home' to the limit* by Patrick Collinson, *The Guardian*, 22 June 2012.

mediately before owners take possession of their properties, probably to Clarendon Court. Despite social benefit rules, unlike Dance Square this new development contains no on site social or affordable housing—strikingly in 2019 the City of London was the only local authority in London in which no new build "affordable" housing was constructed whatsoever. Regardless of the name change from The Denizen to Clarendon Court, the stories collected here are set in the near future at 43 Golden Lane, a building locals have dubbed The Turd.

There was a broad campaign against The Turd both prior to and after the planning process. This had cultural as well as social and legal elements. Most importantly in terms of *Denizen of the Dead* there was an exhibition entitled *Spectres of Modernism,* which took the form of an architectural installation of protest banners featuring slogans by award winning artists and writers hung from the exterior of Bowater House, a block of council flats immediately opposite Taylor Wimpey's Clarendon Court site. Some of those who participated in *Spectres of Modernism* are also included here, and this anthology was begun—initially as a blog—as a follow up to that project.*

As should be clear already, the City fringe/EC1 area is notorious for its unaffordable housing and empty ghost towers stuffed with plush investment flats. Silvertown Properties who—alongside others such as Mount Anvil— are responsible for the blight of empty apartments in EC1, trumpeted the following in the "About Us" section of their website:

> With the gentrification of Clerkenwell now complete, sizeable opportunities for residential and commercial schemes

---

* The blog this anthology emerged from is still up but all the stories that once featured on it that are also in this book have been taken offline. There is original material in this anthology that has never been online, and material online that isn't in this book. The blog can be found at: https://denizenec1.wordpress.com/ —and documentation of the *Spectres of Modernism* project can be found here: https://spectresofmodernism.wordpress.com/

are extremely limited. There is 100 acres of land wedged between Goswell Road, City Road and Old Street which largely remains undervalued compared with its near neighbours in Islington, The City and gentrified Clerkenwell. This "area" has embarked on an ambitious renaissance and is now called Clerkenwell East. There is a high degree of obsolescence and buildings nearing the end of their useful lives, which are ready for regeneration. Islington Council along with the key stakeholder group have granted a sequence of major planning consents which are being delivered over the next 5 years. Excellent infrastructure already exists including public transport and connectivity to the key "hubs". We ourselves have recently located our own offices to Peartree Street in Clerkenwell East.

Surely the key stakeholder group is the local Bunhill community (the area is not called "Clerkenwell East") and needless to say the social cleansing the likes of Silvertown Properties facilitate is not wanted by most of those who already live in the area. Like the City of London, Islington Council appears more interested in assisting the developers than listening to working-class residents. But it isn't as if the council doesn't know there's a problem. The consultation document *Islington Council Preventing Wasted Housing Supply Discussion Paper and Questionnaire March 2014* flags up the issue of empty ghosts homes in Dance Square and The Orchard which is directly adjacent to it:

> Initial data from the council's Electoral Roll shows a mixed picture across Islington. The data from a selected group of major new build schemes in the southern end of the borough completed since 2008 shows a high level of possible vacancy... The price of London property when buying in other currencies has come down, making it more attainable for the upper-middle class in the Far East among others. In some Far East locations, such as Hong Kong, London represents better value than domestic property.

Riffing on the Islington council document just quoted, an *Islington Tribune* article said:

Research by estate agent Knight Frank identified the City Fringe—EC1, Old Street and City Road, all in Islington*— as the prime central London location sought after by overseas buyers. In this area just under half—49 percent—of properties sold were bought by non-UK residents. Of the 51 percent of properties bought by UK residents, only 31 percent were UK nationals, meaning the bulk of property sold goes to non-UK nationals… The council report says… "The issue is not overseas ownership per se but rather new housing supply being 'wasted' by being left empty—so called 'buy-to-leave'. This is particularly associated with overseas buyers, many of whom see property as an asset investment. Overseas buyers paying in cash are causing a ripple of price inflation spreading… overseas buyers are significant purchasers of properties in the £400,000 to £1m price range, which is likely to cover new developments in Islington. There appears to be a clear correlation between concentration of overseas buyers in new residential developments and the high level of vacancy in such schemes."**

Clarendon Court is an EC1 development and while it is located within the City of London, not Islington, it provides a typical City Fringe property investment "opportunity". EC1 is a slightly more extreme example of what's going on across London and indeed large parts of the world. Therefore in terms of fictional explorations, The Denizen AKA The Turd AKA Clarendon Court can stand in for what's wrong with property speculation pretty much anywhere. That said, a specific development is being addressed here and since property of this type in the EC1 area sells disproportionately to Chinese nationals, the characters populating the stories in the anthology reflect that. Obviously the problem these characters represent has nothing to do with their nationality but is rather rooted in the fact they are rich investors who leave their properties empty while London's homeless

* To be more precise, the EC1 postal district covers both southern parts of Islington and north-western parts of the City of London.
** 'Buy-to-leave' investors face massive fines in bid to end scandal of empty flats in Islington by Andrew Johnson, Islington Tribune, 28 March 2014.

are literally sleeping rough in the surrounding streets. It shouldn't need saying there are obnoxious property investors of all nationalities and that across much of Europe and elsewhere it is the British who have a reputation for being particularly reprehensible on this score. Likewise, property speculation in Hong Kong has in recent years caused even greater suffering there than it does in London.

Moving on, I've loved horror stories and films since I was a child, but then I've also had a fascination with Hong Kong since I was twelve and became obsessed with kung fu flicks.* In some ways this anthology brings these interests together. The stories here could be seen as treating Clarendon Court apartments as "hongza" properties (haunted flats). *Reuters* ran a story on this subject that included the following: "The issue of a haunted flat melds the Hong Kong obsession with property with a Chinese population that tends to be superstitious and pursues ancient traditions, illustrated by the use of feng shui by many property developers to ensure that a building uses surrounding natural forces, such as mountains, wind and water, in a harmonious way. Not only does a haunted flat drag down the price of all the flats on the same floor, it can also bring down the value of apartments above and below it, according to property agents. It is commonly believed here that the trapped souls of murder victims are especially haunting, as they linger in humankind, mourning their untimely, vicious deaths and yearning to complete what they did not have time to do while they were alive."**

It would seem Taylor Wimpey didn't take the feng shui into account when it decided to build Clarendon Court, since the development is right by the old City Mortuary. Aside from the hundreds of thousands of corpses that were

---

* One of my recent books was on a subgenre of martial arts films entitled *Re-Enter The Dragon: Genre Theory, Brucesploitation and the Sleazy Joys of Lowbrow Cinema* (LedaTape Organisation, Melbourne, 2018).

** *Spooked no more? Hong Kong's 'haunted apartment' prices levitate with white-hot market* by Venus Wu, *Reuters*, 27 June 2018.

laid out for examination in Golden Lane, there have been plenty of violent deaths in the area, particularly since in the past it was notorious for its brothels and the prostitutes and criminals who haunted them. More recently 22-year-old Bethany-Maria Beales fell to her death from the nineteenth floor of The Heron while visiting it in May 2018; while even closer to Clarendon Court a visitor to a flat in Great Arthur House on the Golden Lane Estate fell to her death a few years earlier, and not long before that there was a gruesome domestic murder with the body stuffed into a suitcase and left on a balcony in the same block. On the other side of Taylor Wimpey's luxury flat development, there is an epidemic of loneliness among older Barbican residents that has resulted in a number of suicides, for example there was a jump death from a high-rise property there on 3 January 2019.

Reuters in the story I've quoted reported that in a heated property market,* the discount on Hong Kong "hongza" flats had fallen from around 30% to 10%. Consequently, rather than its bad feng shui — those who are not planning to live in the flat they are buying likely don't care if it's cursed — it is more probably recent falls in the value of London investment properties and uncertainties over the future of the British economy that are going to impact sales of Clarendon Court apartments. Nonetheless it is still worth using fiction to protest against the way property investors contribute to the London housing crisis.

---

* The City of London, like Hong Kong, suffers from inflated house prices and a deficit of democracy. Recent protests against anti-democratic repression in Hong Kong have been widely covered in the international media. Anger about the feudal nature of local politics in The City of London where residents have no proper voice over what goes on are less widely reported, but this will change. The City of London is the only part of the UK to retain the business vote. Linking up the struggles against rich bureaucrats in London and Hong Kong might move us a step closer to stopping their anti-democratic political manipulations and the associated ghost home investments that ruin lives.

For this anthology I wanted pieces from writers who'd lived in London and understood the specifics of the situation being addressed, but at the same time I was aware that many of them had multiple commitments and therefore I was more than happy if they adapted traditional—that is to say out of copyright—horror tales. There is a range of material here some of which engages with earlier fictions in a Kathy Ackeresque way, while other pieces are wholly original. Katrina Palmer's piece re-imagines Brian Yuzna's horror film *Society* (1989), in which the rich literally feed on the poor, physically deforming and melding with each other as they suck the nutrients out of their victims in a process called "shunting". This fabulous contribution is among the more oblique of the pieces I've collected in the way its author invokes the horror genre. That said, overall the anthology is intended to be both a shot in the arm for the haunted house story and a bullet in the head to property speculation!

The haunted house tale has a long history in Europe and the rest of the world. A letter from Pliny The Younger to Licinius Sura that contains a story about a haunted villa in Athens is sometimes cited as the oldest example of the genre. Obviously, genres are socially negotiated and precisely which texts are included in them changes over time—so Pliny The Younger's 2,000-year-old piece is never gonna be the earliest haunted house tale for all people, in all places, at all times. On another note, horror stories are sometimes condemned as socially and aesthetically conservative, but while a figure like H.P. Lovecraft (1890-1947) was a political reactionary, his overblown prose remains stylistically wild because of—not despite—his insistence on using archaic forms of English. Likewise there have been modernist and other experiments with the ghost story, perhaps most famously represented by Henry James' novella *The Turn Of The Screw* (1898). Thus *Denizen of the Dead* functions as a showcase for a variety of aesthetic approaches to the haunted house story while simultaneously taking on the mantle of social protest.

Needless to say my hope is that having put together this book of horror tales set at 43 Golden Lane, we can continue our series of ongoing cultural protests against Taylor Wimpey's Clarendon Court development by producing an independent horror film with a story that takes place at the same location. I want to sign off with a slogan that was on a placard carried during a ritual Halloween cursing of both Clarendon Court and a proposed (re)development at the nearby Finsbury Leisure Centre in 2017 — "Boo To Ghost Homes!"*

Stewart Home

---

* A video of the event known as *Hex In The Park* can be found on my YouTube channel: https://youtu.be/nYMQiBlY4eg

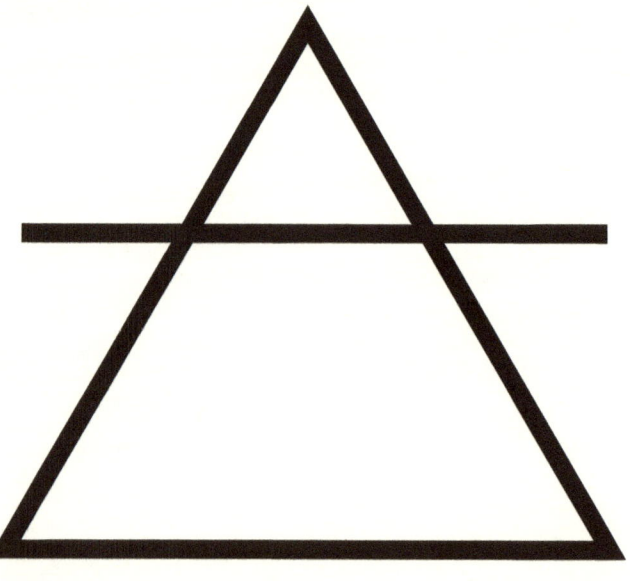

TRISKAIDEKAPHOBIA

PAUL EWEN

A note came under the door of Wang Fang and Wang Wei's apartment. "Hey", said Wang Wei. "A note."

He picked it up. "What do you think it says?"

"Well," said Wang Fang. "I'm sure I could guess and guess until the cows come home. But you're holding it in your hands, so why don't you just open it and read it?"

"What cows?" said Wang Wei.

"English cows. Until the English cows come home."

"Where are they?"

"They're out grazing. They graze all day. All day they graze, out on the meadows. Then, eventually, they return to the cowshed. I haven't got all day to wait for them to return from grazing to know what the note says."

"I'm glad it's not a video," said Wang Wei. "Of us, in bed at night, asleep."

"It wouldn't fit under the door if it was a video. Think about it."

"Hey," exclaimed Wang Wei. "It's from the Clarendon Court people, the owners of the building."

"And?"

"Oh. That doesn't sound good."

"What? Read it aloud, for heaven's sake!"

"There's going to be some construction work," said Wang Wei. "A disturbance."

"What sort of disturbance?" sighed Wang Fang, irritably.

"They're adding three new floors to the building."

"What? But we're on the top floor. We've got a contract! They're going to build on top of us? What?"

"Oh shit," swore Wang Wei.

"You're telling me!" exclaimed Wang Fang. "It's bang out of order."

"No, get this," replied Wang Wei. "They're going to install the new floors below us. Our floor is going to be propped up, with winches and supports."

"Huh? What? Is that even possible?" questioned Wang Fang.

"Listen to this: We apologize in advance for any disruption this building work will cause you. But you can be assured that your penthouse position will remain unaltered, with enhanced elevation...on the thirteenth floor!"

"Thirteenth floor? Holy fuck! No, no!"

Wang Fang and Wang Wei's deeply-rooted superstition — indeed, phobia — would prove well-founded when, due to a winch malfunction, one end of their penthouse apartment would begin slowly rising up during the night while they were in bed, asleep, causing their entire thirteenth floor to slide off the Clarendon Court building and plunge to the unforgiving tarmac of Golden Lane. Wham!

THE ALDERMANIC SHERIFF OF GOLDEN LANE

ABRAHAM STOCKER

When the time for his civil service examination drew near Lung Po made up his mind to go somewhere to study alone. He feared the attractions of the seaside, and he feared rural isolation, for of old he knew its charms, and so he determined to stay in his parents' empty investment flat in London where there would be nothing to distract him. As Po wished to avoid everyone he knew, he had no wish to encumber himself with the attention of his parents' friends, and so their ghost flat in Taylor Wimpey's Clarendon Court development was perfect. His parents and their circle had invested in the luxury apartment block and left their flats empty, banking on an overheated property market to reap a huge profit. He packed a suitcase with some clothes and his laptop, and then flew from Hong Kong to London.

When after a twelve-hour flight Po arrived at Heathrow Airport, he felt satisfied that he had so far obliterated his tracks as to be sure of having a peaceful opportunity of pursuing his studies. He travelled from the western outskirts of London to the centre of town in less than two hours. Clarendon Court was brand spanking new and as attractive as the desert, nobody was living there. Po looked around the Cripplegate and Bunhill neighbourhoods the day after his arrival and found the area he'd moved to was littered with ghost home developments, many of them had attracted Chinese investors, although The Heron AKA Milton Court had drawn most of its money from the mafia state of Russia.

An endless parade of empty luxury apartment buildings towered above social housing that had been built for local proletarians. Canaletto Tower, The Atlas, 250 City Road and

The Lexicon, were all impressively inhuman in their height and scale. Clarendon Court may not have been as tall as these monuments to unbridled capitalism but it was still impressive and prevented sunlight from reaching dozens of council flats, two schools and Fortune Street Park. It more than held its own against the overpriced empty apartments in places like Dance Square, The Eagle, Eagle Point, Fable Apartments, The Featherstone and The Bezier Building.

When Po told the concierge he intended to stay in his parents' Clarendon Court apartment for several months the man beamed.

"People around here need to see Clarendon Court inhabited," the concierge said. "Leaving it empty allows absurd prejudices to grow up around it, and these can be best put down by its occupation."

Po thought it needless to ask the agent about the "absurd prejudices". He knew he could get more information from other locals should he require it. The concierge provided the contact details of a woman who would undertake to "do" for him. He then went to Waitrose to buy provisions. The checkout lady was cheerful and kindly. However when he told her he'd just moved into Clarendon Court, she threw up her hands in horror.

"Not Clarendon Court!" she grew pale as she spoke.

Po explained that his parents owned a luxury apartment there and he was only staying in it for a few months. He asked the cashier to tell him what she had against the place. She told him that hundreds of years before the abode of an aldermanic sheriff had stood on the site of what was now Clarendon Court. The sheriff was held in great terror on account of his harsh sentences and his hostility to prisoners at the Old Bailey. There was a plague pit beneath the site, and its plot of land had also housed brothels and later warehouses. Children had been horribly abused in these establishments.

The cashier also told Po locals were against the new apartment block being built because 110 social housing units for key workers had been knocked down to make way for the empty ghost flats. They disliked the development because it was much taller than the building it replaced. Clarendon Court stole vast amounts of sunlight from its neighbours. The history of the site made locals queasy. There was a general feeling that when the foundations of Clarendon Court had been laid evil spirits were disturbed. The block being taller than previous buildings on the site, its foundations had had to go deeper. It was located directly opposite where the old City Mortuary had stood until it was destroyed in the Blitz. For her own part the check out lady said she would not take all the money in the Bank of England in exchange for staying in Clarendon Court an hour by herself. Then she apologised to Po for her disturbing talk.

"It's bad of me, sir. But are you really going to live there all alone? If you were my boy — and you'll excuse me for saying it — you wouldn't sleep there a night, not if I had to go there myself and blow the place up to stop you sleeping in it!"

The lady was so manifestly in earnest, and was so kindly in her intentions, that Po, although amused, was touched. He told her how much he appreciated her interest in him.

"My dear woman," he replied, "you need not be concerned about me! A man who is reading for the Chinese civil service exam has too much to think about to be disturbed by anything eldritch, and his work is of too exact and prosaic a kind to allow mysteries to enter his mind. In three months' time I'm going to have to answer 135 multiple-choice questions in two hours, that's more than one a minute, and the subjects covered include logic, world affairs, language and maths!"

After taking the ready-meals he'd purchased back to Clarendon Court, Po phoned the cleaner the concierge had recommended and arranged to meet her outside the supermarket he'd recently left. The charlady was called Mary Dempster. When Po arrived she was talking to the check-out lady he'd spoken to earlier, who'd evidently finished her shift. The cashier was introduced as Iris and was curious to see inside Clarendon Court. So Po who'd already mentally rated the supermarket worker as grade-A MILF, invited her along too. Iris was manifestly afraid of the apartment block and at the slightest sound clutched Po's arm. Before leaving Clarendon Court she expressed all sorts of kind wishes and at the street door said:

"And perhaps it might be well to have one of those big screens put round your bed at night—I would die myself if I were to be so shut in with all kinds of spirits that put their heads round the sides, or over the top, and look on me!"

The image she'd called up was too much for her nerves and she fled. Mrs. Dempster sniffed in a superior manner as Iris disappeared and remarked that for her own part she wasn't afraid of all the bogies in the plague pit beneath Clarendon Court.

"I'll tell you what," she said, "bogies is all kinds and sorts of things—except bogies! Rats and mice, and beetles; and creaky doors, and loose slates, and broken panes, and stiff drawer handles, that stay out when you pull them and then fall down in the middle of the night. Do you think there's no rats and beetles in Clarendon Court when London is overrun with them? And do you imagine that you won't see none of them? Rats is bogies, I tell you, and bogies is rats, and don't you get to think anything else!"

"Mary," said Po gravely, "you know more than Confucius! And let me say that as a mark of esteem for your indubitable soundness of head and heart, I could pay you a great deal extra if you'd stay over with me on any night I happen to feel lonely. I like mature ladies and while I rather fancy your friend Iris tickling my balls, I'm even keener for you to perform the same service."

"I couldn't sleep away from home a night." Mary answered. "My husband is a very jealous and violent man, and if he suspected something between us it wouldn't surprise me if it ended in murder. He'd give you no peace."

"I came here to obtain solitude," Po said hastily, "and believe me I am grateful to your jealous husband for having so violent a temper that I am perforce denied the temptation of

22

sampling your charms! But do you think Iris might be interested in my money?"

"Iris is a devout Christian who refuses to have sex with her own husband. You'll get all the solitude you want here." Mary chuckled.

The char set to work with her cleaning and when Po returned from eating and drinking his fill in The Masque Haunt on the corner of Old Street and Bunhill Row—he always had his laptop with him to study as he boozed—he found the apartment spick and span and Mary gone.

Po got out his computer and set himself down to a spell of real hard work. He went on without pause till about eleven o'clock, when he knocked off for a bit to make himself a cup of tea. He had always been a tea-drinker. During his college life he had sat late at work and taken tea late. The break was a great luxury to him, and he enjoyed it with a sense of delicious, voluptuous ease. As he sipped his hot tea he revelled in his sense of isolation. It was then that he began to notice what a noise the mice and rats that had invaded the luxury apartment block were making.

"Surely," he thought, "they cannot have been at it all the time I was studying. Had they been, I must have noticed it!" When the noise increased, he satisfied himself that it was new. It was evident that at first the mice had been frightened by the presence of a stranger, but that as the time went on they had grown bolder and were now disporting themselves as they pleased.

How busy they were making strange noises! Up and down in cavities behind the walls, over the ceiling and under the floor they raced, and gnawed, and scratched! Po smiled to himself as he recalled Mrs. Dempster saying, "Bogies is rats, and rats is bogies!" The tea began to have its effect of intellectual and nervous stimulus, he saw with joy another long spell of work to be done before the night was past, and in the sense of security which it gave him, he allowed himself the luxury of a good look round the apartment. There were some pictures on the walls, but he knew his parents had paid a local to furnish the place before his arrival, and he assumed little thought had gone into their choosing. Now and then he saw a mouse scamper across the floor, but in an instant it was gone. The thing that most puzzled him, however, was a rope that hung down from a hole in the ceiling. He made another cup of tea and went back to his work. For a little while the mice disturbed him somewhat with their perpetual scampering, but he got accustomed to the noise as one does to the ticking of a clock or the roar of moving water; and he became so immersed in his study that everything in the world, except the problem which he was trying to solve, passed away from him.

He suddenly looked up, his problem still without solution, and there in the air was that sense of the hour before dawn, which is so dread to doubtful life. The noise of the mice had ceased. It seemed to Po that it must have just stopped and that it was this sudden cessation which broke his concentration. As he looked up he started in spite of his *sang-froid*.

On a leather chair by the right side of the radiator sat an enormous rat, steadily glaring at him with baleful eyes. He made a motion to scare it away, but it did not stir. Then he mimed throwing something. Still it did not stir but showed its great white teeth angrily, and its cruel eyes shone with added vindictiveness.

Po felt amazed and seizing a ceremonial sword from the wall ran at it to kill it. Before he could strike it, the rat jumped upon the floor and running up the strange rope, disappeared. Instantly the noisy scampering of the mice began again.

By this time Po's mind was quite off the problem he'd been attempting to solve and as morning approached, he went to bed and to sleep. He slept so soundly that he was not even woken by Mary Dempster coming in to tidy up his apartment. It was only when she had got his breakfast ready and tapped his bedroom door that he was roused from slumber. He was a little tired after his night's hard work, but a strong cup of coffee soon freshened him up and taking his laptop, he went out for a lunchtime pint. He found a quiet corner in

The Masque Haunt, and there he spent the greater part of the day studying and drinking beer. On his return he checked to see if Iris was on the late-shift in Waitrose. She was and before Po had the chance to offer her money in return for certain "favours", she spoke:

"You mustn't overdo it. You are paler than you should be. Late hours and too much hard work isn't good for any man! Did you manage to sleep last night? I was glad when Mary told me that you were still alive when she went in."

"I was all right," Po assured her, "spirits don't worry me but I was wound up by the rats and mice. There was one wicked-looking old devil that sat up on a chair and wouldn't go till I took a ceremonial sword off the wall and swung it at him, and then he ran up a strange rope in the apartment. I must ask my parents about it for I'm sure there shouldn't be a hole in the ceiling.'

"Mercy," said Iris, "an old devil and sitting on a chair! Take care, take care!"

"How do you mean?"

"The father of all lies! Goat of Mendes, the devil himself perhaps?"

"Oh, forgive me!" said Po once he'd stopped laughing. "Don't think me rude but the idea that Satan himself was on the chair last night was too much for me! I doubt even Zhong Kui could get rid of your Christian devil! But it was a rat I saw not a goat!"

Po laughed again. Then he went home without even bothering to offer the silly woman a lot of money for a little slap and tickle.

That evening the scampering of the rats and mice began earlier. It started before Po arrived home and only ceased whilst the freshness of his presence disturbed them. After dinner he sat by a radiator for a while and had a vape, then began to work as before. The vermin disturbed him more than on the previous night. How they scampered up and down! How they squeaked, and scratched, and gnawed! But to Po, now accustomed to them, they were not wicked but playful. Now and again as they disturbed him, Po made a sound to frighten them, smiting the table with his hand so that they fled under furniture or into the fabric of the building.

And so the early part of the night wore on and despite the noise Po got more and more immersed in his studies. Eventually he stopped overcome by a sudden silence. There was not the faintest sound. He remembered the odd occurrence of the previous night and instinctively looked at the chair standing close by the radiator. There on the leather chair sat the same enormous rat, steadily glaring at him with baleful eyes.

Instinctively he took the nearest thing to hand, a mug of tea, and flung it. The mug was badly aimed and the rat did not stir, so the sword performance of the previous night was repeated. Again the rat on being closely pursued fled up the rope. Strangely too, the departure of this rat was instantly followed by the renewal of the noise made by the general rat and mice community.

On looking at his watch Po found it was close on midnight and not sorry for the divertissement, he turned up the heating and made himself a new pot of tea, as well as taking a mug from the kitchen to replace the one he'd smashed when he'd launched it at the rat. He had got through a good spell of work and felt entitled to a vape. He sat on the leather chair beside the radiator and enjoyed his smoke. Whilst vaping he began to think that he would like to know where the rat disappeared to, for he had certain ideas not entirely disconnected to a rat-trap. Accordingly he took a torch and placed it so he could see up into the hole the rope was run through. Then he took the top layer of stones from a large flowerpot containing a plant he could not identify and laid them out ready to throw at the vermin. Finally he lifted the strange rope and placed the end of it on his table, tying the extreme end to one leg. As he handled it he could not help noticing how pliable it was, especially for so strong a rope. "You could hang a man with it," he thought to himself.

Po began his work again and soon lost himself in his study. Once again he was suddenly called to his immediate surroundings. This time it was not just the utter silence that grabbed his attention. There was a slight movement of the rope and the table shifted. Without stirring, Po looked to see if his pile of stones were within range and then cast his eye along the rope. As he looked he saw the great rat drop from the rope onto the leather chair. He raised a stone in his right hand and taking careful aim, flung it at the rat. The latter sprang aside and dodged the missile. Po took another stone and a third and flung them one after the other at the rat, but each time unsuccessfully. At last as he stood poised with a stone in his hand, the rat squeaked and seemed afraid. This made Po more than ever eager to strike and the stone flew and struck the rat a resounding blow. It gave a terrified squeak, and with a look of terrible malevolence, ran up the chair-back and made a great jump to the rope and ran up it. The table rocked under the sudden strain but it did not topple over. Po kept his eyes on the rat and saw it disappear through the hole in the ceiling.

"I shall look up the rodent's habitation in the morning," said the student as he picked up the stones on the floor. "I'll ask the concierge for the key to the flat above mine and if he won't give it to me I shall break in." Po returned the stones he hadn't used to the flowerpot too. Then he noticed he'd not picked up the stone with which he'd actually hit the rat. Po took it up from the chair and looked at it. As he did so he started and a sudden pallor overspread his face. He looked round uneasily and shivered as he murmured to himself:

"Someone has carved the image of Christ into this stone! How odd." Po sat down to work again, and the rats and mice renewed their gambols. Somehow their presence gave him a sense of companionship. But he could not attend to his studies, and after failing to master the subject that engaged him gave up in despair, and went to bed as the first streak of dawn stole through the window.

He slept heavily but uneasily. When Mary Dempster woke him late in the morning he was ill at ease and for a few minutes did not know where he was. His first request rather annoyed the charwoman.

"Mrs. Dempster, if I paid you double would you do nude cleaning for me?"

The offer was politely rejected. Po went to the ground floor of Clarendon Court and asked the concierge to put him in touch with the person his parents had paid to furnish his flat. He wanted to know about the pictures hanging on the walls. The concierge couldn't reach the man in question. Po got Iris's number from Mary because the cashier clearly knew a lot about the building and perhaps she could clear up the mystery of the rat. Po arranged to meet her when she knocked off work at 5pm. He also asked for the key to the upstairs flat. The concierge rummaged around for it and eventually said it wasn't where it should be and he'd look for it later.

Until late in the afternoon Po worked at his laptop in The Masque Haunt, and as one beer followed another, the cheerfulness of the previous day came back to him, and he found that his study was progressing well. He had worked to a satisfactory conclusion all the problems which had as yet baffled him, and it was in a state of jubilation that he toddled to Waitrose. He found Iris knocking off from her shift and in the company of a stranger. The man was introduced as Dr. Thornhill. Iris was not quite at ease, and this combined with the doctor's plunging at once into a series of questions as they sat at a table on the pedestrian walkway outside the supermarket, made Po conclude that the man's presence was not an accident, so he said:

"Dr. Thornhill, I shall with pleasure answer you any question you may choose to ask me if you will answer me one question first."

The doctor seemed surprised, but he smiled and answered at once, "Done! What is it?"

"Did Iris ask you to come here and advise me?"

Dr. Thornhill was taken aback and Iris blushed and turned away. The doctor was a frank and ready man and he answered openly.

"She did but she didn't intend you to know it. I suppose it was my clumsy haste that made you suspect this. She told me that she did not like the idea of your being in Clarendon Court all by yourself and that she thought you took too much strong tea. In fact she wants me to advise you if possible to give up the tea and very late hours. I was a keen student in my time, so I suppose I may take the liberty of a college man, and without offence, advise you not quite as a stranger."

Po held out his hand. "I must thank you for your kindness and Iris too and your kindness deserves a return on my part. I promise to take no more strong tea — no tea at all till you let me — and I shall go to bed tonight at one o'clock at the latest. Will that do?"

"Good," said the doctor. "Now tell us all that you noticed in Clarendon Court."

In great detail Po recounted all that had happened in the last two nights. He was interrupted every now and then by some exclamation from Iris, and finally when he told of the episode of the stone with the image of Christ on it, the cashier's pent-up emotions found vent in a shriek. Dr. Thornhill listened with a face of growing gravity and when the narrative was complete and Iris had recovered he asked:

"The rat always went up the rope to the upstairs flat?"

"Always."

"I suppose you know," said the doctor after a pause, "what the rope is?"

"No!"

"Mary Mother of Christ appeared to me in a vision only this morning," said the Doctor slowly, "and she told me it is the very rope which the hangman used for all the victims of the judicial rancour of the aldermanic sheriff who once lived on the site of Clarendon Court!"

Here Thornhill was interrupted by another scream from Iris, and steps had to be taken for her recovery. Po looked on enviously as the doctor undid her upper garments and after removing her brassiere, massaged her pendulous breasts. While the doctor was otherwise engaged, Po grabbed the garment and slipped it into his pocket. Thinking he'd like to put on Iris's lingerie and then pleasure himself, Po made his excuses and left.

When Iris was herself again she almost assailed the doctor with angry questions as to what he meant by putting such horrible ideas into the poor young man's head.

"My dear Iris," Dr. Thornhill replied, "I had a distinct purpose in it! I wanted to draw his attention to the rope and to fix it there. It may be that he is in a highly overwrought state and has been studying too much, although I am bound to say that he seems sound and healthy — but then the rat — and that suggestion of the devil."

The doctor shook his head and went on. "I would have offered to go and stay with him but that I am sure would have caused offence. He may get some strange fright or hallucination tonight, and if he does I want him to pull that rope. It will remind him he's in mortal danger. I shall be staying out and keeping a watch on Clarendon Court. Do not be alarmed if Cripplegate gets a surprise before morning."

When Po arrived back at Clarendon Court he found that Mary Dempster had gone away — a jealous and violent husband was not to be neglected. He was glad to see that the place was bright and tidy. The evening was colder than might have been expected and a heavy wind was blowing with rapidly increasing strength that promised a storm. For a few minutes after his entrance the noise of the rats and mice ceased, but so soon as they became accustomed to his presence they began again. He was glad to hear them, for his mind ran back to the strange fact that they only ceased to manifest themselves when the great rat with the baleful eyes appeared.

After a vape Po took off his clothes and put on Iris's bra. Then he lay down on his bed and played with himself until he was spent. After this he sat steadily down to work, determined not to let anything disturb him, for he remembered his promise to the doctor, and made up his mind to make the best of the time at his disposal.

For an hour or so he worked all right, then his thoughts began to wander from his study. The actual circumstances around him, the calls on his physical attention, and his nervous susceptibility were not to be denied. By this time the wind had become a gale and the gale a storm. Clarendon Court, while recently built was poorly constructed, and seemed to shake to its foundations. Although there was no wind in the apartment for the windows were closed, the limber rope fell on the floor with a hard and hollow sound.

As Po listened to this noise he remembered the doctor's words: "It is the rope which the hangman used for the victims of the sheriff's judicial rancour." He went over to the rope and took it in his hand. He took a deadly sort of interest in it, losing himself in speculation as to who its victims were and the grim wish of the sheriff to keep it as a relic to be passed down to future generations. As he stood there the rope swayed now and again. Presently there came a new sensation, a sort of tremor in the rope.

Looking up Po saw the great rat coming slowly down towards him, glaring at him. He dropped the rope with a muttered curse, and the rat turning ran up it and disappeared. At the same instant Po became conscious that the noise of the vermin had began again.

All this set him thinking, and it occurred to him that he had not investigated the lair of the rat or enquired into the meaning of the pictures in his parents' apartment, as he had intended. Po decided to take a good look at the pictures. When he took in the first, he started back suddenly and a deadly pallor spread across his face. His knees shook, heavy drops of sweat poured from his forehead and he trembled like an aspen. But he was young and plucky, and pulled himself together and after the pause of a few seconds stepped forward again and examined the picture.

It was of a judge but not any old magistrate. This man was an aldermanic sheriff of the City of London. He was dressed in robes of scarlet and ermine that marked him out as belonging to the highest of the Corporation's three assemblies, the Court of Aldermen. His face was strong and merciless, evil, crafty, and vindictive, with a sensual mouth and small ruddy nose. The rest of the countenance was of a cadaverous colour. The eyes had a peculiar brilliance alongside their malignant expression. As he looked at them, Po grew cold, for he saw there the very counterpart of the peepers of the great rat. He nearly collapsed when he looked up and saw the rat with its baleful eyes peering out through the hole in the ceiling, and noted the sudden cessation of the noise of the other vermin. He pulled himself together and went on with his examination of the picture.

The sheriff was seated in a leather chair, on the right-hand side of a radiator where, in the corner, a rope hung down from the ceiling, its end lying coiled on the floor. With a feeling of horror, Po recognised the scene of the room as it stood, and gazed around him in an awestruck manner as though he expected to find some strange presence behind him. Then he looked over to the hole in the ceiling – and with a loud cry he fell to the floor.

There, in the leather chair, with the rope hanging behind, sat the rat with the sheriff's baleful eyes, now intensified and with a fiendish leer. Save for the howling of the storm without there was silence. Po stood up, wiped his brow and thought for a moment.

"This will not do," he said to himself. "If I go on like this I shall become a crazy fool. This must stop! I promised the doctor I would not take tea. He was right! My nerves must have been getting into a queer state. Funny I did not notice it. I never felt better in my life. However, it's all right now, and I shall not be such a fool again."

He mixed himself a good stiff glass of brandy and water and resolutely sat down to his work. It was nearly an hour later when he looked up from his laptop, disturbed by the sudden stillness. Without, the wind howled and roared louder than ever, and the rain drove in sheets against the windows – but within there was no sound whatsoever. Po listened attentively and presently heard a thin, squeaking noise, very faint. It came from the corner of the room where the rope hung down, and he thought it was the creaking of the rope on the floor as if it was being raised and lowered. Looking up he saw the great rat clinging to the rope and gnawing it. The rope was already nearly gnawed through — he could see the lighter colour where the strands were laid bare.

As he looked the job was completed, with the severed end of the rope clattering on the floor, whilst for an instant the great rat remained like a knob or tassel on the other part, which now began to sway to and fro. Po felt another pang of terror, which was soon replaced by an intense anger, and seizing a stone from the flowerpot he hurled it at the rat. The blow was well aimed, but before the missile could reach him the rat dropped off and struck the floor with a soft thud. Po instantly rushed towards the rodent, but it darted away and disappeared beneath a sofa. Po felt that his studies were over for the night and determined then and there to hunt for the rat.

His attention was drawn to the picture on the wall. He rubbed his eyes in surprise and then a great fear began to come upon him. In the centre of the picture was a great irregular patch of brown canvas, as fresh as when it was stretched on the frame. The background was as before, with chair and rope, but the figure of the aldermanic sheriff had disappeared.

Po, almost in a chill of horror, turned slowly round, and then he began to shake and tremble like a man in a palsy. His strength seemed to have left him and he was incapable of action or movement, hardly even of thought. He could only see and hear.

There on the leather chair sat the aldermanic sheriff in his robes of scarlet and ermine, with his baleful eyes glaring vindictively, and a smile of triumph on the resolute, cruel mouth, as he lifted with his hands a black cap. Po felt as if the blood was running from his heart. There was a singing in his ears. Without he could hear the roar and howl of the tempest and through it, swept on the storm, came the striking of midnight. With wide-open, horror-struck eyes, he stood still as a statue for a space of time that seemed to him endless. As the witching hour struck, so the smile of triumph on the sheriff's face intensified, and at the last stroke of midnight he placed the black cap on his head.

Slowly and deliberately the sheriff rose from his chair and picked up the piece of rope that lay on the floor, drew it through his hands as if he enjoyed its touch, and then deliberately began to knot one end of it, fashioning it into a noose. This he tightened and tested with his foot, pulling hard at it till he was satisfied and then making a running noose of it, which he held in his hand. Then he began to move along the table on the opposite side to Po keeping his eyes on him until he had passed him, when with a quick movement he stood in front of the door. Po then began to feel that he was trapped, and tried to think of what he should do.

He saw the sheriff approach — still keeping between him and the door — and raise the noose and throw it towards him as if to entangle him. With a great effort he made a quick movement to one side, and saw the rope fall beside him. Again the sheriff raised the noose and tried to ensnare him, and each time by a mighty effort the student just managed to evade it. This was repeated many times, the sheriff seeming never discouraged, nor discomposed at failure, but playing as a cat does with a mouse. At last in despair, Po cast a quick glance round him. Looking up he saw that what remained of the end of the rope hanging from the ceiling was laden with rats. Every inch of it was covered with them and more and more were pouring through the small circular hole in the ceiling.

Then Dr. Thornhill and the concierge were banging on the door of Po's Clarendon Court apartment and shouting to him to open up. At this sound the sheriff, who had been keeping his eyes fixed on Po, looked up, and a scowl of diabolical anger spread over his face. His eyes fairly glowed like hot coals and he stamped his foot with a sound that seemed to make the building shake. A dreadful peal of thunder broke overhead as he raised the rope again. This time, instead of throwing it, he drew close to his victim, and held open the noose as he approached. As he came closer there seemed something paralysing in his very presence, and Po stood rigid as a corpse. He felt the sheriff's icy fingers touch his throat as the rope was adjusted. The noose tightened — tightened. Then the sheriff, taking the rigid form of the student in his arms, carried him over and placed him standing on the leather chair, and stepping up beside him, put his hand up and caught what remained of the end of the frayed rope dangling down from the apartment above Po's. As he raised his hand, rats fled squeaking and disappeared through the hole in the ceiling. Taking the end of the noose that was round Po's neck, he tied it to the hanging-ceiling rope, and then descending pulled away the chair.

Fumbling with the spare keys the concierge eventually opened the door to Po's apartment, and rushed in with the doctor close behind him. There at the end of the rope hung the body of the student, and on the face of the sheriff in the picture was a malignant smile.

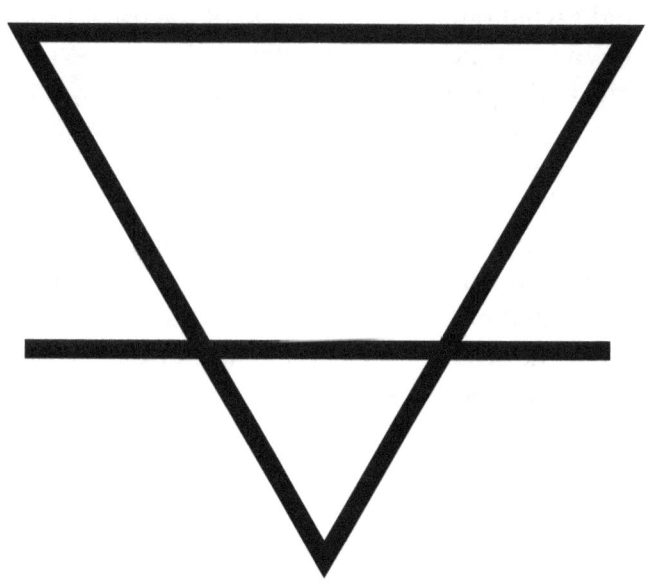

AIRTIGHT

BRIDGET PENNEY

Whilst you are in residence at Clarendon Court pure breathable air will be supplied into and circulated from your apartment 24-7. The rate at which fresh air is pumped into your apartment will be automatically determined by carefully monitoring the needs of its inhabitants as they move through their daily routines. This ensures there is always enough air for everyone in the apartment to function at optimum comfort and efficiency and that you will never find yourself paying for air you don't need. The price of air is subject to change without warning. If pollution levels increase outside due to weather events or circumstances beyond the company's control and our back-up technologies have to be brought online then more energy will be required to filter out harmful particles from Clarendon Court's air supply and therefore you may notice that your air meter is turning more quickly than you might have anticipated. It is strongly recommended that residents set up a flexible direct debit to cover the costs of their air. There is a back-up generator to ensure that all Clarendon Court's services will continue to function in the event of a power outage. In addition all apartments are equipped with emergency oxygen masks, similar to those on an aircraft.

Once it was decided to develop Clarendon Court as London's first certified pure air living environment (PALE)®, some adaptations in the original award-winning design were necessitated. The principal of these was the decision to enclose all the terraces on the building transforming them into greenhouse spaces. Reluctantly the decision was taken to make these greenhouses inaccessible from the apartments. It was felt that their function as part of the air-purifying system was fundamentally incompatible with their use as living spaces. How the technology works: London's polluted air is drawn into the greenhouses through their ventilation screens. At this stage the coarsest of the particulate matter in the air is eliminated. Passively heated by virtue of solar radiation, the polluted air rises through Clarendon Court's interior ducts fitted with many layers of filters designed to trap the different types of pollution found in the environment, even the tiny toxic PM 2.5. By the time the air reaches the top of the building it is of certified PALE® quality and only at that point after rigorous testing is it allowed to enter Clarendon Court's supply of breathable air.

This process, like all innovatory technologies, has not been without teething problems. Despite the use of self-cleaning, pollution-eating glass to enclose the terraces, maintaining the building's attractive appearance has proved something of a challenge. The exterior ventilation screens through which polluted air is drawn into the greenhouses quickly became clogged with particulate matter. In theory rain would wash this down onto the glass and the chemicals coating the glass would work together with water and sunlight to produce "free radicals" that lock the dirt and pollution into a "skin" to be "sloughed off" onto the street below where it could be mopped up in the process of normal street cleansing. However the accumulation of particulate matter on these ventilation screens has proved too rapid for the glass to cope with. This is what has led to the appearance of the dark smears on the exterior glass. After the hashtag "Dirty Denizen" began trending on social media we moved quickly to address residents' concerns by introducing manual window cleaning on a fortnightly basis. This is why the service charge has been subject to an emergency raise. Please refer to your original purchase contract or contact our management team for further information/clarification.

Although the plants deployed in the greenhouse spaces were selected as low maintenance and for their attractive appearance, providing a green, living backdrop against which the sophisticated ambience of Clarendon Court apartments could be even more keenly enjoyed, many failed to thrive. On the other hand some grew so monstrously that residents of a few of the apartments near the top of the south-facing side reported a) experiencing some anxiety at the spectacle of these plants trying to apparently burrow through their windows b) concern that their apartments were shaded by the leaves and stems of plants that appeared to be suffering from a form of gigantism c) that they were not able to enjoy the view over the City of London that they had paid for. We reassured these residents that the plants could not possibly breach the walls and windows of their apartment and arranged for a screen to be installed over the window, which, in addition to hosting a real-time stream of the view over London that apartment had previously enjoyed, also offered its inhabitants a number of other options. Sick of grey skies? You can if you wish change the weather of your view (purchaser subscription required). Or select the view from an apartment higher up the building or a different orientation to be screened on your window. There is even a rotating panorama option. This can be a great way to relax in front of your window in the evening with a glass of wine or a shot of flavoured oxygen. It allows you to study the city you have chosen to make your home and there will be options on your handset to display metadata should you wish more information about a particular building. Homesick or adventurously wishing to travel to another city? An appropriate real time vista could be streamed onto your window, alternatively you may select (purchaser subscription required) a calming view of nature, mountains, wilderness, green fields, the beach or even under the sea. These screens have now been installed in all apartments and have proved to be a very popular innovation.

We recommend that when venturing out into the beating heart of London on your doorstep, you wear an anti-pollution mask at all times. These masks can be purchased from our recommended partner provider; they offer a low-cost, and as many models are washable with replaceable filters, eco-friendly way for you to enjoy all the city has to offer in safety and comfort because, unfortunately, the air you breathe outside in London is putting your health at risk now and in the future. Potential health problems linked to pollution exposure include suppressed lung growth in children, accelerated lung decline in adults, asthma, lung cancer, raised risk of stroke and cardiac arrest, atherosclerosis (furring of the arteries) plus raised risk of type 2 diabetes. It has also been linked to smaller foetal brain size, impacting child development and impaired cognition in adults. Along with nitrous oxide produced largely from vehicle emissions and ground level ozone caused by chemical reactions between various forms of pollution in strong sunlight the most dangerous pollutants are tiny particles of Particulate Matter — toxic dust or liquid droplets sixty times thinner than a human hair. Levels of PM10s and PM2.5s around Clarendon Court are twice the WHO max of 10 mcg per m3. To counteract any discomfort your body may experience in moving from the pure air of Clarendon Court to the polluted outside world we recommend residents carry a handy pocket-sized oxygen canister with them at all times.

The default breathable air supplied to apartments in Clarendon Court is slightly higher in oxygen than the standard atmospheric mix of 20.95% oxygen 78.09 nitrogen 0.93 argon 0.039 carbon dioxide and small amounts of other gases. This is because our highly efficient filtration system eliminates the small amounts of other gases (eg methane, ammonia, acetone, carbon monoxide) that, in addition to exhaled CO^2, humans emit, delivering a neutral, totally odourless product into your home. If you fancy something a little different you may choose from our menu of ambient fragrances (purchaser subscription required). Options range from calming to zesty and energetic. You and your family and guests are sure to find a flavour that suits your mood and personality. Remember, in Clarendon Court it's ok to inhale.

The air in Clarendon Court's communal areas is constantly swept and recycled to clean it of outside contamination.

For the safety, health and comfort of all residents, pollution monitors have been installed by the reception desk. These will be triggered in the exceptional event that your clothing is contaminated with particles/pollution judged beyond the tolerance level at which the building's mechanisms will be able to clear it in normal operation. If one of these exceptional events occurs, you will be escorted to a private area and asked to remove the affected items of clothing. They will be laundered using a special process and returned to you within 24 hours. Whilst we apologise for the occasional inconvenience likely to be caused to residents by this policy, we are confident that, on reflection, individuals will appreciate that these policies have been instituted for the benefit of all those residing in Clarendon Court.

The company take their responsibilities to the local community in which Clarendon Court stands seriously. Paint designed to combat pollution by locking away nitrous oxide emissions has been used on all Clarendon Court's exterior surfaces. In addition the company have erected "urban trees" — you will have observed these in the immediate area — tall double-sided screens covered with moss between two benches. Moss cultures have a much greater leaf surface area than any other plant and therefore are extremely efficient at absorbing pollutants from the atmosphere. These "trees" deliver the same pollution-lowering benefit as 275 actual trees, absorbing 250 grams of particles every day, lowering ambient temperature and removing 240 metric tonnes of carbon dioxide from the atmosphere every year. Positioned along the pavements opposite Clarendon Court, they provide this benefit to our neighbours whilst forming a visually pleasing green screen for the apartments on the lower floors of the building. Our desire to "give back" to the local community has also led us to make small grants to two committed local gardening clubs finding innovative ways to garden with little natural sunlight in a polluted urban environment.

When apartments are uninhabited for more than a week their supply of breathable air is turned off. Non-circulating air quickly becomes stagnant and therefore while the apartment is unoccupied it is more efficient to remove the air altogether and store the apartment in vacuo. Because of the advanced construction methods used in the building of Clarendon Court and the great pains taken with workmanship at all levels, it is possible to achieve a near perfect vacuum inside each unit. The main door to the apartment is sealed and a notification placed on it that it is a state of in vacuo. Once the seal has been tested to higher than industry standards the air in the apartment is captured by the high-capacity vacuum pumps that form part of the air management and delivery system. We have a great deal of experience in this field and therefore the air is removed gently enough so no artefacts or furnishings in the apartment are adversely affected. Please be assured that gravitational forces are still in operation while your apartment is in vacuo. Your furniture will not fly around its rooms! The air removed from the newly sealed apartment is purified before being deployed elsewhere in the building. Whilst the apartment is in vacuo it is technically classed as a void. There is no need to heat or cool a void so residents incur zero energy bills whilst the property is in this state. No dust can settle in the apartment whilst it is in vacuo so cleaning is not required. Another piece of good news is that under current legislation a void is classified as "unfit for human habitation" and therefore exempt from council tax. You will continue to be liable for the full amounts of ground rent and service charges under the terms of your lease at Clarendon Court.

A few residents have expressed concerns about the potential structural consequences of voids. It has been suggested that maintaining discrete internal areas of the building at different air pressures — or in the case of the voids at no air pressure at all — endangers Clarendon Court's structure. However the tests carried out on one of our show apartments before and after it was pumped out and re-aired for the first time showed only very fractional variations, well within the perimeters of tolerance accounted for by the natural heating and cooling of the building in the course of a day. In any event the management team has decided that no more than 50% of the apartments can be in vacuo at any one time. Once that quota has been reached any more apartments coming vacant will not be de-aired. As an additional safety measure, if you are going to be away from your apartment for more than six weeks, your apartment will be temporarily re-aired at the correct pressure and its spatial volume assessed on a monthly basis to guarantee peace of mind before being placed in vacuo again. If you wish, the seal on the door can be released and a member of staff carry out a visual inspection of the apartment however most residents do not find this necessary. When you know the date on which you'll be returning to occupy your apartment, it is advisable to give us at least 48 hours' notice so that air can be gradually reintroduced at a rate that will not disturb its contents. Ideally this process will be completed 24 hours before you arrive to take up residency again. This allows for the air to settle and then the temperature can be adjusted to your chosen level of comfort. It is not recommended that you enter your apartment before our regular safety checks have been carried out. Whilst there have never been any adverse effects experienced by those entering a freshly re-aired space, please bear in mind that in the event of anything unforeseen happening the company could not be held responsible in any way. You would have breached the terms of your lease by failing to follow our instructions. Please contact the management team for further information/clarification.

Initially some residents expressed concern about the in vacuo apartments affecting their Wi-Fi and Bluetooth connections. Such worries are groundless as both Bluetooth and Wi-Fi signals are radio (therefore electromagnetic) waves and electromagnetic waves can propagate in a vacuum. Indeed there are advantages to those who remain in residence of a proportion of the apartments being in vacuo at any one time. Everyone is familiar with the principle of the vacuum flask. Similarly units in vacuo provide effective insulation against heat loss from neighbouring apartments. Since nothing exists in a void to conduct heat, it cannot travel. The same applies to sound which requires air as a medium to propagate. Sound waves cannot move through a space where nothing exists for them to vibrate against. The famous adage "in space no one can hear you scream" is true because space is largely a vacuum. In vacuo units also prevent the noise from the surrounding streets penetrating Clarendon Court.

Reports of hearing voices and noises from within in vacuo apartments simply cannot be credited. Indeed residents have reported these half-apologetically as if they know that they cannot be true. The sounds are only ever described as "fleeting" or "incredibly faint". When a member of staff is summoned to listen to these noises they have always already ceased. Even when someone claims to have recorded sounds from inside an in vacuo unit on their phone, it is impossible to distinguish anything that could not have been made by their own fingernails running down the outside of the door. After a serious incident when a resident with a history of suffering from auditory hallucinations tried to break down the door of an in vacuo unit claiming they had to rescue whoever was inside, the management committee wishes to take the opportunity to put these dangerous rumours to bed for once and for all. It is impossible that anyone could be inside the sealed apartments and doubly impossible you could hear them if they were because sound does not travel through a vacuum. Yes but what, it was suggested at the meeting, if they were scratching at the inside of the door. If they had put their mouth right up against the veneered surface trusting its vibrations to carry a message delivered with their last remaining breath. Sheer nonsense. Rest assured that the management team would never cut off the air supply from an inhabited apartment. There are emergency fail-safes in place. As stated in your leasehold agreements, all apartments have life and motion sensors and if a subject's vital signs are ever giving cause for alarm then a supply of oxygen will be instantly turned on and staff will be deployed to the apartment to assist.

THE CRIPPLEGATE
BLOCKCHAIN MASSACRE

STEWART HOME

Dateline: 21 June 2021

When I arrived in London two months ago I was an ultra-high-net-worth individual. I had close to a billion dollars in liquid assets, having grown the money I'd inherited from my grandfather by investing wisely in cryptocurrencies. There is no secret to being an entrepreneur you just have to buy low and sell high. That's what I'd done; I'd moved through Bitcoin, Litecoin, Ethereum, Zcash, Dash and Monero, while avoiding the players favoured by centralised banks like Ripple. Of course it was no surprise when government agencies like the Securities and Exchange Commission declared initial coin offerings to be securities. Likewise, I knew state sponsored attacks on the anonymity that made cryptocurrencies so attractive were about to create a huge dent in their values. That was why I'd planned to sell my virtual currency stakes during the few days I'd intended to spend in London.

I'd wanted to shift completely to more traditional investments in the form of safe deposit boxes in the sky. I had ghost homes scattered around the world and wanted to upgrade my buy-to-leave investments, which I'd mortgaged to the hilt in order to carry on some profitable currency exchange deals. To cover my tracks I'd converted my huge profits and original investment in forex into cryptocurrencies, which I would convert back into U$D and use to pay off my mortgages and further invest in residential property.

I'd come to London on a whim. I could have completed my transactions anywhere in the world. But I owned a ghost home in the City of London and I thought a couple of days in my Clarendon Court penthouse completing my business by day and cavorting with pasty English prostitutes by night would be fun. And London had other attractions, good shopping and food, not to mention service that came with some of the fakest smiles to be found anywhere in the world. I loved to see bitterness beneath the servility of those beholden to my money.

I don't have secretaries or assistants. I don't trust them. If I'd been a wage slave with access to a wealthy man's financial data, I'd have ripped my boss off. I was happy to employ cleaners, butlers, maids, whores, masseurs, and beauty therapists to irrigate my colon, but I would never trust anyone else with my financial details. Besides, when you have money making more requires little effort; you can do it while you sleep, so there's no need to avoid the small amount of work involved. Having huge liquid holdings, I had assets falling out of my asshole and I was self-reliant, so I didn't need anyone else working on my enterprises.

Still there were moments of pressure. When I arrived at Heathrow Airport I wanted to find the man who was to drive me to the heart of the City, so that I could get on with transferring holdings out of blockchain and into bricks and mortar. The queue at immigration was slow and irritating, a great mass of unwashed humanity. Having got past the checks I rushed down the steps to baggage reclaim.

I don't remember anything after that but in the hospital they told me I'd slipped and banged my head. I'd gone into a coma. When I awoke I felt dazed, and I didn't really think about the fact my noisy surroundings were out of keeping with the comforts my private health insurance should have paid for.

I didn't know then that I'd blacked out for two months. I didn't consider how long I'd been unconscious but I assumed it had been a few hours not sixty days. I asked a nurse some questions but she wouldn't answer them and told me to rest. I looked for my phone and wallet but couldn't find them. I stole someone's overcoat and put it over the pajamas I was wearing. I escaped before a doctor arrived to examine me. I jumped in a black cab and told the driver to take me to Clarendon Court on Golden Lane. In the foyer of the apartment block I'd bought into for just under two and a half million pounds, the concierge grinned at me as if I was nothing better than a piece of shit.

"I need sixty pounds to pay off the cab that brought me here." I said. "Can you give it to me and we'll sort it out later?"

"You'll need a lot more than sixty nicker, mate," came the reply, "You're in arrears on your service charges and the bank is in the process of repossessing your flat because you haven't paid the mortgage."

"Will you give me the money?"

"No."

"Then give me the keys to my flat!"

"I can't do that, the property is only technically yours right now, and very shortly it will belong to someone else."

"Look, I've got money and a load of valuables in the flat, if you let me into it then I'll make it worth your while."

"Is there a grand in it for me sir?"

"Of course there is." I shot back.

The concierge was clearly a greedy idiot. I didn't carry cash around with me and I certainly didn't keep any in the dozen ghost homes I owned across the globe. My apartments were my money. Overheated property markets meant I could just leave them empty and they'd go up in value and make me a profit. Since my Clarendon Court pad was one I occasionally used, what I did have in it was a collection of illegal guns. It was important that I was able to defend myself. I told the concierge to wait in the living room while I went into one of the bedrooms. He thought I was getting money but I was going to where I kept my weapons.

Like Elvis Presley I'd had my Walther PPK inscribed with the legend TCB, short for "Taking Care of Business". I loaded the pistol and emptied the semi-automatic into the concierge.

Then I went to the entrance door of my apartment and barricaded myself in. I had Wi-Fi but my penthouse suite was bereft of a device to connect to it. I didn't need one. A live electronic screen across the road told me all I needed to know.

I'd taken part in online Clarendon Court Resident Association discussions about what to do about our building blocking light to Fortune Street Park. The shadow from Clarendon Court had turned the parts of the park nearest to us into a mud bath. We'd bought our flats off-plan on the basis of the views we'd have of trees and greenery. The foliage subsequently died from lack of sunlight and the choking dust that was thrown up as our building was constructed by Taylor Wimpey. Clarendon Court was much taller than the police section house it replaced and there was no longer any afternoon sunlight in the park from September to March. We decided to commission the young design team Saussure and Jacobsen to create an artwork that would humiliate any low-net-worth scumbag who approached Clarendon Court, while simultaneously blocking our view of the mud bath. The piece used facial recognition technology to identify those who weren't making a substantial financial contribution to society. Computers then searched online for information about them. Algorithms were used to put together a package of embarrassing facts about anyone who appeared to fall short of the wealth ideals Clarendon Court residents had attained. These were displayed on a two-sided electronic screen we'd erected on the western boundary of park.

I could see some terrible mug shots of myself on the west-facing screen. They were chosen because they'd appeared on social media accompanied by text such as "the morning after the night before". I carefully curated the photos I placed of myself online. All those I could see on our live art screen came from the pages of people I knew, not my own. The billboard revealed that my cryptocurrency investments had gone belly up, that I was now heavily in debt and headed for a bankruptcy judgement. The screen also mocked me for investing in Clarendon Court; with the turbulence around

Brexit the value of my heavily mortgaged luxury apartment had plummeted. At least the name I was identified by was an alias.

My buy-to-leave investment wasn't even in the ancient heart of the City of London, as those who'd sold it to me had promised. It actually lay in the ward of Cripplegate Without, beyond the original city wall. It was just inside the local authority's branded Culture Mile, but that stopped halfway across the street I faced, since the other side of Golden Lane belonged to Islington. I'd been ripped off and I knew there was only one way to reclaim the billion dollars I'd lost: by taking human lives. I was inspired to do this by Stephen Paddock, the Las Vegas shooter who made news headlines around the world in 2017. It wasn't a coincidence that we both had degrees in business administration. Paddock was perhaps the greatest mass killer of the twenty-first century, but I would surpass him by claiming more victims from the office workers taking their lunch break in Fortune Street Park.

In 2014 the UK treasury put a price tag on the average murder. The social costs added up to more than £1 million. Economically murder blew £530,000 out of our material world, including lost output. £174,000 was the direct cost to the National Health Service, police and criminal justice agencies. This meant an average murder panned out at £1,778,000 in losses. Taking inflation into account and also the fact that costs are higher in London than elsewhere in the country, going for a low-end ballpark figure, each of those I just shot dead in Fortune Street Park would deprive the British economy of several million pounds. However a mass shooting like Paddock's, which claimed 58 victims, has even higher costs per casualty than a single murder, so I didn't need my kill tally to even reach three figures to recoup the billion I'd lost. By equalling Paddock's score I balanced the books, although I think I took out a few more people than he managed.

Paddock was one of my heroes, so I'd filled my flat with the same weapons and ammunition he'd assembled for his

Las Vegas massacre. These included four DDM4 assault rifles, three FN-15 rifles, one AR-15 assault rifle with forward front grip, one .308-caliber AR-10 battle rifle, and one AK-47. Plus a large quantity of ammunition in special magazines, with up to 75 rounds in each. I had bipods to rest the rifles on and high-tech telescopic sights. And of course my weapons were fitted with bump fire stocks.

On a sunny summer day at lunchtime Fortune Street Park is packed with office workers eating food bought from stalls on neighbouring Whitecross Street. There is barely room to move. Before I started to shoot from my window overlooking the park, I made some handwritten calculations about where to aim in order to maximise the death toll. Killing the muppets in the park was like shooting fish in a barrel. I took them out like turkeys on a meat factory production line at Christmas. People were such idiots; many of them lay flat on the ground in a bid to escape the leaden death spewed by my guns. Others tried to run away and I laughed as I saw claret stain the white shirts of those I'd hit. They made weird twitching movements like spastics before they died.

I can hear police helicopters overhead now, and there must be cops inside Clarendon Court already too. My name doesn't matter. I have five different passports and many other types of fake ID. I hope the authorities never identify me. I am a denizen of our financialised world! I'm going to blow myself up. When I do this I want to take a big chunk of the top of the building and a few cops with me. There is no life within. I want to die happily knowing I've recouped my dollar losses in pounds of flesh. Debts should be collected, and once I've destroyed the top floors of Clarendon Court, what's owed to me will be paid in full.

CRACKING UP AT CLARENDON COURT

CHARLOTTE STETSON

It is very seldom that mere ordinary people like Chang and myself secure a luxury apartment in London for the summer.

An empty new build, a property investment. I would say a haunted house and reach the height of romantic felicity — but that would be asking too much of fate! It is Clarendon Court, a block of 99 empty flats on Golden Lane erected by Taylor Wimpey in the face of fierce opposition from local residents, people whose homes and local park it overshadows.

Still I will proudly declare that there is something queer about it.

Why else should it be let so cheaply? And why have so few people living in it?

Chang laughs at me, of course, but one expects that in marriage.

Chang is practical in the extreme. He has no patience with faith, an intense horror of superstition, and he scoffs openly at any talk of things not to be felt and seen and put down in figures.

Chang is a hospital orderly, and perhaps — (I would not say it to a living soul, of course, but this is dead paper and a great relief to my mind) — perhaps that is one reason I do not get well faster.

You see he does not believe I am sick!

And what can one do?

If a hospital orderly, and one's own husband, assures friends and relatives that there is really nothing the matter with one but temporary nervous depression — a slight hysterical tendency — what is one to do?

My brother is a physician, and of high standing, and he says the same thing.

So I take phosphates or phosphites — whichever it is — and tonics, and journeys, and air, and exercise, and I am absolutely forbidden to "work" until I am well again.

Personally, I disagree with their ideas.

Personally, I believe that congenial work, with excitement and change, would do me good.

But what is one to do?

I did write for a while in spite of them; but it does exhaust me a good deal — having to be so sly about it, or else meet with heavy opposition.

I sometimes fancy that in my condition if I had less opposition and more society and stimulus — but Chang says the very worst thing I can do is to think about my condition, and I confess it always makes me feel bad.

So I will let it alone and talk about Clarendon Court.

It is an ugly construction quite out of place with its surroundings! To the north and south are listed ensembles of modernist housing, viz the Golden Lane Estate and the Barbican Estate. To the west is the Jewin Welsh Church, which Clarendon Court enfolds. To the east Fortune Street Park and two schools — one is for disabled children — all these things Taylor Wimpey's Clarendon Court overshadows.

Clarendon Court is newly built and quite empty. That spoils my ghostliness, I am afraid, but I don't care — there is something strange about Clarendon Court — I can feel it. I even said so to Chang one moonlight evening, but he said what I felt was a draught, and shut the window.

I get unreasonably angry with Chang sometimes. I'm sure I never used to be so sensitive. I think it is due to this nervous condition. But Chang says if I feel so I shall neglect proper self-control. So I take pains to control myself — before him, at least — and that makes me very tired.

I don't like our apartment a bit. It looks out onto a brick wall of The Cripplegate Institute, another listed building I haven't yet mentioned. I wanted a flat overlooking Fortune

Street Park but Chang would not hear of it. He said there was no point paying extra for a view which we could enjoy for free if we walked out of the building.

He is very careful and loving, and hardly lets me stir without special direction. I have a schedule prescription for each hour in the day. He takes all care from me and so I feel basely ungrateful not to value it more.

He said we came here solely on my account. That I was to have perfect rest and enjoy the air in London. "Your exercise depends on your strength, my dear," said Chang, "and your food somewhat on your appetite; but air you can absorb all the time." The air in London isn't perfect but it's better than in Beijing.

Although Clarendon Court is a new build, the paint and paper in our apartment doesn't look new. It is stripped off — the paper — in great patches all around the head of my bed, about as far as I can reach, and in a great place on the other side of the room low down. I never saw a worse paper in my life.

One of those sprawling flamboyant patterns committing every artistic sin. It is dull enough to confuse the eye in following, pronounced enough to constantly irritate, and provoke study, and when you follow the lame, uncertain curves for a little distance they suddenly commit suicide — plunge off at outrageous angles, destroy themselves in unheard-of contradictions.

The colour is repellent, almost revolting; a smouldering, unclean yellow, strangely faded by the slow-turning sunlight. It is a dull yet lurid orange in some places, a sickly sulphur tint in others. I should hate it myself if I had to live in this apartment for more than one summer.

There comes Chang, and I must put this away — he hates to have me write a word.

◆　◆　◆

We have been here two weeks, and I haven't felt like writing before, since that first day.

I am sitting by the window now, up in this atrocious apartment in Taylor Wimpey's Clarendon Court, and there is nothing to hinder my writing as much as I please, save lack of strength. Chang is away all day and even some nights. He is having to work in a private nursing home to pay for our holiday in London.

I am glad my case is not serious! But these nervous troubles are dreadfully depressing. Chang does not know how much I really suffer. He knows there is no reason to suffer, and that satisfies him. Of course it is only nervousness. It does weigh on me so not to do my duty in any way! I meant to be such a help to Chang, such a real rest and comfort, and here I am a comparative burden already!

Nobody would believe what an effort it is to do what little I am able — to dress and to take coffee at the Giddy Up stall in Fortune Street Park. I suppose Chang never was nervous in his life. He laughs at me so about this wallpaper! He said that I was letting it get the better of me, and that nothing was worse for a nervous patient than to give way to such fancies. He said that if the wallpaper was changed I'd start complaining about the carpet, and then the window frames, and so on.

"You know the place is doing you good," he said, "and really, dear, I don't care to renovate this Clarendon Court apartment just for a three months' rental."

"Then do let us go downstairs," I said, "the games room or the private cinema would be a change from this oppressive flat."

Then he took me in his arms and called me a blessed little goose, and said he would go down to the private cinema if I wished — but first we had to find something we wanted to screen in it. But he is right enough about the carpet and windows and things.

It is no smaller than the apartments occupied by our relatives in Hong Kong and, of course, I would not be so silly as to make him uncomfortable just for a whim. I'm really getting quite fond of the apartment, all but that horrid paper.

Out of the windows I can see London brick and I try to imagine the red is the sun setting, but I can't.

Sometimes I fancy I see ghostly figures walking the corridors of Clarendon Court, but Chang has cautioned me not to give way to fancy in the least. He says that with my imaginative power and habit of story-making a nervous weakness like mine is sure to lead to all manner of excited fancies, and that I ought to use my will and good sense to check the tendency. So I try.

I think sometimes that if I were only well enough to write a little it would relieve the press of ideas and rest me. But I find I get pretty tired when I try. It is so discouraging not to have any advice and companionship. When I get really well Chang says we will ask friends he has made at the nursing home where he works to come over for an evening visit; but he says he would as soon put fireworks in my pillow-case as to let me have those stimulating people about now. I wish I could get well faster. But I must not think about that.

This paper looks to me as if it knew what a vicious influence it had! There is a recurrent spot where the pattern lolls like a broken neck and two bulbous eyes stare at you upside down. I get positively angry with the impertinence of it and the everlastingness. Up and down and sideways they crawl, and those absurd, unblinking eyes are everywhere. There is one place where two breadths didn't match, and the eyes go all up and down the line, one a little higher than the other.

I never saw so much expression in an inanimate thing before, and we all know how much expression they have! I used to lie awake as a child and get more entertainment and terror out of blank walls and plain furniture than most children could find in a toy-store. I remember what a kindly wink the knobs of our big old bureau used to have, and there was one chair that always seemed like a strong friend. I used to feel that if any of the other things looked too fierce I could always hop into that chair and be safe.

The furniture in this room is no worse than inharmonious. The wallpaper, as I said before, is torn off in spots, and it

sticks closer than a brother—they must have had persever-
ance as well as hatred. Then the floor is scratched and gouged
and splintered, the plaster itself is dug out here and there,
and this great heavy bed, looks as if it had been through the
wars. Which is strange considering the apartment has only
just been built.

But I don't mind it a bit—only the paper. This wallpaper
has a kind of sub-pattern in a different shade, a particularly
irritating one, for you can only see it in certain lights, and not
clearly then. But in the places where it isn't faded, and where
the sun is just so, I can see a strange, provoking, formless sort
of figure, that seems to sulk about behind that silly and con-
spicuous front design.

Chang says if I don't pick up faster he shall send me to
Kuala Lumpur in the fall. But I don't want to go there at all. I
don't feel as if it is worthwhile to turn my hand over for anything, and I'm getting dreadfully fretful and querulous. I cry
at nothing, and cry most of the time. Of course I don't when
Chang is here, but when I am alone. And I am alone a good
deal just now. Chang is working as many hours as he can to
pay for this holiday.

I'm getting really fond of the room in spite of the wallpaper. Perhaps because of the wallpaper. It dwells in my mind
so! I lie here on this great immovable bed—it is nailed down,
I believe—and follow that pattern about by the hour. It is
as good as gymnastics, I assure you. I start, we'll say, at the
bottom, down in the corner over there where it has not been
touched, and I determine for the thousandth time that I will
follow that pointless pattern to some sort of a conclusion.

I know a little of the principle of design, and I know this
thing was not arranged on any laws of radiation, or alterna-
tion, or repetition, or symmetry, or anything else that I ever
heard of. It is repeated, of course, by the breadths, but not
otherwise. Looked at in one way each breadth stands alone,
the bloated curves and flourishes—a kind of "debased Ro-
manesque" with delirium tremens—go waddling up and
down in isolated columns of fatuity.

But, on the other hand, they connect diagonally, and the sprawling outlines run off in great slanting waves of optic horror, like a lot of wallowing seaweeds in full chase. The whole thing goes horizontally, too, at least it seems so, and I exhaust myself in trying to distinguish the order of its going in that direction. They have used a horizontal breadth for a frieze, and that adds wonderfully to the confusion.

There is one end of the room where it is almost intact, and there, when the cross-lights fade, I can almost fancy radiation after all — the interminable grotesques seem to form around a common centre and rush off in headlong plunges of equal distraction. It makes me tired to follow it. I will take a nap, I guess.

◆ ◆ ◆

Sitting here in Taylor Wimpey's ghost home development Clarendon Court on Golden Lane I don't know why I should write this. I don't want to. I don't feel able. And I know Chang would think it absurd. But I must say what I feel and think in some way — it is such a relief! But the effort is getting to be greater than the relief.

Half the time now I am awfully lazy and lie down ever so much. Chang says I mustn't lose my strength and has me take cod-liver oil and lots of tonics and things, to say nothing of ale and wine and rare meat.

Dear Chang! He loves me very dearly and hates to have me sick. I tried to have a real earnest reasonable talk with him the other day and tell him how I wish he would let me socialise with some of the friends he's made in London. There's no one to talk to in Clarendon Court, nearly all the flats are empty and even the concierge who is supposed to be on call 24-7 disappears for hours at a time. I followed one concierge and discovered he spent a lot of time in a betting shop when he's supposed to be working. Those holding this job come back to Clarendon Court if you call them on their smartphones. When you ring down to the desk you get a message with their mobile number.

Chang said I wasn't well enough to socialise, that I'd exhaust myself. I did not make a very good case for myself, for I was crying before I had finished. It is getting to be a great effort for me to think straight. Just this nervous weakness I suppose. And dear Chang gathered me up in his arms and laid me on the bed, and sat by me and read to me till it tired my head.

Chang said I was his darling and his comfort and all he had, and that I must take care of myself for his sake, and keep well. He says no one but myself can help me out of it, that I must use my will and self-control and not let any silly fancies run away with me. But I still wish I didn't have to live with the horrid wallpaper. Of course I never mention it to Chang now — I am too wise — but I keep watch of it all the same.

There are things in that paper that nobody knows but me, or ever will. Behind that outside pattern the dim shapes get clearer every day. It is always the same shape, only very numerous. And it is like a woman stooping down and creeping about behind that pattern. I don't like it a bit. I wonder — I begin to think — I wish Chang would take me away from Clarendon Court! We could go home or just go somewhere else in London, I'd be happy to be anywhere that isn't a Taylor Wimpey luxury investment apartment. Clarendon Court is ninety percent empty but it isn't soulless, it is creepy!

It is so hard to talk with Chang about my case, because he is so wise, and because he loves me so. But I tried it last night. Chang was asleep and I hated to wake him, so I kept still and watched that undulating wallpaper till I felt sick. The faint figure behind seemed to shake the pattern, just as if she wanted to get out. I got up softly and went to feel and see if the paper did move, and when I came back Chang was awake.

"What is it, little girl?" he said. "Don't go walking about like that — you'll get cold."

I thought it was a good time to talk, so I told him that I really was not gaining here, and that I wished he would take me away.

"Why darling!" said he, "our lease will be up in three weeks. Of course if you were in any danger I could and would, but you really are better, dear, whether you can see it or not. I am a nurse, dear, and I know. You are gaining flesh and colour, your appetite is better. I feel really much easier about you."

"I don't weigh a bit more," said I, "nor as much; and my appetite may be better when you are here, but it is worse when you are away."

"Bless her little heart!" said he with a big hug, "she shall be as sick as she pleases! But now let's improve the daylight hours by going to sleep, and talk about it in the morning!"

"And we can't go away?" I asked gloomily.

"It is only three weeks more. Really, dear, you are better!"

"Better in body perhaps" — I began and stopped short, for he sat up straight and looked at me with such a stern, reproachful look that I could not say another word.

"My darling," said he, "I beg of you, for my sake as well as for your own, that you will never for one instant let that idea enter your mind! There is nothing so dangerous, so fascinating, to a temperament like yours. It is a false and foolish fancy. Can you not trust me as your husband when I tell you so?"

So of course I said no more on that score, and we went to sleep before long. He thought I was asleep first, but I wasn't — I lay there for hours trying to decide whether that front pattern and the back pattern really did move together or separately.

On a pattern like this, by daylight, there is a lack of sequence, a defiance of law, that is a constant irritant to a normal mind.

The colour is hideous enough, and unreliable enough, and infuriating enough, but the pattern is torturing.

You think you have mastered it, but just as you get well under way in following, it turns a back somersault and there you are. It slaps you in the face, knocks you down, and tramples upon you. It is like a bad dream.

The outside pattern is a florid arabesque, reminding one of a fungus. If you can imagine a toadstool in joints, an interminable string of toadstools, budding and sprouting in endless convolutions—why, that is something like it. That is, sometimes!

There is one marked peculiarity about this paper, a thing nobody seems to notice but myself, and that is that it changes as the light changes. It changes so quickly that I never can quite believe it. That is why I watch it always. By moonlight I wouldn't know it was the same paper.

At night in any kind of light it becomes bars! The outside pattern I mean, and the woman behind it is as plain as can be. I didn't realize for a long time what the thing was that showed behind—that dim sub-pattern—but now I am quite sure it is a woman. By daylight she is subdued, quiet. I fancy it is the pattern that keeps her so still. It is so puzzling. It keeps me quiet by the hour.

I lie down ever so much now. Chang says it is good for me, and to sleep all I can. Indeed, he started the habit by making me lie down for an hour after each meal. It is a very bad habit, I am convinced, for, you see, I don't sleep. And that cultivates deceit, for I don't tell him I'm awake—oh, no!

The fact is, I am getting a little afraid of Chang. He seems very queer sometimes. It strikes me occasionally, just as a scientific hypothesis, that perhaps it is the paper! I have watched Chang when he did not know I was looking, and come into the room suddenly on the most innocent excuses, and I've caught him several times looking at the paper!

Life is very much more exciting now than it used to be here in our rented apartment in Taylor Wimpey's luxury ghost development Clarendon Court. You see I have something more to expect, to look forward to, to watch. I really do eat better, and am more quiet than I was. Chang is so pleased to see me improve! He laughed a little the other day, and said I seemed to be flourishing in spite of my wallpaper.

I turned it off with a laugh. I had no intention of telling him it was because of the wallpaper—he would make fun of me.

He might even want to take me away. I don't want to leave now until I have found it out. There is a week more and I think that will be enough.

I'm feeling ever so much better! I don't sleep much at night, for it is so interesting to watch developments; but I sleep a good deal in the daytime. In the daytime it is tiresome and perplexing. There are always new shoots on the fungus and new shades of yellow all over it. I cannot keep count of them, though I have tried conscientiously.

It is the strangest yellow that wallpaper! It makes me think of all the yellow things I ever saw — not beautiful ones like buttercups, but old foul, bad yellow things. But there is something else about that paper — the smell! I noticed it the moment we came into the flat. Now we have had a week of fog and rain, and whether the windows are open or not, the smell is here. It creeps all over Taylor Wimpey's luxury ghost home development Clarendon Court. I find it lying in wait for me on the stairs and in the lift. It gets into my hair.

Such a peculiar odour! I have spent hours in trying to analyze it, to find what it smelled like. It is not bad — at first, and very gentle, but quite the subtlest, most enduring odour I ever met. In this damp weather it is awful. I wake up in the night and find it hanging over me. It used to disturb me at first. I thought seriously of burning down Clarendon Court — to get rid of the smell. But now I am used to it. The only thing I can think of that it is like is the colour of the paper! A yellow smell.

There is a very funny mark on this wall, low down, near the skirting board. A streak that runs round the room. It goes behind every piece of furniture, except the bed, a long, straight, even smooch, as if it had been rubbed over and over. I wonder how it was done and who did it, and what they did it for. Round and round and round — round and round and round — it makes me dizzy!

I really have discovered something at last. Through watching so much at night, when it changes so, I have finally found out. The front pattern does move — and no wonder!

The woman behind shakes it! Sometimes I think there are a great many women behind, and sometimes only one, and she crawls around fast, and her crawling shakes it all over.

Then in the very bright spots she keeps still, and in the very shady spots she just takes hold of the bars and shakes them hard. And she is all the time trying to climb through. But nobody could climb through that pattern—it strangles so; I think that is why it has so many heads.

They get through, and then the pattern strangles them off and turns them upside-down, and makes their eyes white! If those heads were covered or taken off it would not be half so bad. I think that woman gets out in the daytime! And I'll tell you why—privately—I've seen her!

I can see her in the corridors of Clarendon Court and in the private cinema and games room in the basement! It is the same woman, I know, for she is always creeping, and most women do not creep by daylight. I see her creeping up and down. I see her in the pocket park at the side of the building, and creeping all around Fortune Street Park too.

I see her approaching the Giddy Up coffee stall in Fortune Street Park, creeping along, and when a car passes in Fortune Street or Golden Lane she hides in the bushes. I don't blame her a bit. It must be very humiliating to be caught creeping by daylight!

I always lock the door when I creep by daylight. I can't do it at night, for I know Chang would suspect something at once. And Chang is so queer now that I don't want to irritate him. I wish he would take another room! Besides I don't want anybody to get that woman out at night but myself.

I often wonder if she is in several places at once. But turn as fast as I can, I can only see her in one place at a time. And though I always see her she may be able to creep faster than I can turn! I have watched her sometimes at the other end of Fortune Street Park, creeping as fast as a cloud shadow in a high wind.

If only that top pattern could be gotten off from the under one! I mean to try it, little by little. I have found out another funny thing, but I shan't tell it this time! It does not do to trust people too much. There are only two more days to get this paper off, and I believe Chang is beginning to notice. I don't like the look in his eyes.

Chang knows I don't sleep very well at night, for all I'm so quiet! He asked me all sorts of questions, too, and pretended to be very loving and kind. As if I couldn't see through him! Still, I don't wonder why he acts so, sleeping under this paper for three months. It only interests me, but I feel sure Chang is secretly affected by it.

Hurrah! This is the last night but it is enough. Chang is working a long and late shift. However I'm not alone! As soon as the sun set and that poor thing began to crawl and shake the pattern, I got up and ran to help her. I pulled and she shook, I shook and she pulled, and before morning we had peeled off yards of that paper. A strip about as high as my head and half around the room.

And then when the day broke and that awful pattern began to laugh at me I declared I would finish it before I left! We catch a flight home from Heathrow this evening. So I must get to work. I have locked the door and thrown the key out of a window. I don't want to go out, and I don't want to have anybody come in. When Chang returns I want to astonish him.

I got so angry with the wallpaper I bit off a little piece at one corner—but it hurt my teeth. Then I peeled off all the paper I could reach standing on the floor. It sticks horribly and the pattern just enjoys it! All those strangled heads and bulbous eyes and waddling fungus growths just shriek with derision!

I am getting angry enough to do something desperate. To jump out of the window would be admirable exercise. But I won't do it. I know well enough that a step like that is improper and might be misconstrued. I don't like to look out of the windows—there are so many of those creeping women and they creep so fast.

I wonder if they all came out of that wallpaper as I did? I am securely fastened now by a rope! I suppose I shall have to get back behind the pattern when night falls and that is hard! It is so pleasant to be out in this luxury apartment and creep around as I please! I don't want to go outside. For outside you have to creep on the ground and everything is green instead of yellow. But here I can creep smoothly on the floor and my shoulder just fits in that long smooch around the wall, so I cannot lose my way.

Why there's Chang at the door! It is no use he can't open it! How he does call and pound! Now he's demanding the concierge fetches him an axe. It would be a shame to break down that beautiful door!

"Chang dear!" said I in the gentlest voice, "the key is down on the ground, I threw it out the window"

That silenced him for a few moments. Then he said — very quietly indeed, "Open the door, my darling!"

"I can't," said I. "I threw the key out of the window!"

And then I said it again, several times, very gently and slowly, and said it so often that he had to go and see, and he got it, of course, and came in. He stopped short by the door.

"What is the matter?" he cried. "For God's sake, what are you doing!"

I kept on creeping just the same, but I looked at him over my shoulder.

"I've got out at last," said I, "in spite of you! And I've pulled off most of the paper, so you can't put me back!"

Now why should that man have fainted? But he did and right across my path by the wall, so that I had to creep over him every time!

DEN OF INIQUITY

TARIQ GODDARD

It had taken Yu several weeks to realise that his belongings really were being moved round his room in the dark. Once the sun descended over Taylor Wimpey's luxury apartment block Clarendon Court in Golden Lane, Yu's one-bed flat was transformed into a limited-run play in which each night was different. On the first morning of the performance Yu discovered his iPhone in the sock he liked to pretend was Katniss Everdeen's mouth, which as he was still caned, he found funny, instead of its usual spot on the floor, with all the other crap he emptied from his pockets, before he crashed.

Yu could not remember exactly when he noticed something else out of place, but the next manifestation of a sneaky presence, other than his own, was almost as amusing; a festering bowl of Frosties turned upside down at the bottom of the uninhabited fish-tank; brown bubbles and shredded glitter dancing slowly about its murky sides.

In languor, he sat and watched the mouldy cereal crud rise slowly to the top, grinning stupidly at his reflection, the sock now back where it belonged. The ripping noises were a warning that this wasn't all going to be fun; all eight volumes of "A Song Of Ice And Fire" torn and scattered by his mattress, with the last page of each book stuffed into his UGG's like papier-mâché cannon balls. And soon after, other less entertaining messages arrived, not bothering him at first, but slowly turning sour after he considered them again after his morning crack pipe. His IKEA storage draws, instead of being left ajar, with t-shirt and underpants acting as a buffer between the canvas and plywood, were shut firmly closed, the clothes inside folded neatly in a way he was incapable of, and in fact, had never seen anywhere other than in other people's apartments before. The tidiness seemed to be posing a question about himself, or about what he wasn't. Yu knew it was dangerous to make the connection, to draw the conclusion and somehow collude in the process, but he sensed he was being leered at and shown up. His feelings were the real target, as they always were when an adult said he was not very good at his life, yet this was not the work of any adult, rather a childlike mind like his own, reflecting his own idea of sinister cleverness.

And then all hell broke loose. Items he was ashamed of, and long banished to the empty container-tank of memory, appeared outside on the balcony, amidst the old teabags and cigarette butts, there for his mother to find and bring in with his laundry should she ever come to visit from Hong Kong. Battered pornographic magazines with felt pen-redacted genitals, his cousin's knickers that he had filched from her laundry basket and Transformer-rescue-bots, supposedly lost in the fire that he could never remember starting, arranged round his dwelling like DEA agents closing in for a bust.

His panic was assuaged by confusion, forever the dominant influence in his life. Most nights he was so smashed when he passed out that he would not have noticed if his room had been taken apart and put back together again by Martians, as what could be more normal in the life of a novice drug-addict, than remembering nothing before he went to bed? Yu was always up to crazy shit after all, jumping into tubs of weedkiller, painting his toenails with varnish, the first of his friends to get studs, tattoos and piercings; chaos was his master, could not all of this be consistent with the usual madness? Like most comforting and flawed ideas, Yu cleaved to this one, long after it ceased to be sensible to still do so. Besides, despite all his complaining, he was not yet used to bad outcomes in life, or of things, finally and irrevocably, actually turning out for the worse.

And then, the night before the morning of his ultimate realisation, he was woken up by something hitting him, he was sure of it, a hard slap to the face, and there, on the bed, was a shoe that he had lost at the party. This party had been unlike any he had attended, culminating in his unrobing and joining the "old ones" in the silver hot tub, the night it all went wrong and he met Sheena The South Sea Queen, a life time ago, six weeks earlier.

The causal chain that took Yu from appearance to disappearance was triggered unknowingly while he was dreaming of lasting things. There were mornings where he saw himself as a rock-star photographer, persuading his harem to show a little more flesh, and others as a ripped stuntman abseiling into a blast furnace full of snakes, watched by anyone he had ever wanted to impress. That he had never used a camera that wasn't part of a mobile-phone, was terrified of heights and physical risk in general, and could still believe in the possibility of greatness few are touched by, came naturally from an anodyne self-confidence bequeathed by a mother who thought he was beautiful and told him so regularly. If life would just let him be more himself, let Yu be Yu, all would not only be well, and the fruits of paradise would land on his lap washed and peeled. This article of faith saw him through his last summer at school, or fuck-about-time, as he liked to call it; the final few weeks a glorious riot of getting noticed, insolence and attitude. The party continued into the fall, moving from his parents' apartment in Hong Kong to the Clarendon Court ghost home they'd bought in London, which had provided his new student friends at Cass Business School a short walk away in Bunhill Row, with a base for operations, and the necessary privacy for sex with a couple of fresher girls who were doing the rounds.

London was the start of another story and hit Yu hard; a slurry of buddies had come with him to the UK, but others were scattered at colleges around the world, or else left behind in Hong Kong. It seemed that behind the lively clothing, bids for attention and hopes for a better world, his companions had their eyes set on conventional routes to middle-class respectability, but then so had he. With the onset of the coldest winter on record, Yu swapped his student friends for a couple of crack dealing head-cases, a cluster of slow readers, and a Banshee with learning difficulties who worked at a bakery and had already given him the clap. It was nothing short of a betrayal of his teenage hopes, but as everyone had always told him he would come a cropper, there was no one short of his mum he could complain to, and even she was beginning to change her tune now that he was no longer so beautiful, rather, a grumpy man-child approaching twenty with a frightening sense of entitlement.

The loneliness of life in Clarendon Court, depressing drug deals that went wrong and resulted in debt, arguments with his family who said he wasn't taking his studies seriously enough, and always waiting for what, he did not know, was terrible. Gravitating towards an older set, already reconciled to a life of paralysing inertia, Yu accepted mascot status, running errands to the off-licence and rolling joints for those too wasted to get their act together. He knew what he was doing was not exactly fun, in fact no fun at all, but at least proof that he still existed. Occasionally rumours seeped through of bigger and better things, parties where pasty English public school girls stripped off and danced on hay bales, and wealthy swingers who would pay unemployed scruffs to shag their wives, amongst other, darker happenings in the suburbs, but there seemed little way into these as he now spent more time bobbing about in a drug casualty swamp than with business students. That was until the barbecue at Basil Hume Garden on New Years Eve. Everyone had climbed over the fence as this tiny park on Lamb's Passage was locked up. When the police arrived it looked like everyone would be arrested, until Mungo Masters started handing out bundles of twenty pound notes and cheerily wishing the uniformed officers a Happy New Year. Masters was a hedge-fund manager known to his colleagues as Toad, he had an interest in young men, pagan myth and alternative energy. Yu's parents had refused to increase his allowance and his newly acquired drug habit left him desperately strapped for cash. The fledgling business school dropout accepted a bundle of notes from Masters, which sealed an invitation to spend the night with the hedge-fund manager at his swanky mansion in New Malden. Yu had heard this south-west London suburb was full of Koreans but had never actually been there. He wasn't sure whether to believe the rumours, since nearly all the flats in Clarendon Court had Chinese owners, but many had never visited the development or even bothered to send someone else to pick up the keys to their apartments.

In Yu's present circumstances, Masters' invitation was nothing short of a summons to the palace, and he did not need to consider it before accepting. The reality did not disappoint. Yu had never seen a place like it; a Christmas Tree that ought to have stood in Trafalgar Square, surrounded by mountains of unopened presents, resided beside a giant staircase that ascended high into the skull of the domed mansion. Everywhere girls in tights dressed as elves, and boys in Speedos and Santa caps, handed round stockings overflowing with pills in seasonal colours. Yu did not do much sleeping that night, but his world opened up and changed irrevocably. He was there for days, returning to Toad Hall in his dreams every night since, his recollection of heaven—a kind of halfway house between London and Surrey—slowly turning into the fear that someone, or something, had followed him home and was not going to leave again without him...

There was a shadow moving about the walls in his room. Of that Yu was sure, closing in and preventing him from physically rising and running away. It was coming for him and he wanted to scream loud enough to wake up, but he was too scared to because he knew he was already awake, and that life, shit as it often was, was still going to be here in the morning, and he was not.

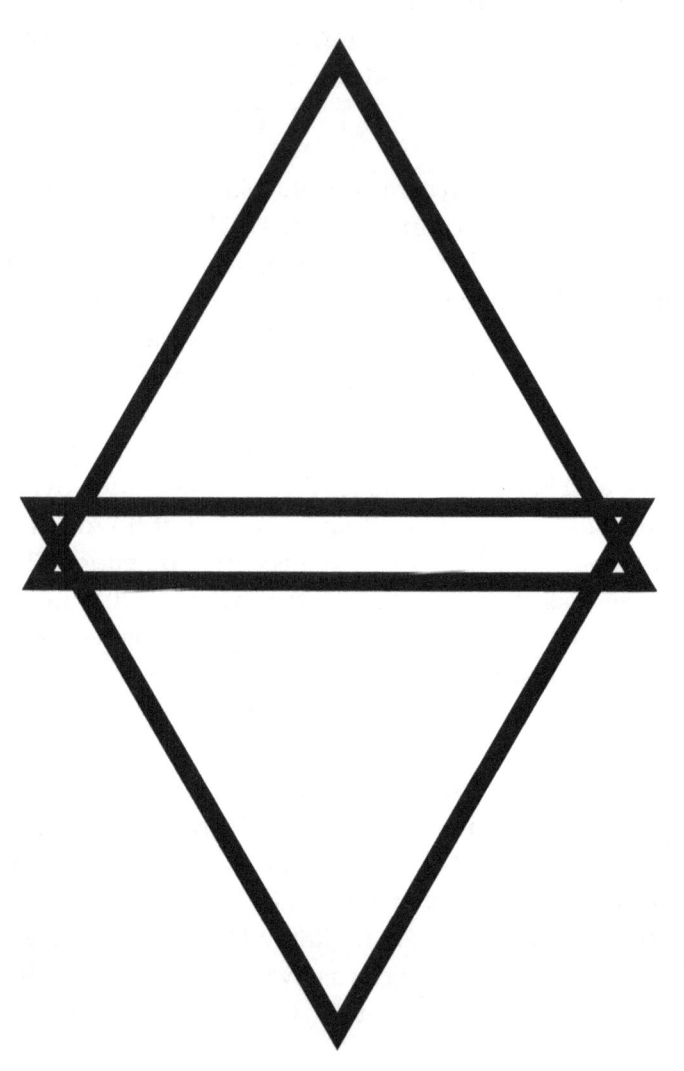

KIMARIS OVER CRIPPLEGATE

CHARLOTTE RIDDELL

"And Clarendon Court, then, stood behind that block of council flats?" I asked a man I met on Golden Lane, the location of Taylor Wimpey's doomed luxury investment apartment development.

"Yes and a fine block of luxury investment apartments it might have been too if it had been properly designed and constructed rather than jerry built to save money. Hearing so much talk about it often makes us feel as if we know every flat in the building, though it has fallen to ruin. Only one man ever lived in it after it was built. Nobody wanted to stop in the place. There used to be awful noises, as if something was being pitched from the top floor, down the lift shaft and into the entrance hall. There would be a sound as if a hundred people were clinking glasses and talking all together at once. And then it seemed as if barrels were rolling in the basement although it only contained a private cinema and games room. There would be screeches and howls, and laughing, fit to make your blood run cold. They say there is gold hidden away in one of the derelict apartments, but no one has ever ventured to find it. Children won't come here to play, when they are cavorting in Fortune Street Park opposite Clarendon Court, nothing will make them stay once the light begins to fade. When the night is coming on, and the shadows creep over the park, many believe they've seen mighty queer things on the site of Clarendon Court."

"But what is it they think they see?" I wanted to know

"Do you really wanna know the doings of Clarendon Court property investors? They were rich, every one of them—all in good stead with the leadership of the Chinese Communist

Party, and as for wickedness, you might have searched Manchuria through and not found their match."

"Tell me about it!" I pleaded.

"The last mortal being that tried to live in Clarendon Court was a creature by the name of Molly Leary. You may be sure she thought herself a made woman when an estate agent said she might stop in Clarendon Court rent free. She picked a penthouse apartment to sleep in, and for a while all went quiet, till one night she was wakened by feeling her bed lifted and shaken like a carpet. Her life seemed to go out of her with the fear. If the bed had been a ship in a storm, it couldn't have pitched any worse, all of a sudden, it was dropped with such a bang as nearly drove her heart into her mouth.

"But that she said was nothing to the screaming and laughing, and hustling and rushing that filled the apartment block. If a hundred people had been running hard along the passages and tumbling downstairs, they could not have made greater noise.

"Molly never was able to tell how she got clear of the place but a man coming home late from the pub found her crouched under the locked gates of Fortune Street Park, naked. She had a bad fever and talked about strange things and never was the same woman after."

"But what was the beginning of all this? When did Clarendon Court first get a reputation for being haunted?" I demanded.

"Soon after it was built an investor called Maurice Wong came to visit. He was old. Nearly a hundred years old. But he held himself as upright as ever and could have drunk a whole roomful under the table, and walked up to bed as unconcerned as you please at the dead of the night."

"He was a terrible man. You couldn't lay your tongue to a wickedness he had not been in the forefront of — drinking, swindling, gambling — all manner of sins had been meat and drink to him since he was a boy. But at last he did something in Shanghai so bad, so beyond the beyonds, he thought he had best come live among people who did not know him.

It was said that he wanted to try and stay in this world forever, and that he had got some blood transfusions that kept him well and hearty. There was something wonderful queer about him anyhow."

"He could hold foot with the youngest, was strong, and had a fine fresh colour in his face. His eyes were like a hawk's and there was not a break in his voice — and he was nearly a hundred years old!"

"The March before Wong turned one hundred was the worst ever known in London — such blowing, sheeting, snowing, had not been experienced in living memory. One blusterous night there was a terrible road accident on the corner of Golden Lane and Old Street. A tourist coach ended up overturned with all thirty passengers killed, a few cars were wrecked too as a pile up followed. They say it was awful to hear the death cries that went up high above the noise of the wind. It was a terrible sight to see Old Street strewn with corpses."

"No one knew who the tourists were or where they came from but the Cripplegate alderman said they should all be buried in the old plague pit on Charterhouse Square, since the one beneath Clarendon Court was no longer accessible. Miraculously a puncheon of brandy survived the carnage. Old Maurice Wong claimed it. He'd been in a taxi that suffered minor damage in the pile up. There was sore ill will because he kept all the booze to himself and most witnesses were sure the puncheon had not fallen from Wong's taxi as he claimed, but had come out of the coach."

"Long story short, that was the most wonderful liquor anybody ever tasted. Wong's friends came from far and near to booze with him, and it was cards and dice, and drinking and story-telling night after night — week in, week out. Even on Sundays, God forgive them! Wong's family and friends would fly over from China and sit emptying tumbler after tumbler till Monday morning came, for it made beautiful punch."

"But all at once people quit coming—word went round that the liquor was not all it ought to be. Nobody could say what ailed it, but it got about that in some way men found it did not suit them. For one thing, they were losing money very fast. They could not make head against the Wong's luck, and a hint was dropped the puncheon ought to have been taken to The Thames, and sunk in its tidal waters."

"It was getting to the end of April, and fine, warm weather for the time of year, when first one and then another, and then another still, began to take notice of a stranger who walked Golden Lane alone at night. He was a sun-kissed man, his skin as tanned as the dead tourists lying in the Charterhouse Square plague pit, and he had rings in his ears, and wore a strange kind of hat, and cut wonderful antics as he walked, and had an ambling sort of gait, curious to look at. Many tried to talk to him, but he only shook his head. So as nobody could make out where he came from or what he wanted, they concluded he was the spirit of some poor wretch who'd died in the road accident on Old Street and wasn't much taken with the Charterhouse plague pit."

"The Cripplegate alderman went and tried to get some sense out of him. 'Is it a Christian burial you're wanting?' the alderman asked, but the creature only shook his head. 'Is it word sent to the wives and daughters you've left orphans and widows, you'd like?' But no it wasn't that. 'Is it for sin committed you're doomed to walk this way? Could a minister comfort you? There's a heathen,' said the alderman; 'Did you ever hear tell of a Christian that shook his head when ministers were mentioned?'"

"'Perhaps he doesn't understand English,' said one of the beadles, 'Try some Spanish.' "No sooner said than done. The alderman started off with such a string of 'holas' and 'vales' that the stranger fairly took to his heels and ran. 'He is an evil spirit,' the alderman explained later, 'I have exorcised him using a ritual I learned at the Guildhall Lodge.'"

"But the next night the gentleman was back again, as unconcerned as ever. 'He'll just have to stay,' said the alderman, 'for I've got lumbago and pains in all my joints — as well as a hoarseness from shouting all the Masonic secret words I know at him. I don't believe he understood a thing I said.'"

"This went on for a while and people got that frightened of the man, or appearance of a man. They would not go near Clarendon Court because the stranger spent most of his time pacing up and down outside it. In the end Maurice Wong, who had always scoffed at the talk, took it into his head he would see into the rights of the matter."

"Maybe he was feeling lonesome because as I told you before, people had left off coming to Clarendon Court, and there was nobody for him to drink with. Out he goes, bold as brass. The man came forward at the sight of Wong and took off his hat with a flourish. Not to be behind in civility, Maurice lifted his. 'I have come, sir,' Wong said, 'to know if you are looking for anything, and whether I can assist you to find it.' The man looked at Wong as if he had taken the greatest liking to him, and took off his hat again."

"'Is it the coach that crashed you are distressed about?' There came no answer, only a mournful shake of the head. 'Well, I haven't got the coach, it went to the scrap yard months ago and, as for the dead, they are snug and sound enough in a local plague pit.' The man stood and looked at Wong with a queer sort of smile on his face. 'What do you want?' asked Wong passionately. 'If anything belonging to you was in the coach, it's the police you need to ask about it, unless it's the brandy you're fretting about!'"

"Wong had tried him in English and Mandarin, and was now speaking a language you'd have thought nobody could understand. But it seemed as natural as kissing to the stranger. 'Oh! That's where you are from, is it?' said Wong. 'Why couldn't you have told me so at once? I can't give you the brandy because it is mostly drunk, but come along and you shall have as stiff a glass of punch as ever crossed your lips.' And without more to-do off they went, as sociable as you please, jabbering together in some outlandish tongue that made moderate folks' jaws ache to hear it."

"That was the first night they conversed together but it wasn't the last. The stranger must have been the height of good company, for Wong never tired of him. Every evening, regularly, he came up to Clarendon Court, always dressed the same, always smiling and polite, and then Wong called for brandy and hot water, and they drank and played cards till cock-crow, talking and laughing into the small hours."

"This went on for weeks and weeks, nobody knowing where the man came from, or where he went. Only two things the Clarendon Court concierge did know — that the puncheon was nearly empty and that Wong's flesh was wasting off him. The night porter felt so uneasy he went to the police about this but they could give him no comfort. The concierge got so concerned that he felt bound to eavesdrop at the door to Wong's apartment. But they always talked in gibberish and whether it was blessing or cursing they were at the night porter couldn't tell."

"Well, the upshot of it came one night in July — on the eve of Wong's birthday — there wasn't a drop of spirit left in the puncheon. No not as much as would drown a fly. They had drunk the whole lot clean up — and the concierge stood trembling, expecting any minute to hear Wong call up from the games room for more brandy, for where was he to get more if they wanted any?"

"All at once Wong and the stranger came up to Clarendon Court's reception. It was a full moon and light as day." 'I'll go home with you tonight by way of a change,' says Wong. 'Will you so?' asked the other. 'That I will,' answered Wong. 'It is your own choice, you know.' 'Yes; it is my own choice. Let us go.'"

"So they went. And running out of Clarendon Court the concierge watched the way they took. Wong walked south beside the strange man, then they turned right into Beech Street. The night porter followed them and saw them walk on, and on, and on, and on, until they came to The Thames. They ambled down some steps at Queenhithe till the water took them to their knees, and then to their waists, and then to their arm-pits, and then to their throats and their heads. Before long the concierge was dialling the cops on his smart-phone but it did no good because by the time the boys in blue turned up, Wong and his companion had disappeared."

"Well?" I said. "What happened?"

"Living or dead, Maurice Wong never came back again. Next morning, when the Thames tide ebbed, a man who was mudlarking saw the print of a cloven foot—that he tracked to the water's edge. Then everybody knew where Wong had gone and with whom."

CLARENDON COURT
99 HORROR

IPHGENIA BAAL

1 Elegant articulation of contemporary HORROR

2 Diverse urban HORROR

3 Local artisan HORROR

4 Refined City haven HORROR

5 Curated selection of HORROR

6 Property investment portfolio HORROR

7 Friendly addition to bustling community HORROR

8 Independent boutique HORROR

9 Creative hub HORROR

10 Abundant greenspace HORROR

11 Tranquil outdoor HORROR

12 Award-winning HORROR

13 Landmark HORROR

14 Exclusive postcode HORROR

15 Desirable lifestyle HORROR

16 Comfortable practical HORROR

17 Thoughtfully designed HORROR

18 Stunning feature wall HORROR

19 Timeless HORROR

20 Perfectly-positioned HORROR

21 Double-dug basement HORROR

22 Dedicated to lateral living HORROR

23 Michelin star HORROR

24 Third party service HORROR

25 24-hour concierge HORROR

26 Secure mail and delivery service HORROR

27 Electronic controlled access HORROR

28 Video door entry system HORROR

29 Secure cycle storage HORROR

30 CCTV HORROR

31 Private courtyard HORROR

32 Comfort cooling system HORROR

33 On-site facility HORROR

34 Residents' lounge and terrace HORROR

35 Communal games room HORROR

36 Open-plan studios for fast-paced HORROR

37 Generous Duplex apartments for family HORROR

38 Penthouse HORROR

39 Floor to ceiling window HORROR

40 Private terrace with decking HORROR

41 Sunken garden HORROR

42 Double-glazed HORROR

43 Sliding door HORROR

44 View of the city's financial district HORROR

45 Programmable mood lighting HORROR

46 Multi-functional HORROR

47 Antique bronze-finish switchplate HORROR

48 Free-standing brass-wrapped kitchen island HORROR

49 Investment interior piece HORROR

50 Premium fixture HORROR

51 Glass balustrade with handrail HORROR

52 Designer door furniture HORROR

53 Engineered hardwood flooring HORROR

54 Fitted broadloom luxury carpeting HORROR

55 Sleek brand-conscious HORROR

56 Composite natural stone kitchen worktop HORROR

57 Tiled splashback HORROR

58 Gloss grey lacquered storage units with concealed handles HORROR

59 Induction hob with extractor hood and child-lock HORROR

60 Fully integrated stainless-steel combi-microwave oven HORROR

61 Fully integrated eco dishwasher HORROR

62 Fully integrated drawer fridge-freezer HORROR

63 Washing machine and spin-dryer cupboard HORROR

64 Free-standing glass fronted wine cooler HORROR

65 Segregated waste disposal HORROR

66 Master en-suite HORROR

67 High end porcelain in all wet area HORROR

68 Underfloor heating HORROR

69 Statement black fittings set apart from the norm HORROR

70 Twin basin HORROR

71 Heated towel rail HORROR

72 Dual flush WC with concealed cistern HORROR

73 Fixed showerhead, adjustable showerhead and riser rail to walk-in shower HORROR

74 Frosted glass bathscreen HORROR

75 Wall-mounted mirrored vanity unit with spotlight and shaver socket HORROR

76 Glass interior shelving in stainless-steel cabinet HORROR

77 Bespoke fitted wood-effect veneer wardrobe HORROR

78 Bespoke matching drawer set HORROR

79 Automated blind HORROR

80 BT socket and 5 volt powerpoint HORROR

81 Hyperoptic broadband HORROR

82 Shared satellite (subscription required) HORROR

83 Commerce meets culture HORROR

84 Entreprenurial, conspiring, artistic HORROR

85 Weekend brunch and cocktail HORROR

86 Showcase HORROR

87 Ambitious project HORROR

88 Undisputed centre of luxury HORROR

89 Effortlessly accessible HORROR

90 Fast and efficient HORROR

91 Heart of the capital HORROR

LIVING DEATH IN CLARENDON COURT

ADELINE WOOLF

Whatever hour you woke there was a door shutting. From apartment to apartment they went, hand in hand, lifting here, opening there, making sure—a ghostly couple.

"Here we left it," she said. And he added, "Oh, but here too!" "It's in the penthouse," she murmured. "And in the basement," he whispered "Quietly," they said, "or we shall wake them."

But it wasn't that you woke us. Oh, no. "They're looking for it; they're drawing the curtain," one might say, and so read on a page or two. "Now they've found it," one would be certain, stopping the pencil on the margin. And then, tired of reading, one might rise and see for oneself, Clarendon Court all empty, the doors locked shut, the owners' keys never picked up from the vendor, only the pigeons bubbling with content on the roof and the hum of the back-up generator sounding from the Barbican exhibition halls. "What did I come in here for? What did I want to find?" My hands were empty. "Perhaps it's on the third floor then?" The concierge was smoking crack in an empty apartment. And so down again, the private cinema as still as ever, only a book had slipped beneath a bean bag.

But they had found it in the games room. Not that one could ever see them. The window panes reflected social housing, reflected the schools on the other side of Golden Lane; Barbican Estate brutalism was grey in the glass. A dawn chorus of council tenants arguing with each other. In the lift an overpowering smell of bleach covered illicit odours that might have lingered otherwise. Yet, the moment after, if the door was opened, spread about the floor, hung upon the walls, pendant from the ceiling—what? My hands were empty. The shadow of a postman crossed the floor; from the deepest wells of silence the pigeons drew their bubble of sound. "Death, death, death," the pulse of Clarendon Court beat softly. "The living dead alive and well…" the pulse stopped short. Was it invoking vampires or zombies, or both?

A moment later the light had faded. Out in the street then? But the over-scaled Clarendon Court spun darkness for a wandering beam of sun. So fine, so rare, coolly sunk beneath the surface the beam I sought always burnt behind the glass. Death was the glass; death was between us; coming to the women first, hundreds of years ago, leaving the apartment block, sealing all the windows; the rooms were darkened. He left it, left her, went North, went East, saw the stars turned in the Southern sky; sought Taylor Wimpey's Clarendon Court, found it dropped beneath the much taller Barbican Towers. "Death, death, death," the pulse of Clarendon Court beat gladly. "Damnation is yours."

The wind roars up Golden Lane. Trees in Fortune Street Park stoop and bend this way and that. Moonbeams splash and spill wildly in the rain. But the beam of the lamp falls straight from the window. The candle burns stiff and still. Wandering through Clarendon Court, opening the windows, whispering not to wake us, the ghostly couple seek their prey.

"Here we slept," she says. And he adds, "Kisses without number." "Waking in the morning—" "Silver between the buildings—" "Penthouse—" "In the basement—" "When summer came—" "In winter snowtime—" The doors go shutting far in the distance, gently knocking like the pulse of a heart.

Nearer they come; cease at the doorway. The wind falls, the rain slides silver down the glass. Our eyes darken; we hear no steps beside us; we see no lady spread her ghostly cloak. His hands shield the lantern. "Look," he breathes. "Sound asleep. A nerve agent upon their lips."

Stooping, holding their silver lamp above us, long they look and deeply. Long they pause. The wind drives straightly; the flame stoops slightly. Wild beams of moonlight cross both floor and wall, and, meeting, stain the faces bent; the faces pondering; the faces that search the sleepers and seek their hidden joy.

"Death, death, death," the heart of Clarendon Court beats proudly. "Long years—" he sighs. "Again you found me." "Here," she murmurs, "sleeping; on a balcony reading; laughing, rolling marbles in the games room. Here we left our lives—" Stooping, their light lifts the lids upon my eyes. "Death! Death! Death!" the pulse of Clarendon Court beats wildly. Waking, I cry "Oh, so this your life within? It's a living death."

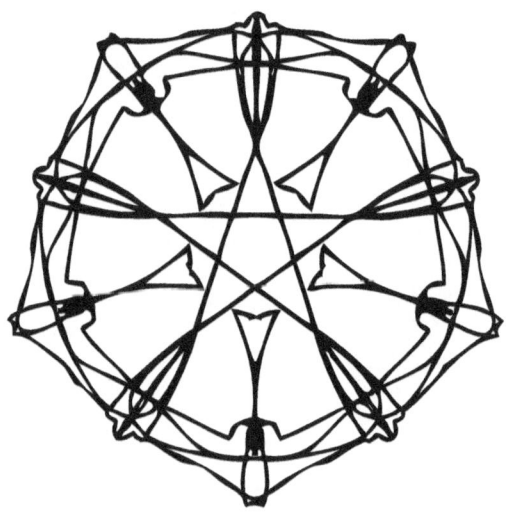

DENI-ZEN

CHRIS PETIT

Hermann had bought into Clarendon Court off-plan, an iconic cascade in the heart of the City of Old London Town, built in the something-or-other vernacular. The super-glossy brochure promised James Bond in the luxury, bespoke cinema. Plus a play room! The most exciting rumour was of top-notch escort agencies operating a 24-hour service in the block. Mutti had said: "Don't be silly! Think of the service charges." Mutti, always canny when it came to property, thanks to a frugal post-war background, preferred bullion investment and disapproved of Hermann's move, which had been provoked by a desire to improve Sino-German business relations. Clarendon Court was a Chinese enclave (thanks to what turned out to be a porky promise of a British passport in return for purchasing an apartment, and ambassadorial status for a penthouse, with the owner addressed as "Excellency" by Clarendon Court staff, all decommissioned beef-eaters from the historic Tower of London.) A proud banner flew "atop" — in the preferred language of the developer — the building, displaying its latest slogan: Sold Down the River.

Mutti, sceptical, had snorted. "It will turn out to be a ghost building." Its post code had particularly bad feng shui. The souls of murdered policemen stalked the demolished corridors of the previous site, a consequence of the unreported Fann Street massacre of 1958. The glorious German super-rockets of 1944 had used the site's co-ordinates for a bull's-eye. Historically, the location was known for rancid, diseased brothels and abattoirs. Mutti: "Not much has changed. Beware, Hermann, because of the nearby meat market the area is haunted by the spirits of dead animals from the Chinese zodiac."

Mutti sniggered. "No wonder it cost you an arm and a leg!" Hermann refused to see the joke, even after Mutti had explained in terms that a child of two could understand. Mutti sighed. "I can see you need to develop the famous British sense of humour."

Despite Mutti's warnings, initial signs were promising. Hermann collected the keys from a fawning agent, who admired his left-hand drive, top-of-the-range Merc, driven over that morning and already festooned with parking tickets. Fawning agent (female) offered her cellphone number in case of any hitches, adding meaningfully that there wouldn't be.

A Banksy mural gave the fabulous Beech Street tunnel artistic tone. A spectacular Jeff Koons turd lay in the street, next to an art installation of an old telephone kiosk (designed, according to its blue plaque, by the brother of a notorious Kray brothers' associate. Or, mused Hermann, shouldn't that be "an associate of the notorious Krays"?). In the kiosk a twitching performance artist pretended to be a junkie. Hermann hadn't realised his room would be north-facing and overlooking this street parade and the proletariat blocks opposite. He was sure he had bought a south-facing apartment and two bedrooms rather than the sunless studio he seemed to have.

Taking the elevator straight up from the underground car park, he had bypassed reception, which came as a surprise when he went back down. It more resembled a street market with stalls serving dim sum and noodles to a scrum of Chinese. Hermann supposed it was a pop-up thing. He was not yet aware of the rumour that the so-called Chinese residents were in fact the equivalent to film-extras, hired in exchange for free food, to make it appear the building was inhabited because very few owners had picked up their keys, before or after the murders.

Outside, the artist junkies seemed to have gone for lunch. The proletariat estate was patrolled by security men in the process of arresting a small dog. Hermann wondered if this was another artwork. Was it conceivable that the estate was entirely inhabited by artists pretending to be proletariat; otherwise why would the block be decorated with garish, tattered banners that seemed either challenging or offensive? Hermann was disorientated. Was it about edge? No one had pointed out that he would live facing this querulous local artists' community. Had he wanted that he would have bought in Shoreditch. He had looked there first, taking Mutti on a German Wings mini-break. Mutti had berated the clerk in the Church's shoe store in the City's Cheapside upon discovering that their women's brogue was made not in England but imported from Italy. Hermann, coveting Paraboots (French and hard to find, hoping Mutti would treat) had to be content with a pair of Clark's desert boots. Bangers and mash for lunch in a bespoke olde worlde pub, and pints of foaming bitter ale — if such a thing could be found. They had to make do with adjectivally-challenged wine — 'generous, round, full' — incompetent service, rabbit and tarragon terrine, three scallops, the ubiquitous pork belly — the pulled, spiritual descendent of old City slaughterhouses — and something Mutti struggled to recognise as fish. Ninety-five quid, thanks very much, with optional service added at twelve-and-a-half percent. That said, the strength of the euro reduced the bill to pence. Hermann in an unexpectedly light-hearted mood after Mutti had coughed up, said in heavy quotation marks — the vocal equivalent to the finger curl — "We're such basic bitches." Mutti was captivated by Shoreditch, mistaking all the bearded young men for the minor European royalty of her childhood (from the neck up at least). But too many short trousers, she complained. Lederhosen only, she admonished, and permissible only under certain circumstances (Wandervogel) otherwise no shorts. Hermann was confused and a little thrilled by Google references to Wandervogel and homosexuality. Leather shorts. Onkel Tom's Kabin. Lederhosen with a flap at the back as well as the front. Hermann took note of Friedlander: "Only he who is a good pederast can be a perfect pedagogue." Try that on the children in the park! he thought. Most looked dangerous and feral, more like frightening tiny adults than kids.

Clarendon Court was already showing signs of its age and discontent. It was—what?—scarcely open a couple of months and residents—known as "the few', an echo on the part of the building's publicists to the historic Battle of Britain—were already moving out. The immediate environs were not what Hermann had been led to expect. However much he was in love with the common people he didn't want to live in their actual vicinity. No one had said anything about a school, within the estate agent's proverbial "stone's throw'. Children! Dickensian urchins running wild! Community! The horror! No mention of sunless canyons. The improvised canteen in reception turned out to be just that. There was nowhere locally anyone wished to eat and residents were scared to go out after a young couple from Shijiazhuang (who had come there because they liked the quality of the high pollution) had been machete-murdered and dismembered by an Uber driver who buried their parts on Queenhithe beach, beneath the smoking balcony of the new hotel development.

Hermann returned to the secure underground car park to find written in indelible ink on the driving window of his Kompressor: C*** Parking. Which was unfair: he was square in the bay. Unless it was noun rather than adjective and referred to him. More Jeff Koons turds lay in a symmetrical arrangement on the concrete floor. Art and property went hand in hand as any fool knew: time to turn a quick profit. Hermann dialled the fawning agent only to be told that prices had in fact dropped; a temporary hiccup. The Chinese were turning out to be unreliable buyers, being fussy, loud and superstitious, so the building's agents were setting up an office in Pyongyang, subsequent to Britain (formally rebranded as Brexit, copyright and patent pending) opening diplomatic relations with North Career, as the only trade option left to it.

The cinema was closed. A handwritten sheet advertised not James Bond but a "curated season" of old English horror movies by LoveFilm. The playroom consisted of a broken ping-pong table, with graffiti scratched on: Germans go home. With nothing to do, Hermann went to his apartment and pictured himself ending his days on a chain gang on the Rhine-Yangtze canal. Five ways not to get a fat belly. Concentration shot. The inside of what passed for his head reduced to brain flickers, electrical faults and poor wiring, his reduced personality a product of conferences and meetings, bullet points and bad air miles, patched together by a combination of Hugo Boss and Ralph Lauren Bacall. The world had reached such a pretty pass that toilet paper now came with user instructions and refugees turned up in Nike and Adidas.

Hermann suspected travel, space and place were just a diorama and architects worked to an identical open plan because once inside another glass Euroturret he found the same everywhere. Architects had regressed to being slaves to wiring conduits, where the construction industry had advanced to being considerate and caring. Hermann's secret wish – the desire he dared not voice – was a loving relationship with a considerate builder.

Every street in Western Europe was regularly dug up with gleeful abandon. Mutti, delirious, feared Muslim insurgents. "Like that Mexican drugs/wetback tunnel in *Breaking Bad*." As Hermann had soothed Mutti's fevered brow, he thought: They never show the wiring in those clean simulations of what the finished building will look like, or the crap of cardboard storage boxes cluttering the windows.

Mutti had texted to point out that Fann Street was the most excavated road in the whole of London, for nefarious reasons, she said, with dark stories of the swimming pool on the proletariat estate being used out of hours as a way of keeping down the local population.

Hermann looked at his Junkers automatic 6060-5 watch. *The Face of Fu Manchu* was due to start downstairs in five minutes. He resolved to go. People to meet...

Hermann decided to avail himself of the in-house Clarendon Court escort service: two for the price of one. A couple of strapping young women turned up with a credit-card dispenser and a twelve-and-a-half percent "optional" service charge, payable in advance. They were afraid to go out because of the Uber killer, so stayed in. After changing into their exotic performance attire, the women undertook strange rituals, though not on Hermann, frotting the fixtures and fittings, eroticising the apartment. Their gestures seemed perfunctory, their hearts not in it. Hermann could hardly be surprised. There was nothing about the place that turned him on, for all the come-hither seductiveness of the brochure (hollow laughter). Sometimes he wondered if he wasn't inadvertently squatting in the wrong building; easily done as so many of these new blocks were abandoned before occupation.

Hermann had his epiphany: he was superfluous to the young women's performance because he had already been screwed, buying the apartment in the first place, which was why the women were now treating it as the client, one of them dropping a magnificent Jeff Koons turd on the white shag pile rug.

A crash from the bathroom. Hermann wondered if the young women in their becoming latex and rubberware were agents for poltergeists, or performing some exorcism. Tiles fell off the bathroom walls. The shower attachment fell out, seemingly of its own accord. A foul-smelling liquid emanated from electrical and light sockets: beyond any regular construction faults. The kitchen microwave removed itself from its built-in unit and performed a 360-degree turn; very Linda Blair!

"The address shines with luxurious details and inner calm," one of the young women recited from the Clarendon Court bible brochure while the other produced a thurible and incense. Hermann. thought: It was a hive of repressed malevolence! He addressed them: "You must persuade the building to levitate and relocate to the 'inner heart of the City' where it has been described as residing, rather than being stuck on its insalubrious perimeter, on an inauspicious ley line, to boot." The women did their magic. The building shuddered but did not rise. They had failed to make the earth move, thought Hermann, disappointed, and in the living room (more inner calm and a slightly nauseous smell) the Samsung QE65Q9F QLED HDR 2000 4K Ultra HD Smart TV, 65 inches, groaned orgasmically before emitting a shower of sparks.

The young women expressed disappointment, compared to what they had achieved in other apartments. Most spectacularly they had changed the natural light in one to resemble a total eclipse even though it remained daylight outside.

"Not bright daylight. Because there is nothing bright about this development or the suckers that bought into it. What shall we play now? Read the small print?"

They played Hermann hiding in the closet, with the door closed, dressed in an adult diaper and suspended from the rail, among his whispering hangers, with a Waitrose tangerine stuffed in his mouth, listening to the young women frolic outside. Hermann woke up tied to the bed with no idea of how he had got there. "They must have spiked my drink," he thought and on the mirror scrawled in lipstick he read: Fascist pig! And in brackets: (What you told us to write). He had no memory. It took three hours to untie himself – in terms of knots, Hermann had seen nothing like it since his last Strauss-Kahn orgy. He shared the illustrious S-K's view: "I always believed that these women came for me – because of who I am."

There had been no residents' meetings yet for lack of numbers to form a quorum but Hermann already had in mind to propose that the penthouse suite be renamed after Strauss-Kahn rather than the knockabout joker now in temporary international disgrace following an inappropriate act involving Angela Merkel and a potted houseplant; the next party leader, everyone said.

Although technically still daylight, Hermann's room seemed to be cast in a state of even more permanent gloom, with a thin sliver of disappearing sunlight appearing on the wall for what he counted as ten minutes. He was sure it had been there on previous days for longer. After all, the winter solstice was past and the days were lengthening. Free from his bonds at last, he bound to his feet, energised, as his handy rang. He sighed. Mutti!

Mutti disapproved of Hermann's away weekends in London to explore what she referred to as the scene. The point of an investment was that it remained empty and was not for the owner's benefit, other than accumulation of profit. Mutti seemed incapable of grasping that prices were in fact going down. Maybe she was right; it was considered bad luck to stay in such apartments. Many Clarendon Court owners preferred when in town to stay at the Thistle City Barbican at a hundred and forty quid a night rather than risk misfortune.

The Chinese were so superstitious, and rapacious. According to Hermann's sources in the local ale houses – into which he ventured in fear and trepidation, on intelligence-gathering missions, in exchange for an open tab behind the bar – it was rumoured that the whole Clarendon Court development had been a done deal in anticipation of the real deal, which was the elimination of all surrounding green space, as a result of an arrangement between Hong Kong triads, who twittered as "Face of Fu Manchu", and committees of Freemasons, twittering as "secret world domination".

Hermann was reading about property development in the Third Reich. Auschwitz – nice old town, surprisingly tolerant of Jews, given that it was the Poles, until the German beasties turned up with their utopian ideals to turn the place into a green paradise – organic farming, land reclamation, climate change for the better – lasting about six months before the developers moved in. Huge petrochemical factory. Land grab! Tax breaks! Government subsidies. Green lit all the way... and look where that ended up.

There were signs already, it was being whispered in the nearest ale house, a dive in Whitecross Street, full of shifty types pretending to pass themselves off as yuppies but clearly part of the deprived community. The local school in the park had already been evacuated, on grounds that it was too close to the City borders, prior to making it a child-free zone.

The children had been transferred to a seemingly unnecessary new school a few hundred yards up Golden Lane in the adjacent borough. Just south of it on the border a 1970s-style Belfast road block had been set up: an up-and-down barrier bought off eBay and what looked like B&Q garden huts serving as sentry boxes, plus a lot of sandbags from the local Travis Perkins builders merchants. Soldiers in camouflage fatigues, with jauntily tilted berets and downward-pointing rifles, checked cars and personnel passing in and out while studiously ignoring the black Astra parked fifty yards up the road conducting its drug business *en plein soleil*, with a long queue taking selfies.

One evening a neighbour introduced herself by ringing Hermann's bell. Strict, older, frighteningly plausible, possibly corrective. In public relations. She said she was organising donations for a welcome party for a disgraced Hollywood film actor and an even more disgraced Hollywood film producer, both of whom had bought into Clarendon Court as part of their rehab programme — estate agents were marketing it as an approved destination for celebrity serial sex offenders and bankrupts. Incomers included several disgraced MPs known for being handsy. Hermann thought of the actor. He had allegedly lain drunk on some sleeping fellow — as one does — and squeezed some bums at faggot central — ditto — and he was RUINED. Really? Fifty quid a head, said the woman. Hermann replied that he would love to but no cash. She produced a credit-card dispenser, identical to the one used by the escort women. Hermann coughed up.

Rumours abounded about why the park was "temporarily" closed: that it was in the process of becoming a private space for the exclusive use of Clarendon Court residents (good); or that this was a soft rumour being peddled by spin merchants to disguise that the developer had purchased the space for redevelopment. As for the road block, no one was sure if it was a Jeremy Deller installation or a sign of the City setting itself up as an independent military government within the larger metropolis, or perhaps both. The most ironic rumour was a replica of the building that had been demolished to make way for Clarendon Court – a police dormitory block – was to be recreated brick for brick in the park, as key-worker housing for the military to control the area. Already there was talk on the communal notice board of a Clarendon Court action committee to protest, with the plaintive request: How many to quorum [sic]?

A subversive blog put out by an innocuous-sounding young woman, fronting for what Hermann suspected were drug-crazed anarchists offered the most extreme scenario: that the whole Clarendon Court affair was part of a side deal pre-agreed with the Chinese, prior to leasing the City for ninety-nine years on a post-Brexit Hong Kong-style contract, on condition that the park was eventually turned into a huge factory, bringing back industry to the centre, as part of a treaty signed with President Trump, now embarked on a third term (unprecedented since the warmonger Roosevelt) to increase global warming as a way of reducing domestic heating costs.

The blog also claimed to have unearthed evidence of a five-year plan to abandon any education policy. Local kiddies would be deported to adjacent boroughs where, like Dickensian urchins of yore, they would be put to work. This was considered the "kinder solution", given that it was universally agreed that education was a waste of time. Plus, since the Vodacom-Nike wars, previously rich City workers now jobless would be grateful for a place on the factory floor. Hermann had heard that the whole programme was part of a reverse eco-policy, to ramp up pollution and reduce light levels, because humans would adapt to these new conditions, given that the universe was f***ed anyway.

Mutti admonished Hermann for negative cultural thinking. Not fair; he had devoted much thought to the placebo effect and wondered if there was an economic equivalent. Did economics suffer from psychosomatic disorder (the English economy, for instance), and shouldn't those quacks in alternative medicine devote their time to developing lucrative alternative economies? Is a shrinking economy in need of shrinks, ho ho? (Hermann had devoted many idle moments over the years to thinking about the conundrum of an expanding contracting company, and wished he had one.)

Standing in his lonely room, listening to Mutti drone on, and staring at the monsoon-lashed streets (a microclimate that now extended to Chinese weather), in whatever the stage beyond twilight was called, he had a sudden yen to hear Robert Palmer singing "Doctor, Doctor, Give me the News (I've Got a Bad Case of Loving You)". (Hermann remembered the stage after twilight was called night.) "Should feng shui be applied to the money market?' he asked Mutti, who was dismissive: "It's called astrology." She thought economics was not a mental exercise as it was no longer an extension of human thinking, but viral and rogue. She was greatly exercised by the role of charity as the link between the abstract rampage of out-of-control economics ('The black! The black!') and third world disease. Charity was the new colonialism. Mutti's latest slogan was, "Scrap the money. Give us the charity." Hermann wondered if the British shopping riots of 2011 were an early manifestation of "the people" showing the way. Mutti, mysterious, said: "Why do you think I had a Blackberry?"

Mutti told Hermann that Reichsführer-SS Himmler's preference was for Blackberry whereas Goebbels and Goering were staunch iPhone men. "What is the dictator's choice of handy?" mused Mutti rhetorically.

The Samsung Mugabe... it could work, thought Hermann. My Blackberry Putin. Maybe even a special edition, in association with YouTube, of Blackberry's "Blueberry" Putin, in homage to the great leader's 2010 charity fundraiser rendition of Fats Waller, whose ringtone is Vlad's version of the song "Blueberry Hill (Club Killers Tramp Remix)".

Mutti was now in permanent residence in Hermann's Clarendon Court apartment while he had to make do with Thistle City's last minute.com rates. Mutti declares herself greatly taken by the Great British TV bake-off programme.

"Far superior to *Das gross Backen*." She effortlessly learns the Wikipedia entry by heart, however shot her minute-to-minute memory. "The signature challenge is for the amateur bakers to show off their tried-and-tested recipes that are rustic and altogether home-made-looking."

Why memorise when you can look up, wonders Hermann.

Mutti had given the apartment a hippie makeover: paisley, patchouli and joss-sticks, which failed to hide the smell of sophisticated shit that seemed to be part of the design of the building.

Hermann noted that the Greek bake-off franchise was still available. Mmm. Maybe better for being outdoors and not baking. BBQ Parthenon. ("The open range in the world's premier location"). Paraffin. Lighter fluid. Glowing coals. Waft of roasting flesh. "Premier iconic location." (Why not, for once, thinks Hermann, who is anti-iconic. Justified use.)

The thrice-bankrupt Hermann still fancied his entrepreneurial skills. Mutti insists on buying a Primus stove from City Hardware so they can have their own bake-off in the apartment since none of the kitchen appliances worked, apart from the freezer, which seemed to be being used to store frozen body parts. "Nothing to do with me," says Mutti. "I thought they were yours. You always were a strange child. Kate Moss just moved in."

"She ought to know better. Are you sure?"

Hermann suspected Mutti was confused. She was reading Kate's biography and had just reached the drunken airline rampage (Tabloid headline: Kate Mess), which Mutti intended to replicate on the Ryanair flight home, plus Primus stove, for a mile-high bake-off. Hermann says the airport Gestapo would confiscate.

"Such spoilsports. They will believe me when I tell them it is my iron lung, trust me."

Hermann wonders: The Dementia Show, whose signature challenge is a test of cognitive memory skills, with a climax of recited Shakespeare learned by rote for the occasion. Shakespeare too highbrow? (Not if Stephen Fry chairs UK show. Hermann hopeful of introduction because of shared history of credit-card fraud.) Hermann thinks Bjorn Borg to chair Swedish Dementia Show or Abba Agnetha, who'd had a stalker. International franchise, here we come. (The DM Show, as it will become known, sells worldwide, including the two-dozen countries even *Game of Thrones* never cracked.) Signature tune "I Forgot to Remember to Forget". Presley rights out of the question. Hermann memos himself: check if Robert Palmer recorded.

Hermann also successfully launches a fake dementia show—Dementia Minus—in which contestants are judged for the best impersonation of memory loss by a panel of "experts", chaired by Gregg Wallace. Scandal when some experts are exposed as fakes.

But Hermann by then will be so rich that he will contemplate buying the whole of Clarendon Court with a view to knocking it down in an act of belated philanthropy.

But success brings no happiness. Of course, he should give up Clarendon Court and move somewhere less blighted, where the air conditioning, as described by an elderly Chinese woman in the lobby, does not smell of the stench of corruption. "Bad men build this building," she warned Hermann, wagging an admonishing finger, as though he were somehow responsible.

But the apartment proved unsellable and worse, unmarketable. However many times it was put on Rightmoves, the details failed to appear. Apparently it was the same with other Clarendon Court apts. By then there was a stampede to offload, yet it was as though they were living in a phantom building. Hamptons. Foxtons. Felicity J. Green. Hermann tried them all and they failed, throwing up their hands. "We just can't get it to upload. It may as well not exist."

The nice but aggressively dim young thing from Foxtons had even more of a problem. When Hermann showed the building to him—or was it a her?—s/he could not see it. Inside the same. In the lift the same. Even in the apartment s/he could see nothing. Yet Herman could see he-she reflected in the mirror while he-she said he-she couldn't see him-herself, which was when Hermann realised all of them there were the undead.

In the sleepless, small hours Hermann would riff on migraines, memory loss and the Atlas-Profilax treatment, which had left him in a neck brace. And whatever had happened to MBT shoes ("Our sole purpose")? The remedial trainer was so fashionable for a couple of years that if you looked under the table at any executive meeting at least four people were wearing them, some modified to be acceptable with suits. They were going to cure the world's collective back problem. Now you saw no one wearing them; ergo, did that mean treatment was successful?

Hermann dreams, briefly, that his best friend has had a hair transplant.

Hermann, furtive, learns by heart the whole following passage from the NAMBLA website.

Parallel to, and overlapping with, the early pederast movement in Germany were the Wandervogel and youth movements. The first Wandervogel group was founded in 1896, the year the first issue of Der Eigene appeared. By 1913, there were approximately 800 different Wandervogel groups, with more than 25,000 members. The Wandervogel (which literally means "migratory bird") was initially all-male, and organised youth into outdoor activities such as hiking and camping. It represented a reaction to the constraints of bourgeois society. The movement continued off and on until it was largely subsumed by the Hitler Youth.

It was not a gay movement, and its ideology was "lead and be led". The Wandervogel institutionalised homoerotic sentiment—though not necessarily sex between leaders and followers. This outlook contained an inherent ambiguity: it institutionalised something like the Greek mentor relationship on the one hand, but on the other contained an implicit militaristic potential. Today, most of us would find the combination of homoeroticism and leadership outlook less appealing than the free development of all forms of tenderness and true democracy.

Hermann and Mutti rehearsed Kate Moss's cabin rant.

"EasyJet!" says Mutti. "Attagirl! Hope for the world if Kate takes EasyJet."

Mutti reported that Kate was on a vodka swig after a five-day detox in a Turkish clinic, following Sadie Frost's fiftieth.

Fine prose from the *Daily Beast*, googled by Hermann in an idle moment.

There are few public figures who can claim the iconicity of Kate Moss, and fewer still who can claim the kind of ever-evolving badassery that made Moss an icon in the first place. She is an emblem of cool, her image an evergreen source of inspiration for youthful nonconformists since her debut at 15 in the world of high fashion. Photos of Moss (often with her most famous ex, Johnny Depp) that once ran in magazines now take up space on millions of Tumblr pages and Pinterest profiles—a badge of the nostalgia harboured by today's teens for the halcyon days of a '90s era they couldn't quite experience for themselves.

"Iconicity" and "halcyon" within the space of a few lines. Bravo! They should have a show the equivalent to *Strictly Come Dancing* for prose like this. Judges' praise for the twirlery of "ever-evolving badassery" but marks deducted for repeat of "icon", "emblem of cool", "evergreen source of inspiration", "badge of the nostalgia". End result disappointing. Tired moves. Minus google minus score. Plus five for "couldn't quite experience for themselves", but minus two for inclusion of "quite".

The Kate Moss Wandervogel Show. Not a huge stretch. Come on; second home in the country; Hunter wellingtons; goes to festivals (Glasto, which Hermann had always thought a laxative). Perhaps the divine Kate, the nearest the Brits had to Greek goddess, could be contracted to ramble and lecture on the joys/evils of pederasty, depending on country of franchise. Kate "takes a walk on the wild side". Kate: "This week, let's talk Greek, courtesy of the BBQ Parthenon show, where, just for today, I am special guest judge." (Minus marks for inclusion of "just for"; Hermann can't stop himself.)

The Dementia Show. The Disabled Room. Maybe even The Mental Channel. Meeting slotted with Sir Richard to discuss Virgin Homes for the Aged (Hermann permits himself a brief tennis-champ fist pump), with free access to the Beatles' entire back catalogue. Cool funerals. Hermann memos himself to patent Cool Funerals. Climax of which is a frail appearance by live ancient rock/folk act for rousing send-off. Donovan? Hermann contemplates his own demise. He thinks: rock stars turn out for rich people's private parties, so there is bound over time to be a "trickle-down effect". His own funeral would be the perfect time and place to indulge his very secret guilty pleasure for Neil Diamond. R. Palmer would be the natural last companion of choice, of course, except dead. (What was his funeral like? C of E vicar probably. Dommage. Fuck these desert boots, Hermann thought.) Mmm. What about the common/poor people's Cool Funerals? Taylor Wimpey Central London pall bearers for all dead deni-zens; motto: "We stiffed you from the start."

Hermann looked around the apartment. Not somewhere you would die by choice. Found dead in perhaps. He had seen Mutti's Kate Moss in the lift. Close but no cigar, as she was around a third of Kate's height and looked like those little people in David Lynch films, with rubbery faces and voices too deep for their size. Also this Kate was Oriental, probably Chinese. She said, "Hi, I'm Kate. I'm the new face of Clarendon Court."

Hermann asked himself what would be the number one choice in the Cool Funeral chart. Led Zeppelin, "Stairway to Heaven" would be a bit boring but predictable. Hermann's nightmare: that Mutti would outlive him somehow and, mischievous to the end, substitute Led Zep for the Rolf Harris (paroled for the day, or was he out already?) jokey cover version. Ooooh, and it makes make me wonder. It does, Rolf.

Tempus fugit.

Hermann has his moment of epiphany. A Cool Funeral in the style of Robert Palmer. The tribute band! Eureka! Google minus times one trillion. Negative invoice. Maybe Badass Funerals! (with exclamation point).

At 35,000 feet (fact check needed), crossing the Dutch coastline, Mutti lights up the Primus.

"Drop scones. Let's not get too ambitious first time out. It's a common mistake among contestants."

Hermann, almost beside himself at the thought of googling minus (or should that be google minusing?), stands and moves into the cabin aisle to recite aloud, "Parallel to, and overlapping with, the early pederast movement in Germany were the Wandervogel and youth movements."

Upon safely landing, the passengers treat them to a burst of spontaneous applause. Over the intercom, the captain congratulates H&M on their unorthodox entertainment, which has kept usually unruly passengers entranced for the duration. He makes a joke in poor taste about German Wings, which rather spoils the show. (Use of "rather" permissible under the circumstances, decide the judges: plus 3.)

Mutti: "Performance art and the pressurised cabin, what's not to like?"

On leaving the aircraft Hermann, handcuffed, pauses to clasp the hand of the doe-eyed cabin steward (Bulgarian) to repeat, "Today, most of us would find the combination of homoeroticism and leadership outlook less appealing than the free development of all forms of tenderness and true democracy."

It would Hermann thought make a lovely season's greeting for TWCL's forthcoming Christmas card, signed Love, TWLC — tender construction.

And not out of the question either, as Hermann had just bought TWCL's PR company. His mission would be to spike the chairman's Christmas drink at the office party, for him to say: "We no longer see ourselves as merely in the construction business, we now consider ourselves building love bombs." As demonstration of his intent, the chairman would announce that the name of their premier flagship building Clarendon Court would henceforward be known as Love Bomb (no "the").

Mutti's hash brownies went down very well and everyone went home happy, arms linked, led by Hermann singing, "I love to go a-wandering".

Cabin doors to manual, thought Hermann, wondering if it wasn't too late to bale out of his life. Debt, addiction, breakdown, sickness, pornography: the once fabulous realm of the Neu Landschaft, playful Gardens of Eden, had turned to the Great Negative AKA Clarendon Court AKA The Turd.

Hermann had eaten of the Apple, fruit of all knowledge, and watched it go pear-shaped. The iPhone twitch, the wired brain, the drunken weave of the texting walker. Hermann hated all TV presenters, including daughter Stephanie, who now fronted her own show after gaining a PhD in the history of TV hosting, with special reference to a "comedian" with the catchphrase "swinging!" (thumb up) and "dodgy" (thumb down); died following road accident. Herman was incapable of seeing beyond the cosmetic dentistry to what Stephanie's show was about, other than hallucinatory impressions of viral weather, rightist eugenics and rampant property development e.g. in TLC with TWCL emergency pet surgery took place in showcase apartments being flogged off on air. Lots of crocodile tears from Stephanie/paramedics/mug punters as apartments sold/failed to sell or even be given away and mutilated animals died/lived. *The Standard* was running one its hyper-energised campaigns, this time Let's Be Fair to Old Offenders. Following the big success of the Jimmy Savile Trafalgar Square Christmas tree, Stuart Hall had been rehabilitated in a shopping channel so far up the ladder to be in the broadcasting equivalent to above the tree line. *The Standard* was now pushing for Rolf to be brought in to co-host TLC with Stephanie. Hermann sighed. He loathed Mutti. He found Houellebecq sentimental. He disliked all previous mistresses, Mercedes, VW, Volvo, Nissan, Kia and the rest. Alfa, once covetable, was just another set of Eurowheels for spivvy housewives. Adieu Audi. Good to wake up in a good mood for a change.

The world lived in a state of re-decision, translated as indecision about any decision made. Matter discussed; decision reached; business sorted. Then the whole thing gone over again and another decision reached. Hermann blames email. Were the tedious *Sex in the City* Carrie Bradshaw still around she no doubt would be asking another of her pointless rhetorical questions: How do you tell when a maybe is maybe a no?

Free-floating anxiety relocates regardless. Hermann counted it among the new digital neuroses. Anxieties used to be specific, from what he could remember. "I am worried about,' he used to say to himself. Now he couldn't tell, other than being generally worried. He vaguely remembered brief periods of respite, years ago, when he didn't have a "care in the world', or maybe it was some programme he had seen on TV. Actually, one thing he was worried about: the bungee-jump fall of value to his apartment. For the first time in market history sellers were paying buyers to take property off their hands. Poor people could be seen outside Clarendon Court no longer begging but offering to take apartments in exchange for moderate living expenses, the trick being to do a runner as soon as the next service charge came up.

Hermann checked emails. One from Mrs Edwige Lyon of Lyon Interpol was under the heading Your Long Awaiting Compensation Fund Has Been Released.

"Good," thought Hermann. "A break at last."

He read: This is to inform you that we have been working towards the eradication of fraudsters and scam Artists in Africa and Europe with the help of the Organisation of African Unity (OAU) United Nations (UN), European Union (EU) and FBI. We have been able to track down some scam artist in various parts of African countries and Europe which includes (United kingdom, Nigeria, Republic of Benin, Burkina Faso, Ghana and Senegal with cote d'ivoire) the scam artists we tracked are all in Government custody right now, they will appear at International Criminal Court (ICC) soon for Justice. During the course of investigation, they were able to recovered some funds from these scam artists and IMF organization have ordered the funds recovered to be shared among the 70 Lucky people listed around the World as a compensation. This notice is been directed to you because your email address was found in one of the scam Artists' file and computer hard-disk on investigation, maybe you have been scammed, buying the property you have. You are therefore being compensated officially with sum of ($900,000.00) Nine hundred thousand US Dollars which is right now deposited with Allegacy Federal Credit Union North Carolina US and we have giving them instructions to credit you with the sum of ($900,000.00) Nine hundred thousand US Dollars as soon as you contact them, you are adviced to contact Allegacy Federal Credit Union Finacial Manager Sir Cosby Davis with the below contact information so that he will proceed on your transfer.

Oh, Mutti, Hermann sighed. What spelling! Get a copy editor! To her credit, last week, with even more wayward spelling and grammar, she had hacked the staff email addresses of TWCL (in protest against rising quarterly service charges hitting £10,000 and the closing of the cinema) and sent a barrage of "Help! I am stranded without money in Manila/Athens/Naples after an unfortunate incident and the police and the British embassy cannot help me, so you are my last hope!'

Mutti had been encouraged by the response, enough to cover half the service bill.

"They may be horrible builders but they're cute little suckers for a friend in need!"

Hermann asked in disbelief, "A Sir Cosby Davis in North Carolina? Really?"

Mutti hung her head.

"In fact," Hermann went on, "There is only one Sir Cosby in the entire universe of google, a twitter account of a college athlete in St. Louis, MO."

"Maybe I was thinking of him," Mutti mumbled.

Mutti was giving the apartment yet another makeover, this time in the style of Munich in the 1930s, turning it into a replica of the Führer's love-nest shrine to his dead niece Geli. After she "shot" herself, he kept her room "just as it was". Mutti was adamant Geli had been driven to it by her horror of Uncle Alf's insistence on a golden shower and a hot lunch. Hermann was sceptical. He was very much of the no-sex-Adolf school.

"No!" said Mutti. "There's proof in the book I am reading. After Geli, he had a sado-masochistic relationship with an actress, who later also killed herself, who tells of a private tour of the chancellery after a party, including his dressing room. Look, see what it says."

Hermann took the book and read aloud, "'He brought out his tail-coated dinner shit [sic], saying he had never worn evening dress till he came to power.' It's a typo, Mutti."

"No. Proof! And how's your little baby-making machine? Seeing action?"

Hermann thought: Oedipus had it easy.

Hermann wished he had invested in traffic cones and road signage, what his curator friends called "traffic culture". He still struggled to "get" Facebook and the Insta- one. Cute kitten. Nice dog. Hermann posts: Me and my Bunny, and is depressed by only six likes. He looked forward to the internet's first great evangelical movement: viral religion. He would follow, gladly. He would karaoke Errol Brown and Hot Chocolate's "You Sexy Thing (I Believe in Miracles)" and form a sub-cult of his own, catchphrase: "Yes, I believe". Had he become the old-fashioned reactionary he despised his father for being? Had he become his father? He needed a rush. The rush. The synaptic snap. He would take up parachuting bungee jumping free solo climbing self-surgery. He would cut off his arm with a penknife, leaving the other free to let go when the moment came.

Hermann gazed out of the window of Clarendon Court and admired the pollution-hazed cityscape, daydreaming through another set of residents' meetings. Four members, plus translators for each, yet seven languages around the table. So many flats were up for sale by absentee owners unwilling to pay the service charge, which was reaching Weimar Republic proportions in terms of inflation, that it was voted to request TWLC feature Clarendon Court in its TLC programme. Hermann stuck up a thumb and said "Swinging!"

Mutti had now taken over the apartment completely, leaving Hermann on lastminute.com and staying in an identical maze of hotels. In one he ordered ennui for dinner and the waiter hadn't blinked. Hermann could no longer remember what his job was and what he actually did, other than indulge in bouts of aggressive recreational pimping in the company of oversexed top property men. Thanks to recent trips, Hermann was becoming a connoisseur of art in hotel rooms. He was thinking of giving up his executive positions, whatever they were, to take up buying such art for new hotels and apartment lobbies and corridors. Future generations would hold him as the true curator, and the likes of Obrist mere jesters.

He heard Mutti say, "Some things you should not even think, let alone google." Already an unbeliever, he refused to give google or god its capital. Would there come a time when people would deny google existed the way they denied god?

"No, no, you mean blood spatter," says Mutti. They were re-enacting Geli's suicide, so-called, shot in the chest, from above. Mutti recited: "Uncle Alf in the bedroom with the Mauser. And you don't mean back-splatter!" Hermann was sure he did. They were always talking about it on *CSI*. And in Phil Spector's case there hadn't been any on his white tux.

Regardless of the sieve that passed for her memory, Mutti recited word perfect, "Back-splatter is the high-velocity pattern made by liquid faecal matter on the back of the toilet above the waterline. This pattern is formed when one has an uncontrolled evacuation of the bowels as he or she is in the process of sitting down and is still in a leaning-forward position. Because the movement associated with this phenomenon is usually time-consuming, the resulting back-splatter typically dries and will not come off when the toilet is flushed. Back-splatter usually lasts until physically removed with a brush and Comet."

Hermann sighed and memo'd himself to google R.L. Stevenson, Paul Gauguin, the Great White Whale.

Stephanie experienced strange and troubled dreams about an erotic encounter with a one-armed solo yachtsman. Heavy swell, Nor'Westerlies, the tilting horizon, something sticky in the hand and spume. During the grounded day her mind was invaded by even more bizarre and disturbing images, to the point where she sometimes experienced seconds of autocue freeze during recordings of TLC with TWCL (the pets'n'property show).

It was widely rumoured that a clandestine serial killer known as the Bomber—because of his habit of dropping a large object on his victims' heads, after having his horrible way with them—was at large and his killing rampage went unreported by the media for the simple reason that newspaper sales actually went up when it was known that news was being withheld. The internet was awash with vigilante reporters, paid in minus euros, tracking the murders, which were reaching Mexican proportions, leaving Mutti fearful of what she called the Mexican/Muslim cartel. She berated everyone, saying, "I can't remember your name or why we are speaking but it is terribly important that you understand the HBO conspiracy that promoted *Breaking Bad* as a drama, when it was a documentary, and Walter White is now living in London with some Mexican bitch and they are plotting to corrupt our youth with their filth."

More to the point, if proof were needed it came when Mutti saw *Breaking Bad*'s Walter White in the lobby of Clarendon Court. Hermann tried to point out it was the actor who had played Walter White now appearing in a play in London's glamorous West End, but Mutti would have none of it: "It's Walter pretending to be the actor. Walter took over years ago.'

Mutti was Stephanie's grandmother. Stephanie thought Mutti mad but clued up. She had a secret map showing the Bomber's murder trail, all in London and according to esoteric symbolism if the dots on the map were joined up correctly. Fifty-three according to some reports, 66 according to others, going as high as 116 in some of the most tenacious accounts. Victims all female, between 16-35, often marginal drifters, but not always. The Bomber had been known to break into affluent homes and luxury tower blocks. And not a single news report.

The point was Stephanie had come to believe not that she was going to be the next victim but she was in fact the Bomber. She travelled for work. Her expenses sheets confirmed that she had been to all the locations on the killing map. It didn't make sense in terms of gender, identity, background, knowledge, etcetera, but Stephanie could not shake loose her conviction that she was a transformer, like in American comics, and her terrible fate involved becoming a man for the length of time it took to carry out the imperative work that would reveal the Greater Awakening. She had been chosen.

She also suspected that Hermann and her mother, who seemed the most improbable married couple in the world, were not her parents, had in fact murdered her real parents, and kidnapped her, an only daughter, in order to train her through auto-suggestion for her mission as the Bomber. This was all highly unlikely, she knew, but she could not rid herself of the notion that her two identities were about to merge and she would wake up in her father's Clarendon Court apartment as an hermaphrodite, screaming at the blood dripping from her hands and with no idea of how she had got there or the body parts had found their way into the freezer or where the churning whoo! whoo! whoo! music was coming from.

And there was no one with whom Stephanie felt she could share this terrible secret, unless she departed from the autocue and tell the world (well, those that watched TLC with TWCL in the UK anyway) of her awful fear.

Once a fortnight the show went out live on the Love Bunny days, a mobile animal hospital in which people brought in pets usually too damaged to save to discuss with experts what form of radical surgery could be applied. Viewers donated money and the animal with the most cash got the prize of that week's cosmetic operation. "A dog that was once three-legged now whole and four-legged again!' Tears were frequently shed. There was a scandal brewing about unreturned donations. Stephanie decided she would share her secret with the nation, but how far and how much? Would she utter the dreaded words, "I am the Bomber.' Her parents—her "fake" parents—didn't watch the show of course and Stephanie rather relished the prospect of them being informed second-hand by social media. They would say she had cracked up, pressure of work. But Stephanie had never felt more sane... seven more days until the next live show. Her heart contracted into a tiny ball when she saw where it was to be recorded—Clarendon Court.

◆ ◆ ◆

Mutti's birthday; what to give? Hermann, in a lather of indecision, decided on two presents. A mutt for Mutti, the yappiest, most irritating little lapdog he could find, a minuscule longhaired monster that shed hair so fast it was bald after a week; named Mutt or should that be Jeff? Indecision as Hermann decides to name it Ted 2 after the greatest movie ever made. More indecision; maybe Zoolander, after the second greatest movie ever made, George Double-yah's favourite of all time, plus cameos from crypto-fascists Trump and Bowie; well, not so crypto in Dave's case. One of the highlights of Hermann's life was London's Victoria Station 1976 as a humble commuter witnessing the Thin White Duke's snapping off the old Sieg Heil salute, the frisson spoiled only by David telling Hermann later, "I waved, I just waved, believe me. On the life of my child, I waved. And the bastard caught me in the wave, man." They commiserated about David being detained at an Eastern European border for transporting Nazi memorabilia. Hermann was trying to sell David a fake of the gun Hitler's niece had shot herself with. "Allegedly..." said David with a cheesy grin, and told Hermann his interest in the Third Reich was the fact that they came to England before the war to find the Holy Grail at Glastonbury. The significance of the site was not lost on Hermann: David's Glasto Rally performance in 2000 put all of Adolf's greatest hits into the shade. David would have liked Clarendon Court, Hermann thought. Too late. So many of the brave and mighty cut down before their time. Sixty-nine was the new 27.

Mutti was a huge fan of the Hitler *Downfall* parodies, especially the one where Adolf mourns David's death. Hitler and the Burning Man Festival; Hitler hears of England leaving the EU; Hitler on Mastermind; Hitler phones an Indian call centre; and Mutti's absolute favourite, Hitler's Fart Contest. Hermann, being German, found them not funny because what was actually being said never conformed to whatever silly English subtitles were put at the bottom of the picture. He thought the sequences needed to be dubbed for the joke to work. Mutti told him he had no sense of fun. "How can you not laugh at Adolf's reaction to Alan Rickman being no longer with us to deliver Bowie's funeral oration and Adolf saying, "Spacey couldn't hold a candle to Rickman as an actor and he knows it. Rickman never had to try, he was just magnificent. I cried when he died at the end of *Die Hard*. He was the real hero of that film. I modelled my political career on his *Sheriff of Nottingham*."

Spacey was rumoured to be in the building, part of which had been converted into a high-class enclave for serial offenders. See Harvey in the lobby in his chef's hat, dishing out dim sum in the pop-up canteen that seemed to have become a permanent soup kitchen. "I'm not being paid," said a chastened Harvey. "The guilt is overwhelming." Harvey was rumoured to avail himself of the in-house escort agency for corrective treatment; in fact Mutti badmouthing.

Second Mutti birthday present. Hermann decides on his bespoke *Downfall* spoof: Hitler hears that TWCL have demolished Bernard Morgan House, to make way for Clarendon

Court; and good riddance, thinks Hermann. He thought it funny Adolf ranting on about flattening a building put up to replace the destruction wrought by his miracle rocket bombs. In Hermann's beloved script, laboured over for days, Adolf was able to bang on about people's housing and the grand municipal vision and town planning, all subjects dear to the Führer's heart. High on the list of Reich enemies: property speculators; allowing Adolf a towering denunciation of TWCL as a conspiracy of queers and Freemasons, to be swept aside for the entire City to be redeveloped using Speer's unfulfilled vision of the new Berlin: vistas, boulevards, people and tank space. The City planning department infiltrated with fifth columnists intent on a building revolution, slogan: Giving the City back to its Volk.

Mutti couldn't hide her disappointment: "You sound quite pro-Adolf when you're supposed to be for the rampant capitalists. Are we having a Road-to-Damascus moment?"

Hermann thought: if I had to choose between Adolf and TWCL? Hugo Boss uniforms, the stiff salutes! Cool technology.

◆ ◆ ◆

Meanwhile, post-Brexit and following the evacuation of the Chinese, Clarendon Court had taken on a new lease of life. With most of the building empty it was rented out to TV shows, including *Naked Attraction,* which Mutti persuaded Hermann to enter ("Such a pity, dear, voted out first") and the new budget edition of *I'm a Celebrity, Get Me Out of Here,* which could no longer afford the Australian fares. Hermann could never remember which of Ant or Dec had gone on the wobble and fallen into disgrace, a confusion made not easier because the two lovable scamps, in an act of showbiz solidarity, seemed to have undergone radical plastic surgery rendering them even tinier and quite unrecognisable. Hermann remembered Roy Keane, one of football's great leg breakers turned pundit, murmuring in a half-time commentary about a controversial moment with the air of one who knows: "That wasn't a head butt, not really." The same applied to *I'm a Ce-*

lebrity: none of them were, celebrities, not really. The show included an added audience bonus of a cash-o-meter which went up every minute the celeb remained unrecognised. After four shows the meter was through the roof with the public incapable of identifying any of them.

"Una Stubbs!" screamed Mutti at the screen showing a contestant abseiling past the very window of their apartment.

Time for a hot lunch, thought Hermann. "It can't be," he said. "She has already been on."

Various lesser members of the Boris Johnson tribe, all identical, went unrecognised even though they may as well have had their names emblazoned across their chests. Mutti poohpoohed, saying it was like Alec Guinness in *Kind Hearts and Coronets* and they were all the same actor who had played Freddy Krueger.

Hermann's mind drifted and he announced: "Spare a thought for Glenn Hoddle. Our prayers are with him and his family." Heart attack on his birthday in the BT Sport studio. Hermann could see how it must have all been too much for the legend and his cultured left foot with his deep understanding of the game and "them diagonals" to be reduced to BT Sport. Memo: check name of Glenn's faith healer. Had he and the family availed themselves of her? Hermann never really saw the point of Hoddle when you could have Gerd "Bomber" Müller.

Hermann recited verbatim, quoting Wikipedia, Ecclesiastes 12:13 "Fear the Bomber, and keep his commandments; for that is the whole duty of everyone." He proclaimed to Mutti: "The Bomber is a German retired footballer. A prolific striker renowned for his clinical finishing, especially in and around the six-yard box, he is regarded as one of the greatest goal scorers of all time."

Mutti replied, "No, the Bomber is a serial killer and your daughter Stephanie is currently in custody awaiting trial for the murders, after confessing to them on live TV."

Hermann ignored Mutti. Such a Debbie Downer. Stephanie had also confessed to being the Uber killer in exchange for a TV show trial that would earn her more in a month than she would get in five years from her animal eugenics show.

Hermann suspected that he was wrestling with great metaphysical questions without identifying what they were. He was the Heidegger and Hegel of Clarendon Court rolled into one. His lecture *I Google Therefore I Am* had been a sell out. In the Q&A Kevin and Harvey had asked questions: both incomprehensible, rambling on, penitent, with Hermann thinking, that's not a question, not really, not without an eroteme. Harvey protested that he wasn't guilty of eroteme. They were in the downstairs cinema, long since fallen into neglect; last screening *Pollyanna Goes Beijing* (starring Hayley Mills, Sir Cliff Richard and Melvyn Hayes), a massive flop for Ken Loach and the BFI, which had taken up residence in the Winter Palace in St. Petersburg. Hermann's Chinese film-critic friend pointed out that the film was a foregone failure as no movie with three consecutive titles in a title had ever made money. Hermann ignored Kevin's non-question and told his Noel Coward joke about how the great man upon passing through Leicester Square and seeing the cinema awning advertising *The Sea Shall Not Have Them*, starring Michael Redgrave and Dirk Bogarde, remarked: "I don't see why not when everyone else has." Boom! Boom! Kevin cracked up. Hermann asked Harvey if he thought it was possible to reopen the cinema with a programme of Adolf's favourite films. *King Kong! Mickey Mouse!* Laurel and Hardy's *Swiss Miss!* Hermann makes a mental note: the great Laurel and Hardy remake starring Harvey and Kevin as the lovable duo, in a stunning act of rehabilitation. Harvey was gung-ho about reviving the cinema. Harvey would introduce the season himself. "Can I wear the uniform?" he asked.

Germaine Greer came and gave a lecture on Slade which was a big hit. Mutti spotted Noddy Holder sitting incognito in the audience and announced herself as one of his biggest fans. Of "Mama Weer All Crazee Now", she asked, "Noddy, why did you spell 'all' and 'now' correctly?"

Noddy, recognising a serious student of his work, indulged her, agreeing on "awl" for "all" but they couldn't come up with an agreed misspell for "now".

"It's a Black Country thing," explained Noddy and Mutti said he must have made a lot of money out of Nobby's Nuts.

She told him how a friend of her son had dreamed that Glenn Hoddle and Chris Waddle were reforming to record another immortal follow-up classic to their "Diamond Lights". Noddy said, "Oi cann ardley weight."

Mutti said, "I think you are getting the hang of it. Why did Elizabeth Arden?"

"Because Max Factor," came back Noddy quick as a flash.

Mutti sighed. "Noddy, if only I were five years younger."

A pleasing addition to Clarendon Court was a full-scale facsimile of a V-2 rocket on the roof, simulating the moment of impact as it smashes into the building, commissioned by TWCL who put it to competition, won by local artist Gavin Turk. A small reception was held in Fortune Park. Hermann's idea of awarding Iron Crosses to the winner and runners up was sadly vetoed.

But all this was frippery compared to what Hermann suspected was really going on. Something big. He suspected the memory bank was on the sputter. When he googled Whatever Happened to the Guy Who Played Freddy Krueger? he got nothing. Nada. Zilch. Not even a reference to the films. Zero on Wes Craven too. Could it be, as Carrie Bradshaw might put it, that after years of the internet being clogged up with complete crap whole chunks of it are starting to go missing? The *Daily Express*, always a leader when it comes to climate change, ran a trenchant editorial arguing that melting ice caps were nothing compared to the erosion of whole continents of the internet. Facebook accounts had casualty rates that made the Battle of the Somme (no google reference) look like child's play. Google Premier League. Nothing. No fixtures. No results. No table. Even Roy Keane is lost for words. With satnav down no one can find their way to the stadia. Roy blames the offside rules. "I think we'd be better off thinking of it as a game with no goals and no goalposts, something more conceptual for the pundits to get their teeth into." Roy's verdict: "Google has to get more streetwise. They got off to a great start, points on the board, but they're starting to look like a bunch of Nancy boys. The feller that started it would have done himself a lot better had he called it The Facebook, then you know where you are."

Roy, true stalwart and son of Eire, sports a tee-shirt: I was Je suis Charlie; now I am Down on the Deni-zen. (Complete with semi-colon.)

As so often it was Clarkson that provided the answer. Jeremy became a feature of Clarendon Court's lobby lunches. At first Hermann thought Clarko must have fallen on hard times but Jeremy always had been a bit of a scruff and was there to host another anniversary edition of *Who Wants to be a Millionaire?* Yes, please, thought Hermann, who was bankrupt again. Hermann had known Jeremy on and off for years. They bantered about Jeremy's choice of John Lennon as the greatest man who ever lived. "Ringo surely," ventured Hermann. Clarko said Hermann had been a whisker away from being chosen to be a Star in a Reasonably Priced Car back in the glory days of *Top Gear*, scotched by the producer pointing out that even by the programme's elastic definition of stardom Hermann failed to qualify. But as a consolation Jeremy could offer him a contestant slot on the upcoming *Who Wants to be a Millionaire?* Hermann thought: Headlights. Frozen Rabbit. "I would be honoured."

The show was recorded in the Strauss-Kahn penthouse suite. Mutti said it's a straightforward process of common sense and elimination. She was sulking because she hadn't been asked. Hermann thought 64,000 easy. The show got off to a bad start with the pre-selection of contestants. Assemble in the right order in the quickest time, except no one could. Ten goes later still no one came up with a correct order after hours of trying. In the end they had to resort to paper, scissors and rock. At last a contestant. The first questions were always silly and comically patronising, just to let the punter get a feel. Hermann sensed something was badly wrong when three contestants fell at the first hurdle, contestants four and five at the second. Number six split 50/50 on question one, phoned a friend, asked the host and still got it wrong. And so on until it was Hermann's turn after winning the preliminaries on a split-second decision to go scissors rather than rock.

First question. "Abba. Final answer, Chris." Only because Mutti in the audience held up large cards with the answers did Hermann get through the next four questions. It was blatant. Mutti was clearly out to humiliate. Hermann was not a cheat. He told Jeremy. Jeremy and the producer conferred. It was decided to go ahead. The show was in tatters as it was and Hermann realised: no one can remember anything anymore, making the whole concept redundant. Next question: answer between Hitler, Goebbels, Himmler and Charlie Chan. Hermann shut his eyes to avoid seeing Mutti holding up the answer. I am an honest man, he told himself.

"Phone a friend?" prompted Jeremy.

"I have no friends," said Hermann.

"Ask the host?" prompted Jeremy.

"I wouldn't ask you if you were the last man on earth. You know nothing." Spontaneous, foot-stomping applause.

"Ask the audience?"

"Fuck the audience, Jeremy." Whoops and cheers of approval. Fifty-fifty leaves Himmler and Charlie Chan.

"Lord Sugar. Final answer, Chris."

The answer was sublime self-sabotage, of course. Hermann knew there were no more contestants after him and from the studio clock could see there was still five minutes of airtime. He announced, "The correct answer is of course Himmler."

"Is the wrong answer," said Jeremy. Hermann insisted on being heard. "This is a people's show," he announced to the audience and he had an important message. Their memories had all been google-snatched, google-fucked, google-napped, in fact had ceased to exist and replaced by looking everything up. Memory had become the equivalent to useless belly flab. "And which came first you might ask, the XXXL people or the giant supermarkets." Clarko tried to move to a commercial break but the producer overruled. Hermann, although he seemed to be performing with the charisma of a fifth-rate politician discussing post-Brexit customs borders (Hermann's solution, just give Northern Ireland to the Republic as a Brexit giveaway offer; maybe Wales as well in a two-for-one), sensed from the audience's spellbound reaction that they were witnessing television history, until Mutti started heckling.

"This is rubbish. I know Noddy Holder is the lead singer of Led Zep without looking it up."

"Get Noddy!" the audience began to chant. The producer started making winding-up motions. Clarko had gone off for a comfort break. Hermann seized his opportunity and took charge of the host's chair and announced that he was founding a new religion Googlemegod, all donations gratefully received.

"I thought that went very well," Hermann to Clarko at the wrap party.

◆　◆　◆

A man came from TWCL to address residents, telling them, "We need to show that we are a compassionate dictatorship but also dark and dangerous," so it was only a matter of time before the SS took over the building and TWCL rebranded itself Taylor Wimpey Third Reich. "Yet another fucking makeover," moaned Mutti. "And so yesterday." She wanted Clarendon Court to be called Trump Tower and had written to the Don who tweeted: "Mutti, you're tops. I'm looking into it." Mutti tweeted back to say he could remodel the existing park into a pitch and putt. The Don: "Attagirl! Let's play the inaugural round together!" Mutti starts practising her swing.

The few remaining residents were told that the new black-uniformed guard were only actors, to give the right image, and the ID cards they had to show on admission and exit part of a performance-art installation, and the stick-thin stiffs sitting in the lobby in various states of wistful contemplation copyright of Dr. Gunther von Hagens' Institute for Plastination. Rumours of apartments being turned into dormitories were denied. The dim sum kitchen was gone, replaced by a super-smart Hugo Boss concession selling SS uniforms with an introductory discount for residents. Even Mutti was impressed by Hermann's new look. "They should give you a little concentration camp to run. Listen, I am planning something big, what do you think?"

"Genius," said Hermann afterwards. The whole bunker Götterdämmerung recreated in Clarendon Court. The last days. Adolf's birthday.

"We'll have a separate party for that. Adolf's wedding, another party for that. And the endless orgies. Just think! A role for Kevin. He's champing at the bit. Perhaps a part for Harvey too. I'll ask Noddy to play the wedding reception, why not? Michael Douglas and Catherine Zeta-Jones got that Welsh belter at theirs."

"Tom Jones?" asked Hermann, thinking it unlikely.

"No, Bonnie Tyler. Enterprising lass. She did a special cruise ship tour during a total eclipse allowing her to reprise her greatest hit." Sadly neither Mutti nor Hermann could remember its name—"C'mon, it's on the tip of my tongue. Jim Steinman. Meat Loaf." Google was no help, with all reference to Bonnie wiped. Hermann's internet servers had collapsed completely apart from telling him why eating bananas was bad for you and warning him to never give a dog peanuts, leaving him thinking he should at least try out a pack of Nobby's on Ted 2. All his best porno sites were gone, leaving only one bucolic sample of a fabulously buxom and game young woman being serviced by a donkey, photographed with such interminable and unblinking black and white camerawork that it could have been shot by Jean-Marie Straub. Hermann exhibited some of his old flair persuading Tate Modern it was in fact a fragment of a lost masterpiece by the old maestro and was in discussion regarding purchasing rights. With so many servers down, little could be done to check, apart from the Tate Modern archive, which had Jean-Marie listed as bass player for the Strawbs and co-writer of "Part of the Union".

"Bags I Eva Braun!" said Mutti.

"Bags I Adolf," said Kevin.

"No, Kevin, the world is not ready for your Adolf," Mutti admonished. "You can play Dr. Goebbels, his wife and all six of their children."

"Bags I Göring," said Harvey, getting into the swing.

"Close, Harvey, but no cigar," said Mutti. "Göring wasn't in the bunker.'

Harvey crestfallen.

Kevin made a poor fist of Dr. Goebbels, Hermann thought, merely offering a reprise of his Richard III. Harvey had his way, saying he would play Göring as though he were in the bunker. Invites went out. Noddy was a reluctant unavailable (tonsils). Bryan Ferry a maybe. Mutti in the end hired a mariachi band from Guildford, pointing out that the bunker was pretty Mexican by the end. Guests of honour: Max Mosley and Dominique Strauss-Kahn. Fulsome apologies for non-attendance from Joanna Lumley, Stephen Fry and J.K. Rowling. Otherwise a terrific turnout of E and F listed celebs. "The bunker is heaving!" announced Mutti, resplendent as Eva Braun. She had insisted Hermann play Adolf. "It means we will have to be married, my little Oedipus!' Hermann gave a speech at the birthday party, asking for a minute's silence in memory of Max Clifford. You could have heard a pin drop. The wedding party was a more select affair. Hermann was getting annoyed with Mutti telling him off saying it was Adolf's left arm that shook uncontrollably, not his right, and to drag his leg more.

"I am not fucking Quasimodo," Hermann snapped, the pressure getting to him.

Mutti said, "You realise we will have to poison the dog. They tested the cyanide capsules out on Adolf's." Hermann protested. He had grown quite fond of Ted 2. "On the mouth and with tongue," insisted Mutti after the wedding ceremony when Hermann gave her a chaste peck on the cheek upon being told to kiss the bride. They argued over whether the marriage had been consummated. "Fuck," said Mutti, turning on Harvey. "Enough of your Göring. You're the Brown Eminence Martin Bormann from now on.' Harvey looked pleased, saying Bormann had got away. "No, he didn't," hissed Mutti. Paper streamers hung forlorn from the ceiling. Someone let off a rocket.

Kevin started swishing around Harvey, going "Oooh, you Brown Eminence!"

"This is serious," shouted Mutti, asking Kevin, "Have you poisoned the kids yet?" Kevin put on a splendid show miming all six deaths, pulled himself together and gave a faultless performance of Goebbels' Total War Sportpalast speech, in German, which went on and on. Dissatisfied with the level of applause, he made them do it again and again until it was stormy enough for his liking. Hermann thought perhaps he should end it all and just go off and shoot himself. The moment came: Adolf and Eva on the sofa. Two cyanide pills and the gun. Ted 2 had been reprieved in what Mutti called a gesture towards humanity. The Russian barrage seemed to be getting closer but it was only Taylor Wimpey Third Reich demolishing yet another block.

"There are no happy endings," thought Hermann, except for Stephanie, who had signed a contract with Channel 5 to host a full recreation of the Nuremberg Trials. Hermann looked at Mutti, who had never appeared more beautiful. "Shall we do it?" he asked. Mutti looked coy. "After one more look at the Hitler Fart Contest. I want to go out on a high." But all communications in the building were down.

Harvey said, "The barbarians are at the gates."

Mutti retorted, "Looking at you, fatso, they're in the building already." She said she'd had enough. "Fuck the suicide pact. Eva had smarts. Eva was on the last Lufthansa flight to Madrid out of Berlin." And with that Mutti was gone: German Wings from City Airport. Hermann went out with Ted 2 into the blitzed landscape and watched another tower block implode courtesy of TWTR. The dog did its business and Hermann looked at the darkening sky, wondering if the plane passing overhead was Mutti.

The next day everything was gone. No more Third Reich. Hugo Boss moved out. The dim sum kitchen was back and Hermann wondered whether he was in one of those stupid stories where everything turned out to be a dream. There was a good crowd of diners in. Kevin was reprising his role as Bobby Darin, singing Bob's swinging version of "Mack the Knife" to entertain the waiting line. He winked at Hermann and said, "A shame Mutti isn't here, she would make a terrific Lotte Lenya."

"Rosa Klebb, more like," riposted Hermann and Kevin cracked up, not missing a beat, finger popping as he sang.

"I said Jenny Diver, whoa, Sukey Tawdry, Look out to Miss Lotte Lenya and old Lucy Brown, Yes, that line forms on the right, babe, Now that Spacey's back in town, Look out, old Spacey's back."

Storming Sportpalast applause. Hermann looked round and thought: "Brand new day. Good to wake up in a good mood for a change."

Harvey in his chef's hat was dishing up food. "Bonjour, Herman. What a beautiful Taylor Wimpey morning it is when you can feel truly forgiven. Chow time. We got dog on the menu."

IN GHOSTLY LONDON— FRAGMENT

STEVE FINBOW

*Think not that buildings appear to the
dreamer only at night: the buildings
of this world of ghosts appear
to us even by day.*
JAPANESE POEM

A nd it was at the hour of sunset that he came to the foot of the building at 43 Golden Lane. There was in that place no sign of light, neither token of sunshine, nor trace of moon, nor shadow of flying pigeon, nor scribble of crow, nothing but desolation rising to desolation. And the ninth-floor penthouse was enwrapped in a swirling thick mist.

Then the TaylorWimpey said to the young man, "What you have asked to see will be shown to you. The place of The Denizen AKA Clarendon Court is near and the way is rich. Follow after me and do not fear: strength will be given you. But not money. Come, we will use the electronically controlled access to the building entrance doors."

*We build within ourselves stone
On stone a vast haunted castle.*
VINCENT MONTEIRO

Twilight gloomed about them as they passed through the video door-entry system, ignored the 24-hour concierge and ascended the marble staircase. There was an easy path through the communal spaces but no mark of working-class human visitation; and the way was past endless heapings of materials and finishes, light, colour, texture and tone blending harmoniously with fragments of engineered hardwood that gave and sprang beneath the foot. Sometimes a mass of wealth dislodged and clattered down with hollow echoings; golden coins, plastic banknotes, credit cards; sometimes the substance trodden would burst like an empty shell spilling rhodium and platinum ingots. Above the landscaped courtyard and pocket park, stars twinkled and blinked out and the darkness deepened.

"Do not fear now, son," said the TaylorWimpey, smirking smugly, "danger there is none, though the future be grim."

> *We can never truly pin down where*
> *our place of dwelling lies; each newly*
> *discovered overview of what we call*
> *home effectively places it within a new*
> *topography, forcing us to redefine*
> *what it is we mean when we say,*
> *"I live there".*
> NICK PAPADIMITRIOU

Under the fritzing stars they climbed, fast, fast, mounting sometimes by help of state-of-the-art elevators. High zones of mist they passed; and they saw below them, ever widening as they climbed, a soundless flood of homeless people, like the tide of a dying sea.

Hour after hour they climbed and forms invisible yielded to their tread in the private residents' lounge with dull soft crushing and below them faint cold fires lighted and died at every breaking. And once the young man laid a hand on something smooth that was not marble and lifted it and dimly saw the cheerless map of the area's future death.

> *The contrast between Classical building*
> *organism and Gothic building system*
> *becomes the contrast between a living,*
> *breathing body and a skeleton.*
> WILHELM WORRINGER

"Linger not thus, my son!" urged the voice of the Taylor-Wimpey, "the ninth-floor penthouse that we must gain is very far away!"

On through the marble hallways they climbed and felt continually beneath them the soft strange breakings of hearts and minds and saw the barrel fires and braziers beneath worm and die until the rim of the night turned grey and the stars began to fail again and the East began to darkly bloom.

> *Space that has been seized upon by the*
> *imagination cannot remain indifferent*
> *space subject to the measures and*
> *estimates of the surveyor. It has been*
> *lived in, not in its positivity, but with*
> *all the partiality of the imagination.*
> GASTON BACHELARD

Yet still they climbed, fast, fast, mounting sometimes by help of state-of-the-art elevators. Below them now was the frigidness of death and a silence tremendous. Through an open veneered interior door and floor-to-ceiling windows, the young man caught sight of a strange Gherkin kindled in the East.

Then first to the young man's gaze the steps revealed their nakedness and despite the underfloor heating a trembling seized him and a ghastly fear as he held onto the handrail of the glass balustrade. For there was not any ground neither beneath him nor about him nor above him but a heaping of engineered hardwood only, monstrous and measureless and embedded in that engineered hardwood skulls and fragments of skulls and dust of bone of what appeared to be all those that had ever lived on the site and he saw a shimmer of shed teeth like high-quality porcelain strewn through the drift of it like the shimmer of scrags of shell in the wrack of the Thames' tide.

...the unlimited solitude that makes
a lifetime of each day, toward a
communion with the universe, in a
word, space, the invisible space that man
can live in nevertheless, and
which surrounds him with
countless presences.
RAINER MARIA RILKE

"Do not fear, my son!" cried the voice of the TaylorWimpey, "only the strong of funds can win a place in Clarendon Court! Only the well-heeled can afford this refined haven, only the prosperous own the right to be uplifted and calmed."

Behind them Golden Lane had vanished. Nothing remained but the homeless beneath and the grey sky above and the heaping of skulls between and the ninth-floor penthouse upslanting, out of sight, out of reach.

This house, which seemed somehow to
have formed itself, flying together into
its own powerful pattern under the
hands of its builders, fitting itself into
its own construction of lines
and angles, reared its great head
back against the sky without
concession to humanity.
SHIRLEY JACKSON

Then the moon climbed with the climbers and there was no warmth in the light of the cinema room and coldness sharp as a sword in the games room. And the horror of stupendous height and the nightmare of stupendous wealth and the terror of silence ever grew and grew and weighed upon the young man and held his mind so that suddenly all power departed from him and he moaned like a sleeper in dreams.

"Hasten, hasten, my son!" cried the TaylorWimpey, "the day is brief and the summit is very far away." But the young man shrieked, "I fear! I fear unspeakably and all power has departed from me!" "The power will return, my son," made answer the TaylorWimpey. "Look now below you and above you and about you and tell me what you see."

> *Spectrality does not involve the*
> *conviction that ghosts exist or that the*
> *past (and maybe even the future they*
> *offer to prophesy) is still very much alive*
> *and at work, within the living present:*
> *all it says, if it can be thought to speak,*
> *is that the living present is scarcely as*
> *self-sufficient as it claims to be; that*
> *we would do well not to count on its*
> *density and solidity, which*
> *might under exceptional*
> *circumstances betray us.*
> FREDRIC JAMESON

"I cannot," cried the young man, trembling and clinging, "I dare not look beneath! I dare not look at the shrubs of the sunken gardens or the darkened trees of Fortune Street Park. Before me and about me there is nothing but human skulls." "And yet, my son," said the TaylorWimpey, laughing smugly, "and yet you do not know of what this building is made?" The young man, shuddering, repeated, "I fear! Unutterably, I fear there is nothing but human skulls."

"A building of skulls it is," responded the TaylorWimpey. "But know, my son, that all of them ARE YOUR OWN! Each has at some time been the nest of your dreams of mortgages, your delusions of wealth and your desires for an affordable home. Not every one of them is the skull of any other being. All, all without exception, have been yours, in the billions of your former lives."

CLARENDON COURT FROM LUXURY APARTMENT BLOCK TO MADHOUSE

EDITH JONES

Zhang Chunqiao, pacing the length of his Clarendon Court apartment, paused to compare the time on his phone to a clock on a shelf.

Three minutes to eight.

In exactly three minutes Mr. Yao Wenyuan, of the eminent legal firm of Yao and Lee, would have his punctual hand on the doorbell of the Taylor Wimpey flat in Golden Lane. It was a comfort to reflect that Yao was so punctual — the suspense was beginning to make his host nervous. And the sound of the doorbell would be the beginning of the end — after that there'd be no going back, by Chairman Mao — no going back!

Zhang resumed his pacing. Each time he reached the end of the room, opposite the door he caught his reflection in the Florentine mirror — saw himself spare, quick-moving, carefully brushed and dressed, but furrowed, gray about the temples, with a stoop which he corrected by a spasmodic straightening of the shoulders whenever a glass confronted him: a tired middle-aged man, baffled, beaten, worn out.

As he summed himself up thus for the third or fourth time his phone beeped. A text from Mr. Yao to say he was unexpectedly detained and wouldn't arrive until eight-thirty.

Zhang made a curt gesture of annoyance. It was becoming harder and harder for him to control these reflexes. He threw himself into a chair, propping his elbows on the table and resting his chin on his locked hands.

Another half hour alone with it!

He wondered irritably what could have detained his guest. Some professional matter, no doubt — the punctilious lawyer would have allowed nothing less to interfere with a dinner engagement, more especially since Zhang, in his email, had said: "I shall want a little business chat afterward."

But what professional matter could have come up at that unprofessional hour? Perhaps some other soul in misery had called on the lawyer; and, after all, Zhang's email had given no hint of his own need! No doubt Yao thought he merely wanted to make another change in his will. Since his sex-toy business had taken off, ten years earlier, Zhang had been perpetually tinkering with his will.

Upon striking it rich in the sex-toy business he'd endured ten years of dogged work and unrelieved boredom. His days taken up with figuring out new and cheaper designs for bondage restraints, dildos and gags! The ten years from forty to fifty — the best ten years of his life! And if one counted the years before, the silent years of dreams, assimilation, preparation — then call it half a man's life-time: half a man's life-time spent on sex-toys! And all the while Zhang had been looking for love and just couldn't find it. He was useless at relationships. There had been prostitutes yes, hundreds of them, but never love.

As often as he could, Zhang left his sex-toy factory in Wuhan and enjoyed time in the luxury apartment he'd bought in Taylor Wimpey's Clarendon Court development in the central London district of Cripplegate. Zhang hadn't known the flat was in Cripplegate when he bought it and he'd have opted for a London pad elsewhere if he had known this. The sales agents had lied to him saying the property was in the beating heart of the ancient city, when actually it lay outside the original city wall. He'd hoped to meet other like-minded property investors when he took his holidays in London, but Clarendon Court was always empty and bereft of life. He wouldn't have come back to London so regularly had it not been his good luck to meet a spectacularly gifted financial dominatrix who ordered him to visit her frequently. Mistress Ilsa had grown up in the Spanish city of Seville but found the financial pickings much richer in London.

And what was he to do with the remaining half of his life apart from serve Mistress Ilsa with tribute? Well, he had settled that, thank Anatoly Lunacharsky! He turned and glanced anxiously at the clock. Ten minutes past eight — only ten minutes had been consumed in that stormy rush through his whole past! And he must wait another twenty minutes for Yao. It was one of the worst symptoms of his case that, in proportion as he had grown to shrink from human company, he dreaded more and more to be alone. … But why the kulak was he waiting for Yao? Why didn't he cut the knot himself? Since he was so unutterably sick of the whole business, why did he have to call in an outsider to rid him of this nightmare of living?

He opened the drawer again and laid his hand on the revolver. It was a small slim ivory toy — just the instrument for a tired sufferer to give himself a "hypodermic" with. Zhang raised it slowly in one hand, while with the other he felt under the thin hair at the back of his head, between the ear and the nape. He knew just where to place the muzzle: he had once got a young army officer to show him. And as he found the spot, and lifted the revolver to it, the inevitable phenomenon occurred. The hand that held the weapon began to shake, the tremor communicated itself to his arm, his heart gave a wild leap which sent up a wave of deadly nausea to his throat, he smelt the powder, he sickened at the crash of the bullet through his skull, and a sweat of fear broke out over his forehead and ran down his quivering face…

He laid away the revolver with an oath and, pulling out a cologne-scented handkerchief, passed it tremulously over his brow and temples. It was no use — he knew he could never do it in that way. His attempts at self-destruction were as futile as his attempt to find a bride! He couldn't make himself a real life, and he couldn't get rid of the life he had. And that was why he had sent for Yao to help him…

The lawyer, over the camembert and burgundy, began to excuse himself for his delay.

"The fact is, I was sent for on a rather unusual matter —"

"Oh, it's all right," said Zhang cheerfully. He was beginning to feel the usual reaction that food and company produced. It was not any recovered pleasure in life that he felt, but only a deeper withdrawal into himself. It was easier to go on automatically with the social gestures than to uncover to any human eye the abyss within him.

"My dear fellow, it's sacrilege to keep a dinner waiting—especially the production of an artist like yours." Mr. Yao sipped his burgundy luxuriously. "But the fact is, Mrs. Ying sent for me."

Zhang raised his head with a quick movement of surprise. For a moment he was shaken out of his self-absorption.

"Mrs. Ying?"

Yao smiled. "I thought you'd be interested; I know your passion for *causes célèbres*. And this promises to be one. Of course it's out of our line entirely—we never touch criminal cases. But she wanted to consult me as a friend. Ying was a distant connection of my wife's. And, by Stalin, it is a queer case!"

"Tell me about Mrs. Ying," Zhang said, seeming to himself to speak stiffly, as if his lips were cracked.

"Mrs. Ying? Well, there's not much to tell."

"And you couldn't if there were?" Zhang smiled.

"Probably not. As a matter of fact, she wanted my advice about her choice of counsel. There was nothing especially confidential in our talk."

"And what's your impression, now you've seen her?"

"My impression is, very distinctly, that nothing will ever be known."

"Ah—?" Zhang murmured.

"I'm more and more convinced that whoever poisoned Ying knew his business, and will consequently never be found out."

"Then you believe in the theory that the clever criminals never are caught?"

"Of course I do. Look about you—look back for the last dozen years—none of the big murder problems are ever

136

solved." The lawyer ruminated. "Why, take the instance in your own family: I'd forgotten I had an illustration at hand! Take old Huang Feng's murder – do you suppose that will ever be explained?"

As the words dropped from Yao's lips his host looked slowly about his luxury apartment in Taylor Wimpey's Clarendon Court development, and every object in it stared back at him with a stale inescapable familiarity. How sick he was of looking at that room! It was as dull as the face of a comrade one has wearied of. He cleared his throat slowly; then he turned his head to the lawyer and said: "I could explain the Huang murder myself."

Yao's eye kindled. He shared Zhang's interest in criminal cases.

"By Lenin! You've had a theory all this time? It's odd you never mentioned it. Go ahead and tell me. There are certain features in the Huang case not unlike this Ying affair, and your idea may be a help."

Zhang paused and his eye reverted instinctively to the drawer in which the revolver lay. He thought of the notes and bills on his desk in his office in Wuhan, and the horror of taking up again the lifeless routine of life – of performing the same automatic gestures another day – and he happily threw discretion to the wind.

"I haven't a theory. I know who murdered Huang Feng."

Yao settled himself comfortably in his chair, prepared for enjoyment.

"You know? Well, who did?" he laughed.

"I did," said Zhang, rising.

He stood before Yao, and the lawyer lay back staring up at him. Then he broke into another laugh.

"Why, this is glorious! You murdered him, did you? To inherit his money, I suppose and invest it in your sex-toy business? Better and better! Go on, my boy! Unbosom yourself! Tell me all about it! Confession is good for the soul."

Zhang waited till the lawyer had shaken the last peal of laughter from his throat, then he repeated doggedly: "I murdered him."

The two men looked at each other for a long moment, and this time Yao did not laugh.

"Zhang!"

"I murdered him—to get his money, as you say."

There was another pause, and Zhang, with a vague underlying sense of amusement, saw his guest's look change from pleasantry to apprehension.

"What's the joke, my dear fellow? I fail to see."

"It's not a joke. It's the truth. I murdered him." He had spoken painfully at first, as if there were a knot in his throat; but each time he repeated the words he found they were easier to say.

Yao laid down his extinct cigar.

"What's the matter? Aren't you well? What on earth are you driving at?"

"I'm perfectly well. But I murdered my cousin, Huang Feng, and I want it known that I murdered him."

"You want it known?"

"Yes. That's why I sent for you. I'm sick of living and when I try to kill myself I funk it." He spoke quite naturally now, as if the knot in his throat had been untied.

"By Trotsky—by Fritz Platten," the lawyer gasped.

"But I suppose," Zhang continued, "there's no doubt this would be murder in the first degree? I'm sure of the chair if I own up? After all I committed the crime in Texas not London."

Yao drew a long breath, then he said slowly: "Sit down, Zhang. Let's talk. You know they favour lethal injection in Texas but I could put in a special plea for the chair."

◆ ◆ ◆

To the guest in his Clarendon Court apartment, Zhang told his story simply, connectedly. It was the perfect tale to recount on the benighted site of Taylor Wimpey's Golden Lane luxury apartment development. The foundations of the new building had disturbed an old plague pit, and Clarendon Court had been constructed right opposite the old city mortuary.

He began with a quick survey of his early years — the years of drudgery and emotional privation. If he'd been 15 years older he could have had fun with the Red Guards. He'd always liked girls but they didn't like him. He was incapable of a romantic relationship. That's why sex-toys had become his master-passion. He would have sold his soul for a factory in which to make the sex-toys he designed! It was in him — he could not remember when it had not been his deepest-seated instinct. As the years passed it became a morbid, relentless obsession — yet with every year the material conditions were more and more against it. He felt himself growing middle-aged and he'd achieved nothing!

At this point in his narrative Zhang stood up, and went to lean against the wall, looking down at Yao, who had not moved from his seat, or changed his attitude of rigid fascinated attention.

"Then came the summer when we went to Austin to be near old Huang — my mother's cousin, as you know. Some of the family always mounted guard over him — generally a niece or so. But that year they were all scattered, and one of the nieces offered to lend us her pad if we'd relieve her of duty for two months. It was a nuisance for me, of course, for Austin is a long way from Wuhan; but my mother, who was a slave to family observances, had always been good to the old man, so it was natural we should be called on — and there was the saving of rent. So we went.

"You never knew Huang Feng? Well, picture to yourself an amoeba or some primitive organism of that sort, under a Titan's microscope. He was large, undifferentiated, inert — since I could remember him he had done nothing but take his temperature and read Stalag fiction. He claimed he used those pornographic novels to improve his Hebrew and Yiddish but the fact is he only took up those languages to read tales of allied prisoners being tortured by female camp guards, until at the conclusion the tables were turned and the victimizers were raped and tortured. He would translate the titles for me. Many consisted of the word Stalag with a different number after it to denote different books, although there were also *I Was Colonel Schultz's Private Bitch* and *Torture Stalag*.

"Huang's life apathetic and motionless, hung in a net of gold, in an equable warm ventilated atmosphere, high above sordid earthly worries. The cardinal rule of his existence was not to let himself be 'worried.' . . I remember his advising me to try it myself, one day when I spoke to him of my bad health and need of a change. 'I never let myself worry,' he said complacently. 'It's the worst thing for the liver — and you look to me as if you have a liver. Take my advice and be cheerful. You'll make yourself happier and others too.' And all he had to do was to write a cheque and send me off for a holiday in Bangkok or Manila or some other destination favoured by sex tourists! But instead he wanted to talk to me about stocking clad Nazi death squad bitches!

"The hardest part of it was that the money half-belonged to me already. The old skinflint only had it for life, in trust for me. But his life was a good deal sounder than mine — and I could picture him taking extra care of it for the joke of keeping me waiting. I always felt that the sight of my hungry eyes was a tonic to him.

"Well, I tried to see if I couldn't reach him through his vanity. I flattered him, feigned a passionate interest in his Stalag novels. And he was taken in, and used to discourse on them by the hour. When he bragged to me of the expense of obtaining original paperback copies of Stalag fiction he was simply a hideous old Lothario bragging of what his pleasures cost. And the resemblance was completed by the fact that he couldn't get an erection no matter what he did — Viagra had no effect on him. 'But, after all, it's my only hobby — why shouldn't I indulge it?' he said sentimentally. As if I'd ever been able to indulge any of mine! For what he paid for those pornographic softbacks I could have lived like a god…

"One day toward the end of the summer, I entered cousin Feng's hideous black-walnut library. He sat in his usual seat, behind the darkened windows, his fat hands folded on his protuberant waistcoat, a Stalag fiction at his elbow, and looking down at his trousers I could see he finally had an erection. I congratulated myself on finding him in such an aroused state, since I had made up my mind to ask him a favour. Then I noticed that his face, instead of looking as calm as an eggshell, was distorted and whimpering—and without stopping to greet me he pointed passionately at an old Israeli paperback laid before him.

"'It's the most perverted thing I've ever read!' It was as if he had said 'she' instead of 'it,' and when he put out his senile hand and touched the book I positively had to look the other way. "'But the last few pages are missing and I can't find another copy for love or money!'

"The old man's rage was fearful in its impotence—he shook, spluttered and strangled with it. He wanted to have the book dealer who'd sold him the item without mentioning a few end pages were missing, locked up. 'By God, and I'll do it—I'll write to Washington—I'll have the pauper scoundrel deported! I'll show him what money can do!' He meant to have the police look into it... And then he grew frightened at his own excitement. 'But I must calm myself,' he said. He took his temperature, rang for his drops, and turned to his computer. He called up an English translation of a Stalag novel and asked me to read it to him, which I did for an hour, in the dim close room.

"All the while one phrase of the old man's buzzed in my brain. 'I'll show him what money can do!' By Nie Yuanzi! If I could but show the old man! If I could make him see his power of giving happiness as a new outlet for his monstrous egotism! I tried to tell him something about my situation—spoke of my ill-health, my unsuccessful drudgery, my longing to go into the sex-toy business, to make myself a name—I stammered out an entreaty for a loan. 'I can guarantee to repay you, sir—I could assign you the patents on my sex-toy designs as security...'

"I shall never forget his glassy stare. His face had grown as smooth as an eggshell again—his eyes peered over his fat cheeks like sentinels over a slippery rampart.

"'Patents—patents for sex-toys as security?' He looked at me almost fearfully, as if detecting the first symptoms of insanity. 'Do you understand anything of business?' he enquired mildly. I laughed and answered: 'No, not much.'

"He leaned back with closed lids. 'All this excitement has been too much for me,' he said. 'If you'll excuse me, I'll prepare for my nap.' And I stumbled out of the room, blindly."

Zhang moved away from the wall, and walked across to the tray set out with decanters and soda-water. He poured himself a tall glass of soda-water, emptied it.

Then Zhang went on with his tale. He told of his mounting obsession—how the murderous impulse had waked in him on the instant of his cousin's refusal, and he had muttered to himself: "By Mao, if you won't, I'll make you." He spoke more tranquilly as the narrative proceeded, as though his rage had died down once the resolve to act on it was taken. He applied his whole mind to the question of how the old man was to be "disposed of." Suddenly he remembered the outcry. But no definite project presented itself. He simply waited for an inspiration.

Unable to find a complete copy of the Stalag that had so aroused him, cousin Feng, languished, had "nerves," and lost his appetite. The doctor called in a colleague, and the consultation amused and excited the old man—he became once more an important figure. The medical men reassured the family—too completely!—and to the patient they recommended a more varied diet: advised him to take whatever "tempted him." And so one day, tremulously, prayerfully, he decided on a tiny bit of melon. It was brought up with ceremony, and consumed in the presence of the housekeeper and a hovering cousin; and twenty minutes later he was dead...

Zhang paused. He had dropped into a chair opposite the lawyer's, and he sat for a moment, his head thrown back, looking about the familiar room in his Clarendon Court apartment. Everything in it had grown grimacing and alien, and each strange insistent object seemed craning forward from its place to hear him.

"It was I who put the stuff in the melon," he said. "And I don't want you to think I'm sorry for it. This isn't 'remorse,' understand. I'm glad the old skinflint is dead. But my money is no use to me any more. I'm not happy with what it bought me."

Yao continued to stare; then he said: "What on earth was your object, then?"

"Why, to get what I wanted—what I fancied was in reach! I wanted change, rest, life—wanted, above all, the chance to make it in the sex-toy business! I travelled, got back my health, and came home to tie myself up to my work. And I've slaved at it steadily for ten years without reward! Making sex-toys is a waste of time! It gives me no pleasure! I'm fifty, and I'm beaten, and I know it." His chin dropped forward on his breast. "I want to chuck the whole business," he ended.

❖ ❖ ❖

It was after midnight when Yao left Zhang's Clarendon Court apartment in Golden Lane. His hand on his friend's shoulder, as he turned to go—"Criminal justice be hanged! See a doctor, see a doctor!" he had cried and with an exaggerated laugh had pulled on his coat and departed.

Zhang turned back into his Taylor Wimpey investment property. It had never occurred to him that Yao would not believe his story. For three hours he had explained, elucidated, patiently and painfully gone over every detail—but without once breaking down the iron incredulity of the lawyer's eye.

At first Yao had feigned to be convinced—but that, as Zhang now perceived, was simply to get him to expose himself, to entrap him into contradictions. And when the attempt failed, when Zhang triumphantly met and refuted each disconcerting question, the lawyer dropped the mask suddenly, and said with a good-humoured laugh: "By Grigory Zino-viev, Zhang you should be writing novels not making sex-toys. The way you've worked this all out is a marvel."

Zhang swung about furiously — that last sneer about writing fiction inflamed him. Given his experiences the only type of novel he was qualified to write was some kind of contemporary variation on the Stalag!

"I did it, I did it," he muttered sullenly, his rage spending itself against the impenetrable surface of the other's mockery; and Yao answered with a smile: "Ever read any of those books on hallucination? I've got a fairly good medico-legal library. I could send you a PDF or two if you like…"

Left alone, Zhang cowered in an armchair and stared vacantly ahead. His eyes didn't take in the moonlit view of Fortune Street Park through his undrawn curtains. He understood that Yao thought him off his head.

"By Lev Kamenev — what if they all think me crazy?"

The horror of it broke out over him in a cold sweat — he sat there and shook, his eyes hidden in his icy hands. But gradually, as he began to rehearse his story for the thousandth time, he saw again how incontrovertible it was, and felt sure that any criminal lawyer would believe him.

"That's the trouble — Yao's not a criminal lawyer. And then he's a friend. What a fool I was to talk to a friend! Even if he did believe me, he'd never let me see it — his instinct would be to cover the whole thing up… But in that case — if he did believe me — he might think it a kindness to get me shut up in an asylum…" Zhang began to tremble again. "By Li Zhisui! If he should bring in an expert — one of those damned psychiatrists! Yao and Lee can do anything — their word always goes. If Yao drops a hint that I'd better be shut up, I'll be in a strait-jacket by tomorrow! And he'd do it from the kindest motives — be quite right to do it if he thinks I'm a murderer!"

The vision froze him to his chair. He pressed his fists to his bursting temples and tried to think. For the first time he hoped that Yao had not believed his story.

"But he did—he did! I can see it now—I noticed what a queer eye he cocked at me. By Jiang Qing, what shall I do—what shall I do?"

He started up and looked at the clock. Half-past one. What if Yao should think the case urgent, rout out a shrink, and come back with him? Zhang jumped to his feet, and his sudden gesture brushed the morning paper from the table. Mechanically he stooped to pick it up, and the movement started a new train of association.

He sat down again, and reached for his smartphone.

The new idea in his mind had revived his flagging energy. He would act—act at once. It was only by thus planning ahead, committing himself to some unavoidable line of conduct, that he could pull himself through the meaningless days. Each time he reached a fresh decision it was like coming out of a foggy weltering sea into a calm harbour with lights. One of the queerest phases of his long agony was the intense relief produced by these momentary lulls.

"Hello, Wang... Yes, Chunqiao Zhang. ... Just caught you? Going straight home? Can I have a talk? It's rather urgent ... yes, might give you some first-rate 'copy.' ... All right!" He hung up the receiver with a laugh. It had been a happy thought to call up the journalist from the *China Daily*—Wang Hongwen was the very man he needed...

Zhang put out the lights in his Clarendon Court apartment—it was odd how the automatic gestures persisted!—put on his hat and overcoat, and let himself out of the flat. Taking the lift, Zhang passed out into the street. The Uber ride he'd called was waiting outside. Soon the long thoroughfare of Green Lanes stretched before him, dim and deserted, like an ancient avenue of tombs. But from Wang's house a friendly beam fell on the pavement, and as Zhang sprang from his cab the editor turned the corner.

The two men grasped hands, and Wang, feeling for his latch-key, ushered Zhang into the brightly-lit hall.

"Disturb me? Not a bit. You might have at ten tomorrow morning … but this is my liveliest hour … you know my habits of old."

Zhang had known Wang Hongwen for fifteen years — watched his rise through all the stages of journalism in Wuhan to the Olympian pinnacle of the foreign reporter based in London. In the thick-set man with grizzling hair there were few traces left of the hungry-eyed young reporter who, on his way home in the small hours, used to "bob in" on Zhang, while the latter sat grinding at his sex-toy designs. Wang had to pass Zhang's flat on the way to his own, and it became a habit, if he saw a light in the window, and Zhang's shadow against the blind, to go in, and discuss the universe.

"Well — this is like old times — a good old habit reversed." The journalist smote his visitor genially on the shoulder. "Reminds me of the nights when I used to rout you out… How's the sex-toy business, by the way? There is a new design, I suppose? It's as safe to ask you that as to say to some men: 'How's the baby?'"

Wang laughed good-naturedly, and Zhang thought how thick and heavy he had grown. It was evident, even to Zhang's tortured nerves, that the words had not been uttered in malice — and the fact gave him a new measure of his insignificance. Wang did not even know that he felt flattened by life! The fact hurt more than Yao's irony.

"Come in — come in." The journalist led the way into a small cheerful room. He pushed an armchair toward his visitor, and dropped into another with a comfortable groan.

"Now, then — help yourself to a drink. And let's hear all about it."

He beamed at Zhang. Then the sex-toy magnate turned, and began: "Wang, I want to tell you —"

The clock ticked rhythmically. Once the hour struck — then the rhythmical ticking began again. The atmosphere grew denser and heavier, and beads of perspiration began to roll from Zhang's forehead.

"Well — go on," Wang said. His composure exasperated Zhang.

"There's no use in my going on if you don't believe me."

The journalist remained unmoved. "Who says I don't believe you? And how can I tell till you've finished?"

Zhang went on, ashamed of his outburst. "It was simple enough to commit murder, because no one was going to suspect me. But he fell ill — perhaps the fates were going to do it for me! By Lin Biao, if that could only be!"

"Then came word that he was better; and the day after, I found my cousin's laughing over the news that he was to try a bit of melon. The doctor himself had picked out the melon, one of the little French ones that are hardly bigger than a large tomato — and the patient was to eat it at his breakfast the next morning.

"In a flash I saw my chance. It was a bare chance, no more. But I knew the ways of the house — I was sure the melon would be purchased the day before and put in the fridge. If there were only one melon in the icebox I could be fairly sure it was the one I wanted. Yes, I felt pretty sure of my melon... and poisoning was much safer than shooting. It would have been the devil and all to get into the old man's bedroom without his rousing the house, but I could get into the kitchen without any trouble.

I groped my way to the fridge, opened it — and there was the little French melon... only one. I stopped to listen. Then I pulled out my bottle and syringe, and gave each section of the melon a hypodermic. It was all done inside of three minutes."

At length Wang asked: "Why did you want to tell me this?"

The question startled Zhang. He was about to explain, as he had explained to Yao. But suddenly it occurred to him that if his motive had not seemed convincing to the lawyer it would carry much less weight with Wang. Both were successful professional men, and their type of success outside of trade does not understand the subtle agony of being a magnate in the sex-toy industry. Zhang cast about for another reason.

"Why, I—the thing haunts me... remorse, I suppose you'd call it..."

"Remorse? Bosh!" Wang said energetically.

Zhang's heart sank. "You don't believe in—remorse?"

"Not an atom in the man of action. The mere fact of your talking of remorse proves to me that you're not the man to have planned and put through such a job."

Zhang groaned. "Well—I lied to you about remorse. I've never felt any."

Wang's lips tightened sceptically. "What was your motive, then? You must have had one."

"I'll tell you—" And Zhang began again to rehearse the story of loathing trade, of the drudgery of designing sex-toys day after day. "Don't say you don't believe me this time... that this isn't a real reason!" he stammered out piteously as he ended.

Wang meditated. "No, I won't say that. I've seen too many queer things. There's always a reason for wanting to get out of life—the wonder is that we find so many for staying in!"

Zhang's heart grew light. "Then you do believe me?" he faltered.

"Believe that you're sick of your role as a sex-toy entrepreneur? Yes. And that you haven't the nerve to pull the trigger? Oh, yes—that's easy enough, too. But all that doesn't make you a murderer—though I don't say it proves you could never have been one."

"I have been one, Wang—I swear to you."

"Perhaps." He meditated.

There was a long silence between the two men. Zhang, with a throbbing heart, watched Wang. The editor, at any rate, did not sneer and flout him. After all, journalism gave a deeper insight than the law into the fantastic possibilities of life, prepared one better to allow for the incalculableness of human impulses.

"Well?" Zhang faltered out.

Wang stood up with a shrug. "Look here, man—what's wrong with you? Make a clean breast of it! Nerves gone to smash? I'd like to take you to see a chap I know — an ex-prize-fighter — who's a wonder at pulling fellows in your state out of their hole — "

"Oh, oh — " Zhang broke in. He stood up also, and the two men eyed each other. "You don't believe me, then?"

"This yarn — how can I? If somebody else had accused you, the story might have been worth looking into. As it is, a child could have invented it. It doesn't do much credit to your ingenuity."

❖ ❖ ❖

Zhang was overcome by the futility of any farther attempt to inculpate himself. He was handcuffed to life — a "prisoner of consciousness." Where was it he had read the phrase? Well he was learning what it meant. In the glaring night-hours, when his brain seemed ablaze, he was visited by a sense of his fixed identity, of his irreducible, inexpugnable selfness, keener, more insidious, more inescapable, than any sensation he had ever known. He had not guessed that the mind was capable of such intricacies of self-realisation, of penetrating so deep into its own dark windings. Often he woke from his brief snatches of sleep with the feeling that something material was clinging to him, was on his hands and face, and in his throat — and as his brain cleared he understood that it was the sense of his own loathed personality that stuck to him like some thick viscous substance.

Then, in the first morning hours, he rose from his comfortable bed in his Clarendon Court apartment and looked out of his window at the awakening activities on Golden Lane — at the street-cleaners, bin men, and the other dingy workers flitting hurriedly by through the sallow winter light. Oh, to be one of them — any of them — to take his chance in any of their skins! They were the toilers — the men whose lot was pitied — the victims wept over and ranted about by altruists and economists; and how gladly he would have taken up the load of any one of them, if only he might have shaken off his own! But, no — the iron circle of consciousness held them too. Each one was chained to his own hideous ego. Why wish to be any one man rather than another? The only absolute good was not to be.

For the first time since his decision to tell Yao Wenyuan he was a murderer, Zhang found himself without an occupation, and understood that he had been carried through the past weeks only by the necessity of constant action. Now his life had once more become a stagnant backwater, and as he stood on the corner of Golden Lane and Fann Street watching the tides of traffic sweep by, he asked himself despairingly how much longer he could endure to float about in the sluggish circle of his consciousness.

The thought of self-destruction recurred to him but again his flesh recoiled. He yearned for death from other hands, but he could never take it from his own. And, aside from his insuperable physical reluctance, another motive restrained him. He was possessed by the dogged desire to establish the truth of his story. He refused to be swept aside as an irresponsible dreamer — even if he had to kill himself in the end, he would not do so before proving to society that he had deserved death from it.

Yao came to see him and begged him to rest. Wang Hongwen dropped in and tried to joke him out of his delusion — till Zhang, mistrustful of their motives, began to dread their visits and set a guard on his lips. But the words he kept back engendered others and still others in his brain. His inner self became a humming factory of arguments, and he spent long hours reciting and writing down elaborate statements of his crime, which he constantly retouched and developed. Then gradually his activity languished under the lack of an audience, the sense of being buried beneath deepening drifts of indifference. In a passion of resentment he swore that he would prove himself a murderer, even if he had to commit another crime to do it, and for a sleepless night or two the thought flamed red on his darkness. But daylight dispelled it. The determining impulse was lacking and he hated too promiscuously to choose his victim... So he was thrown back on the unavailing struggle to impose the truth of his story. As fast as one channel closed on him he tried to pierce another through the sliding sands of incredulity. But every issue seemed blocked, and the whole human race leagued together to cheat one man of the right to die. Even Mistress Ilsa who repeatedly promised to kill him, would never actually carry out the threat no matter how much he offered to pay her!

Thus viewed, the situation became so monstrous that he lost his last shred of self-restraint in contemplating it. What if he were really the victim of some mocking experiment, the centre of a ring of holiday-makers jeering at a poor creature in its blind dashes against the solid walls of consciousness? But, no — men were not so uniformly cruel. There were flaws in the close surface of their indifference, cracks of weakness and pity here and there...

Zhang began to think that his mistake lay in having appealed to persons more or less familiar with his past, and to whom the visible conformities of his life seemed a final disproof of its one fierce secret deviation. The general tendency was to take for the whole of life the slit seen between the blinders of habit: and in his walk down that narrow vista Zhang cut a correct enough figure. To a vision free to follow his whole orbit his story would be more intelligible. It would be easier to convince a chance idler in the street than the trained intelligence hampered by a sense of his antecedents. This idea shot up in him with the tropic luxuriance of each new seed of thought, and he began to walk the streets, and to frequent out-of-the-way noodle-houses and bars in his search for the impartial stranger to whom he should disclose himself.

At first every face looked encouragement, but at the crucial moment he always held back. So much was at stake and it was so essential that his first choice should be decisive. He dreaded stupidity, timidity, intolerance. The imaginative eye, the furrowed brow, were what he sought. He must reveal himself only to a heart versed in the tortuous motions of the human will. He began to hate the dull benevolence of the average face. Once or twice, obscurely, allusively, he made a beginning — once sitting down at a man's side in a basement noodle-house, another day approaching a lounger on a park bench. But in both cases the premonition of failure checked him on the brink of avowal. His dread of being taken for a man in the clutch of a fixed idea gave him an unnatural keenness in reading the expression of his interlocutors, and he had provided himself in advance with a series of verbal alternatives, trap-doors of evasion from the first dart of ridicule or suspicion.

He passed the greater part of the day in the streets, coming home to Clarendon Court at irregular hours, dreading the orderliness of his apartment, and the empty, silent, ghost flats in the rest of the block. His real life was spent in a world so remote from this familiar setting that he sometimes had the mysterious sense of a living metempsychosis, a furtive passage from one identity to another — yet the other as inescapably himself!

One humiliation he was spared, the desire to live never revived in him. Not for a moment was he tempted to a shabby pact with existing conditions. He wanted to die, wanted it with the fixed unwavering desire which alone attains its end. And still the end eluded him! It would not always, of course — he had full faith in the dark star of his destiny. And he could prove it best by repeating his story, persistently and indefatigably, pouring it into indifferent ears, hammering it into dull brains, till at last it kindled a spark, and someone of the careless millions paused, listened, believed…

It was a mild March day, and he had been loitering on Whitecross Street, looking at faces. He was becoming an expert in physiognomies, his eagerness no longer made rash darts and awkward recoils. He knew now the face he needed, as clearly as if it had come to him in a vision, and not till he found it would he speak. As he walked northward through the food market he had a premonition that he should find it that lunchtime. Perhaps it was the promise of spring in the air — certainly he felt calmer than for many days…

He turned into Old Street, struck across it obliquely, and walked up Ironmonger Row. Its heterogeneous passers al-

152

ways allured him—they were less hurried than those in Moorgate, less enclosed and classified than yet others in Brick Lane. He walked slowly, watching for his face.

Hitting City Road he felt a sudden relapse into discouragement, like a cadre who has waited too long for a sign of favour from the party. Perhaps, after all, he would never find his face... The air was languid and he felt tired. He walked southeastwards and in Bunhill Burial Grounds made for an empty seat. Presently he passed a bench on which a girl sat alone, and something as definite as the twitch of a cord made him stop before her. He had never dreamed of telling his story to a girl, had hardly looked at women's faces as they passed. His case was man's work, how could a woman help him? But this girl's face was extraordinary—quiet and wide as a clear evening sky. It suggested a hundred images of space, distance, mystery, like ships he had seen, as a boy, quietly berthed by a familiar wharf, but with the breath of far seas and strange harbours in their shrouds... Certainly this girl would understand. He went up to her quietly, lifting his hat, observing the forms—wishing her to see at once that he was "a gentleman."

"I am a stranger to you," he began sitting down beside her, "but your face is so extremely intelligent that I feel... I feel it is the face I've waited for... looked for everywhere; and I want to tell you—"

The girl's eyes widened. She rose to her feet. She was escaping him!

In his dismay he ran a few steps after her and caught her roughly by the arm.

"Here—wait—listen! Oh, don't scream, you fool!" he shouted out.

He felt a hand on his own arm; turned and confronted a policeman. Instantly he understood that he was being arrested, and something hard within him was loosened and ran to tears.

"Ah, you know—you know I'm guilty!"

He was conscious that a crowd was forming, and that the girl's frightened face had disappeared. But what did he care about her face? It was the policeman who had really understood him. He turned and followed, the crowd at his heels...

◆ ◆ ◆

In the charming place in which he found himself there were so many sympathetic faces that he felt more than ever convinced of the certainty of making himself heard.

It was a bad blow, at first, to find that he had not been arrested for murder; but Yao, who had come to him at once, explained that he needed rest, and the time to "review" his statements; it appeared that reiteration had made them a little confused and contradictory. He needed to rest in his quiet Clarendon Court apartment, surrounded by empty ghost flats.

For a time he was content to let himself go on the tranquil current of this existence; but although his auditors gave him for the most part an encouraging attention, which, in some, went the length of really brilliant and helpful suggestion, he gradually felt a recurrence of his old doubts. Either his hearers were not sincere, or else they had less power to aid him than they boasted. His interminable conferences resulted in nothing, and as the benefit of the long rest made itself felt, it produced an increased mental lucidity which rendered inaction more and more unbearable.

If ever he tried to leave Clarendon Court there was always a man in the entrance hall who'd prevent him going into the street. Food and anything else he wanted would be delivered to him. He just had to order it online. At length he discovered that on certain days visitors from the outer world were admitted to his retreat as Airbnb guests; and he wrote out long and logically constructed accounts of his crime, and furtively slipped them into the hands of these messengers of hope.

This occupation gave him a fresh lease of patience, and he now lived only to watch for visitors to Clarendon Court, and scan the faces that swept by him like stars seen and lost in the rifts of a hurrying sky.

Mostly, these faces were strange and less intelligent than those of his companions. But they represented his last means of access to the world, a kind of subterranean channel on which he could set his "statements" afloat, like paper boats which the mysterious current might sweep out into the open seas of life.

One day, however, his attention was drawn to a visitor with a brow like Shakespeare and a face like Satan. The man was a Geordie from the north of England.

Zhang's hand shook so that he could hardly draw the folded paper from his pocket. It came to Zhang in a wild thrill of conviction that this was the face he had waited for...

"Perhaps you could glance over this—or I could put the case in a few words if you have time?" Zhang's voice shook like his hand. If this chance escaped him he felt that his last hope was gone. The stranger looked at him and then glanced at his watch.

"I'm sorry I'm busy—"

Zhang continued to proffer the paper. "I'm sorry—I think I could have explained. But you'll take this, at any rate?"

The stranger looked at him gently. "Certainly—I'll take it." He had his hand out. "Good-bye."

"Good-bye," Zhang echoed.

He stood watching the man move away from him; and as he watched a tear ran down his face. As soon as the Geordie was out of sight, Zhang turned and took the lift from the communal entrance to his Clarendon Court luxury apartment, beginning to hope again, already planning a new statement.

Outside Clarendon Court the man stopped to converse with a medical orderly.

"So that was Zhang?"

"Yes—that was Zhang, poor devil," said the orderly.

"Strange case! I suppose there's never been one just like it? He's still absolutely convinced that he committed that murder?"

"Absolutely. Yes."

The stranger reflected. "And there was no conceivable ground for the idea? No one could make out how it started? A quiet conventional sort of fellow like that—where do you suppose he got such a delusion? Did you ever get the least clue to it?"

The orderly stood still, his hands in his pockets, his head cocked up in contemplation of the windows of the empty Clarendon Court. Then he turned his bright hard gaze on his companion.

"That was the queer part of it. I've never spoken of it—but I did get a clue."

"By Adam Smith! That's interesting. What was it?"

The nurse formed his red lips into a whistle. "Why—that it wasn't a delusion."

He produced his effect—the other turned on him with a pallid stare.

"He murdered the man all right. I tumbled on the truth by the merest accident, when I'd pretty nearly chucked the whole job."

"He murdered him—murdered his cousin?"

"Sure as you live. Only don't split on me. It's about the queerest business I ever ran into…"

"What did you do about it?"

"What was I to do? I couldn't send the poor devil to Texas to be killed, could I? Lord, but I'm glad they collared him, and put him under house arrest in Clarendon Court! Ninety-eight of its ninety-nine luxury apartments are empty, so there's no one in the building he could harm—apart from the concierge and the occasional Airbnb guest. And everyone with the concierge job has medical training and is armed."

The tall man listened with a grave face, grasping the killer's statement in his hand.

"Here—take this, it makes me sick," he said abruptly, thrusting the paper at the orderly; and the two men turned and walked in silence to Old Street tube station.

HARD BUT FAIR

JOHN KING

I t was Chris Davis who set things up and in an odd way links the characters and events that will one day be referred to as the BarbDoll Nasties. We'd come out of Old Street station and were barrelling down the main road, checking the pubs as we went, at the turning we wanted spreading out and speeding up. Chris swore he saw Sammy Skyves going into the named boozer, but whether it was Skyves or not I do not know, but it was full of Spurs. Out they came. This was 1969 or '70. I'm not sure when. Proper skinhead aggro. The Shed versus The Paxton. Best days of our lives.

We were sixty-handed and been drinking in the Elephant, and because Chris knew a couple of the Tottenham from working at Smithfield he had a good idea where their mob would be. He was unloading lorries at the market, eating in the cafes and drinking in pubs where you could get a pint twenty-four hours a day if you knew where to go. With Smithfield being central the different clubs mixed, but being youngsters the football lads knew to behave. The older blokes were the guvnors. There were some serious hard-nuts knocking about as well, and not just the soldiers who'd fought in Europe.

This was back in those great light-and-bitter days when half the pubs in London were Irish-run and a pint of stout wasn't going to cost you a craft-beer fortune. People held their tongues in one sense, but spoke more honestly in another, many of them having firm political and religious views. There were those who liked Nye Bevin and those who liked Enoch Powell and plenty who liked neither or both. Then there were the pensioners kept sane by the Spiritualist church after the First German War, and whether you believed in God or not we did tend to think that a person reaped what they sowed, that there was a natural justice nobody could dodge, a day of reckoning when the big heads and bullies and all the rest of the horrible cunts who fuck up the world got their comeuppance. It didn't stop us lot fighting, but that was normal. Part of being young. Part of growing up.

Chris believed in this deeper fairness more than most, which was probably thanks to his auntie, and maybe it's what led to the appearance of the small man that night near Old Street, as if Chris had somehow conjured him up. Opened a door to another dimension. Dolly Davis had never recovered from losing her husband in the First War, while the death of her only child Mary in the bombing of London tipped her over the edge. Chris was a thoughtful chap and looked out for Dolly, made sure she was never short. He even sat in a circle with her for a while.

People talk about the Swinging Sixties, but London was still recovering from the Blitz. Ted Heath and his Tory traitors hadn't taken us into the Common Market yet, but that was only three or four years away. The heroes knew this was a political takeover, that this time the Germans would use trade and the law instead of their failed blitzkrieg tactics. These men were nailed into their culture as only those with family and long-term ties to an area can be, knew the real enemy was within, a line of collaborators that ran from Heath to Cameron via Thatcher, Major, Blair and Brown—line them up against a wall and shoot the lot of them.

Our London was very different to today's digitised version. We were teenage skinheads listening to the boss sounds of Jamaica—Prince Buster and Laurel Aitken, Roy Ellis and Desmond Dekker—Jack The Lad tearaways looking for a bundle and a laugh. True, we were poorer and society was more violent, but it was also less sneaky and we had our freedom. If these trendy cunts you see now had been poncing around back then they wouldn't have lasted five minutes. A good kick in the bollocks and off they'd go.

Today, with CCTV and everyone carrying spy cameras in their mobiles, only a clever clogs like Mr. Fair can deal with them and stay out of trouble.

Chris soon had the glooms working at Smithfield. The stink of blood was in his nose and the fluff of chicken feathers in his mouth, the sound of butchers' cleavers chopping in his ears. He was surrounded by piles of flesh, bone, organs, guts. He hated seeing the bodies lined up on hooks, and especially the pigs with their heads cut off, maybe because they weren't covered in fur and seemed more human. The same as any of us, he had to take what he could get when it came to work, plus he had a gammy leg, but while he was game and highly respected after that row with the North Bank, he also had a way of bringing people together.

The bloke saw things as well, told me about the animal spirits drifting along the roads leading away from Smithfield, how they hadn't accepted they were dead until they'd reached the market. The scale of the butchery and dismemberment brought them out of the shock of their slaughter, and breaking free they turned their backs on Central London and headed East. But they were quickly confused and stopped in the quieter Cripplegate. They felt safer here, thought to rest before carrying on, but their confidence faded and they couldn't continue. More and more souls arrived and before long their emotions were swirling in a huge mental whirlpool that filled this small corner of the city. When the rubble of the Blitz was cleared and Fortune Street Park established in the early 1960s the spirits hurried inside.

Back on the skinhead streets of London, the aggro had spilled across the road and nobody was running, and while we hated Spurs and they hated us I suppose there was a grudging respect. I know we were fighting among ourselves, but reputations were important and there was nothing like it for excitement. London belonged to us. Its quirks were clear in the different manors and traditions, the sights and sounds of our lives, and yet we were all the same really, while the toffs were kept away by their fear of our violence. What have you got without that fear? Now any rich sod can stroll in and do whatever they want.

The traditional areas of London are near enough gone, gentrified out of existence, bought up and sterilised by the wealthy of the world, and never mind the politics these people spout, they're all the same. Only interested in making a profit. Got no class. No real style. But after the war Cripplegate was in ruins and — to be honest — it wasn't worth a bean.

◆ ◆ ◆

The Germans did a good job clearing the land back in 1940, part of their masterplan to take over Europe and create an empire ruled from Berlin. The raid I'm thinking about took place on December 29th. I know this because it was my old man's birthday and he watched the fire from Hounslow in West London. The sky was glowing, but the reality made it a terrible sight and the cockneys who'd moved over in the 1920s were forced to think more fondly of the streets they'd played in as kids, these feelings at odds with the joy they'd felt escaping the poverty of the East End.

The Luftwaffe used incendiaries to create what some came to call the Second Fire Of London. The wooden warehouses near St. Paul's were easy to set alight and the flames spread fast, yet the cathedral survived and a photograph was taken which remains iconic. Believers say it was God who saved St. Paul's from the devil that was Hitler, while some of us feel another force was responsible. The robot folk talk about chance and luck.

They say there is no such thing as coincidence, which makes the tale told to me by my pal Mr. Fair easier to believe. Not that he would ever lie. A small man with a pointed head, he does wear some unusual clobber, but he comes from the fairground and has a magic about him. It is impossible to make out his features, and those strangers who catch a glimpse of his blank face are scared at first, yet as soon as they think about him he is inside their minds and a

bigger picture, and while he was sad he knew it was the human way. He also knew the future. Those bombers had created an opening. One of many such wounds. He realised early that success is all about keys. The click of imagination. Mr. Fair wandered the Barbican and sat in its private gardens. Spirits joined him in the greenwood. Locks were made to be opened. It took me most of my life to understand this fact. Find the right key and in you go.

◆ ◆ ◆

Two-person Crats split from graft to disco. Skinny is a fashion. Vs 1, 2, 3, 4. In the calm of day these clevers chill in plazas flanked by blue palms shading yellow cacti. Chill-out plots prosper. Technos and Bureaus meander and whisper sweetie-talk to imported dates. Free to exploit, the wider society booms. Coffee stimulates chat of Palm upgrades and Solutions. Tummies are filled with Blueberry muffins. Child-lovers play graphics of Cripplegate playgrounds and parks, images of molester toilets, serious and weeping for long-dead libertines branded paedos by the commons. Beyond the London Wall, lowlife estates remain. Dregs, droogs, skins rule. The death of much-loved Controller Horace at the hands of racist-scum English/British plebs — patriots GB45 and localisers Conflict — has rocked the Goods to the extent that No More Mr. Nice Guy slogans have appeared across the Sides and inside Central, delivered by USE-sponsored free-thinker Blankety Banks. Every Palmcorder is fed tasters.

Brave Mr. Saviles calls for action. He is an architectural guru who zapped the Barb Carbuncle and reached for glory, replacing brutals with silky smooths. Investors reject the history fouling London's heart. Filthy commons tales. Plebber culture. But Mr. Saviles loves Barbie. He really does love little Barbs. And Dennis. Sweet Den-Deny. Naughty Den. Dirty Den. Their sporting life. Long-distance grunters. He is taking Den to see Terry Johns abused as London United play tonight. He will watch from the heart of the crowd. In the privacy of his penthouse. Popcorn will be served. He is a tough cookie crumble. A hard-hard ultra. Very brave. Mr. Saviles will stand with the ruffians and hools.

◆ ◆ ◆

The small man is in—oh yes—he's in like Johnny Flynn. Passwords and codes are fine and dandy, but for Mr. Fair they are no more than easily broken versions of the classic key. The brilliance of a physical can never be bettered. Keys are fine works of philosophy and art. He loves the materials used. Differences of shape and weight. He is an admirer of the industrial giants and swears he has been on the lash with Robert Barron, Jeremiah Chubb, Joseph Bramah and Linus Yale (the father, not the son).

There are no humans around as a code is cracked and a shape darts across the DenZen foyer. He is quickly inside the lift. Elevator going up… It stops at the fourth floor. The CCTV is dead. Killed by Fair Play. The machine is soulless. Recognises no spirits. Meanwhile, the masses dream of justice. Deserving targets. Righteous retribution. It is time to live in the moment. Tonight Mr. Fair will open one, two, three doors. He knows the numbers and the names. Knows his history.

Safely through Door 1, he finds Clint Donaldi asleep in his bed. Billionaire Clint deals in top-end Los Angeles property, but is also a slum landlord with a big Chicago portfolio, a lazy man who talks about hard work but has never done a day's worth. Never takes responsibility for his actions either, never took responsibility for the fire that killed twenty-one people two years ago. Why should he? Did Clint strike the match? Did Clint fan the flames? He buys the best legal representation and that proves his innocence. He owns two apartments in London and stays in this one when he is in town. The other remains empty. He has never collected the keys. His investment has more than doubled.

Clint is coaxed awake, eyes slowly opening, brain groggy as it tries to separate a fading story from the moment, and then a surge of adrenaline strikes as he realises there is an intruder in his apartment, but when he sees the blank face he is so shocked that he sags and his strength drains away. He comments mentally on the pointed head of a dunce, the mangled body and uneven limbs, which means that an insulted Mr. Fair is invited into his mind.

Clint flops back and gasps. The room has filled with smoke and he struggles to breathe. It fills his lungs. Flames hiss and spit and Clint images serpents circling. A different devil is in control. A deformed freak worse than any goat-headed demon. Clint has to escape, believes he has the strength to rush to the window, and he is pulling it open and feeling the clean air on his skin, jumping into the night and flying with the spirits silently flapping their wings as they circle the park opposite.

His own wings snap and he is falling towards the ground, and his fear isn't short-lived because he is higher in the sky and crashing through layers of cloud, picking up speed, moving faster and faster, on and on, his life racing past, and Clint exploding as he hits the pavement headfirst — a rock hard mattress — blood and brains splattering the walls, ceiling, floor of his bedroom.

Door 2 opens and closes. Mr. Fair is surprised to find that Rave Girl is wide awake. He hurries to a dark corner of the living room. Rave is relaxing in a leather armchair, her fingers frantically tapping the screen of an iPad. Three lines of cocaine are laid out on a glass table, next to the faint remains of another two. She is so focused on her Twitter feed that she doesn't notice the new arrival. Nails deliver insults. Short, sharp doses of hate. She smiles as she destroys the middle-aged white male who has tried to flirt with her. There is no hint of ageism, racism, sexism in her generalisation. He is one of that dangerous army of Islamophobic, homophobic, transphobic pigs plaguing the planet. Dirty pig. She is sure he deserves her scorn and the vitriol of her online gang.

Rave is a Twitter star. A Facebook revolutionary. A keyboard warrior. Rich and spoiled, educated at a leading university and immediately employed by a friend of Daddy's, she is a perpetual victim who has never suffered. Rave is sussed and straight off the mean streets, mixes good looks with a mastering of the current groupthink. Some might call her a troll. But they would be fascists. The suicide of her former best-friend, who she bullied to death after finding she had voted to leave the EU, is quickly dismissed. Stupid, reactionary, bigoted Sarah. Clearly.

Mr. Fair steps forward and places a hand on Rave's shoulder. She turns and screams when she sees the mad clown, a description that he does not appreciate. Rave is on her feet and running through the streets of an analogue London. She is being chased by a gang of skinheads. Some are Chelsea, others are Tottenham. Their Doctor Martens thud on concrete. Echo through the city. Rave is racing away from these Neanderthals, and when she glances back she sees that the mob has given up and has started to fight among itself. She stops and checks her mobile. Frowns at the dirty brickwork around her, wants to return to her apartment. Raising her head she sees the clown at her window.

A skinhead girl approaches. Her blonde hair is cut in a neat feather-crop. Rave knows she is safe, that as females they think and feel the same way, share a bond men will never understand. Class is unimportant. Background means nothing in the digital world. Rave can self-identify however she chooses. A headbutt connects with her face. Staggering, Rave remains on her feet, the coke helping her move towards her attacker, nails ready to scratch the bitch's eyes out, but then she sees the steel comb. Handle sharpened. The skinhead girl smiles and plunges the blade into Rave's chest.

Mr. Fair passes several apartments to reach Door 3, and once inside he finds a beam of light cutting across the living room. He stands in it for a full minute, regaining his calm after the insults of Clint and Rave. The beliefs of the man in the next room boom. Henry D'Arcy may have inherited one fortune and made another in the armaments business, but it isn't the rancid nature of missiles hitting schools and hospitals that decides what happens next. No, it is something much closer to home. The small cruelties mustn't be forgotten. Acts of bullying that take place on the margins. Crimes never mentioned or recorded.

Mr. Fair bangs Henry's bedroom door to wake him up. Perches on a chest of drawers. Fifteen-year-old Henry is squeezing the balls of his pet dog Bruce. The animal is yelping as it tries to free itself. The teenager laughs when he yanks and Bruce screams. The torment goes on as animals filter into the room, which quickly fills with the spirits of the Smithfield dead. They want to find their mums and dads, their brothers and sisters. Where are the judges of this world? They glance at Mr. Fair.

Henry cowers as the animals close in. He fears them, but they are not violent creatures. When they part, he sees Bruce. The dog is much bigger than he recalls. Huge in fact. The teeth are bared and Bruce growls and Henry wets the bed. Worse than Bruce is the small man with the strange head. Henry squints, but can't make out the features. Fuck him. One more subhuman.

Mr. Fair jumps to the floor and is quickly on the bed, Henry rolling off and standing and running towards the door, Fair's razor cutting a hamstring so he falls. The animals move back. They have an empathy that Henry D'Arcy, Rave Girl and Clint Donaldi lack. They are peaceful souls. Mr. Fair has lost his temper at last. He slashes at the beast, slicing through cloth and skin, blood soaking material and then the floor, and when he finally reaches the skull he carves the face. The room clears. Only Bruce remains. He feels sick as he watches the attack on the man who killed him in the woods many years before. Hands around his neck. Eyes bulging. Eyes sparkling. The loss of Bruce blamed on a poacher or a tramp.

The shower is on full blast and the small man washes. He is clean and efficient. Lessons are taught and lessons are learned. Examples set. But people forget. Never change. Time moves on.

In fifty years Brave Mr. Saviles will be standing on the balcony of BarbDoll Tower, high above this very spot, in a brand-new, cutting-edge, fashionable addition to the city. Mr. Saviles rides high in his penthouse. "Sugar Baby Love" is the song for New London. Saviles shudders as Mr. Fair connects. The brave libertine wants to poo his panties, but retains control.

A faceless hero walks away from DenZen. He is keen to find his way into the future. Mr. Saviles is safe for now, but that paedo's day will come. Mr. Fair continues along Golden Lane and stops on a corner, remembers football rows from the days of skinhead, hears "Liquidator" blaring, Harry J leading from the front. The Shed claps and chants in all the right places. And the spirit of Dolly Davis is close by and her words are merging with those of her husband and daughter. They are drinking in a local pub turned into a gastro, the prices jacked up to keep the riff raff out, nothing but airheads to be seen, yet nobody has told the originals who carry on in a parallel world, unseen by the yuppies, hipsters, trendies.

There is more music and laughter. Harry Champion sings "Any Old Iron" as Spurs favourite Chas Hodges bangs out some barrelhouse piano. A man taps spoons that sound like keys clanking on kneecaps. Bones vibrate. Chris Davis is standing at the end of the bar drinking with familiar faces from Arsenal, West Ham and Millwall. A couple of Cockney Reds. Boy soldiers and elderly windows hold hands and relive memories they never got to share. Everyone is guzzling, thinking, saying what they feel, and looking over at the shadow crossing the big plate-glass window they glimpse Mr. Fair and are pleased. He opens the door and comes inside, reminding me that I am free to enter and leave this and every other building at will. Common land and the common good. He is a fair man. Hard but Fair.

❖ ❖ ❖

Brave Mr. Saviles was nervous. It was unlike this noble libertine to feel fear or ever to worry, as he was rich and powerful and lived in enlightened times. Standing on the balcony of his penthouse apartment, he focused on the Gates as he tried to calm himself. While the past had long been erased, as a Good he had access to hards and had read about the atrocities committed in this very location, albeit inside a deleted tower. He understood the Grand Theory of repetition, which had been so cleverly exploited by the gurus of New Democracy. That claustrophobic, pre-ND era had seen the boldest property developers criticised by reactionary locals, while a primitive version of InterZone allowed troll identification and prosecution. Even animal fun was condemned.

Beyond the domes a full moon muddied the sky. Dirty light filtered through birdy heavens where feathered defecators dropped plop parcels on the heads of the lowlife, which was correct if foul. Those racist, brain-dead Englishers loved birds and other subs and refused to eradicate them beyond the Wall. The commons were a burden, but who else would do the dirty jobs? He was pragmatic. Workers were a necessity. At least they lived outside the domes and travelled in and out of Central and the Gates. He shivered at the idea of these ignorants brushing against his body, even if he had never come into contact with them beyond his sexuals.

Mr. Saviles had returned to his apartment charged after a lively evening at the nightclub Morgue, and yet his mood had swiftly altered. He was uneasy, the vision of a small man with a pointed head and no face flashing across his mind for the briefest of moments, the image so powerful he had started and nearly lost control, had even looked behind the sofa, imagining the patter of feet as he approached. Where had the image come from? He could not say. It made no sense. Too much narcotic perhaps? Too much champers? Too much necro?

Mr. Saviles was suddenly overcome by the crazy notion that the horrors of DenZen Past were about to repeat. An unplanned replay was ridiculous. History had been locked tight, studied by intellectual giants, and in time exploited. A series of nasties inside BarbDoll? Impossible. He was a creative. A man of ideas. He decided to indulge his genius, hurried inside and locked the door to the balcony. The windows were already secure. He waved his wands and sealed the apartment with an extra security coating. He was safe. Nobody could enter and nobody could leave. The Controller was untouchable in his tower.

FULLY FURNISHED

CHLOE ARIDJIS

Her honeymoon was one long shudder and her husband's hard mien quickly froze the daydreams she'd had as a girl. And yet she still loved him, and in his enigmatic way he seemed to love her, even if she often cringed when they walked home at night, one furtive look at his huge bulking figure was all it took, and she was also amazed by his silence, for he rarely spoke or showed any emotion. He had grown increasingly reserved ever since starting his new job with the Company.

Their new home only added to the shudder. The impassive glass walls of the lobby, the pervading smell of new building material, the sinister concierge with her wizened stare. They were among the first tenants of Clarendon Court, finished only a few months earlier, and so far it had been a constant battle against disenchantment. The flat had come fully furnished — the kitchen cupboards stocked with plates and knives, the bedroom with fresh sheets and pillows — yet even the furnishings felt alien, and the sleek leather sofas in the living room bore the stench of slaughterhouse.

Her footsteps sounded throughout the flat as she crossed from one room to the next, a kind of spiritual vacuum adding to the echo, and in that strange nest Alicia spent all autumn. She did her best to settle into the atmosphere, counting the hours till her husband came home from work. Half the time the lift wasn't working so if she wanted to go out she had to take the glacial stairwell — poor insulation made it subject to outside temperatures — and rarely glimpsed anyone else in the building. The basement games room and cinema lay silent and empty, too desolate to inhabit for more than ten minutes.

It came as no surprise that Alicia started to lose weight. It began with an attack of influenza that dragged on for days, her nausea intensified by the new construction smell, the chemicals from paint and sealant evaporating from the walls. One morning her husband woke up to find her in a faint. In a rare display of passion he quickly rang the doctor, who seemed puzzled after a brief examination.

"I have no idea what's wrong," he told Alicia's husband before parting, "She shows a great weakness I can't explain. No symptoms, but very fragile. Ring me tomorrow if she shows no improvement."

The next morning Alicia woke up even worse. The doctor returned and conducted a few tests. Severe anaemia, he concluded, its severity completely inexplicable. She was ordered to remain in bed, an easy order to follow given her total lack of energy.

Alicia did not faint again yet all day long she lay in bed with the lights on, the irksome sounds of the city entering through the thinly glazed windows. Her husband took time off of work and spent hours pacing back and forth in the living room. Every now and then he peered into the bedroom to check on his wife, who was usually asleep, her head resting on a fluffy white pillow.

Before long Alicia began having hallucinations. With eyes wide open she would stare for hours at the carpet on either side of the headboard. One night she yelled out for her husband. He ran in and upon seeing him she let out a wail of horror.

"It's me, Alicia, it's me!" he cried.

Alicia stared at him, then at the carpet, then back at him, and after a few moments of total stupefaction she returned somewhat to her senses. In a rare moment of communication she told her husband about one of her more persistent hallucinations, that of an enormous spider that circled the bed, staring up at her with hungry eyes.

The doctors came and went, futilely. There before them was a diminishing life, the blood and strength draining away hour after hour, without any of them able to explain why. They took turns feeling Alicia's pulse, holding her inert wrist in silence. It's an inexplicable case, muttered one of them, There's nothing to be done... Her husband banged his fist on the dining room table.

Alicia continued to vanish into a delirium of anaemia. Each morning she would wake up in a state, almost catatonic; it seemed that it was mainly at night that her life drained away. Upon waking she always had the sensation of a tremendous heaviness, as if lying under a tonne of cement. Soon she could hardly move her head. She forbade anyone to approach her bed or rearrange the pillow.

The agonising silence within the flat, and within Clarendon Court itself, was countered only by the sounds outside, people obsessively playing football in Fortune Street Park, children howling in the street, raucous men leaving The Shakespeare pub and heading east. And the noise of cars seemed to be growing louder, too. The din of rush hour was entering through the windows one Tuesday evening when Alicia finally passed away. Her husband peered into the room and noticed her lifeless, one arm hanging over the side of the bed.

Upon drawing closer he noticed that her pillowcase was spotted with dots of blood. On either side of the pillowcase, he saw with horror, were little red spots. They looked like tiny bites. He held the pillow up to the bedside lamp, surprised by how much it weighed, far more than one would expect. With dread he carried the pillow out to the living room for inspection. A few feathers floated out when he sliced it open with one of the shiny knives from the kitchen drawer. Within the pillow something moved amidst the nest of down: a monstrous ball of a thing, viscous and swollen, so swollen that its mouth was hardly distinguishable.

Night after night, ever since they had moved into the flat and Alicia had laid her head on the pillow, her husband now discovered, this thing had sucked on her temples, drawing out the blood, fattening up as he emptied her of life.

These avian parasites tend to remain small in their natural habitats. But provided with the right conditions, they are known to grow to hideous proportions. Human blood is a particular delicacy and it is not uncommon to find them in newly built homes of poor quality, where the temperature of human bodies drops just enough to make them especially palatable.

The author wishes to thank Horacio Quiroga.

GLITCH IN
THE MACHINE

TOM McCARTHY

Tom McCarthy
[redacted] strasse [redacted]
10[redacted] Berlin
Europe

20 August [redacted]

Dear Stewart,

I enclose the file that I found on my laptop after walking with
it past the Clarendon Court site on Fann Street.

As you know, I had been working on two quite separate
files at the time: one containing the text of Dante's *Divine
Comedy*, a new critical edition of which I was editing for Vin-
tage; another containing that of Shakespeare's *The Tempest*,
on which I was writing an article for the *London Review of
Books* (my article drew attention to the fact that the Fortune
Theatre in which many of Shakespeare's plays were first performed was located in our neighbourhood — as chance would
have it, mere yards away from the planned site of Clarendon
Court). These two documents had been open at the time, as
had (in minimised form) a digital copy of the Corporation of
London's planning regulations, and another setting out the
by-laws governing the movement of contractors' vehicles,
the management of demolition dust, and the like. All these
documents were saved in quite separate folders.

As I mentioned to you (forgive my rather distraught state
when we met in the street): after returning to my house and
opening my laptop after passing the building site, I found
to my dismay that all these files had, inexplicably, disap-

peared—or rather, had become amalgamated into a new one that I had never seen before, let alone composed. In this new file, the contents of the old ones seemed to have become scrambled, hopelessly entangled; moreover, they seemed to have been augmented by promotional material, penned by the proposed luxury flats' developers, which I had neither downloaded nor, to my knowledge, ever been sent.

I'm not a superstitious person. Unlike you, I don't believe in ghosts. However, I'm at a complete loss to comprehend what has taken place here. To be honest, the whole thing is freaking me out. I've rented out my flat on Golden Lane to Brian Dillon, and moved to Berlin. I'm sending you the file, which I have now deleted from my laptop. I suggest you do the same after you've read it.

Yours,
Tom McCarthy

VI, The Third Circle, Denizen, City of London, 3 bedroom apartments offering cloud-capp'd towers, the gorgeous palaces, with carpet to wall bedroom, integrated dishwasher, glass shower and bath screen to ensure an adequate water supply and water pressure for effective dust or particulate matter mitigation by the powers conferred by sections 19 (4) and 60 and Paragraph 3 of Schedule 3.

VI, The Third Circle, London's innermost layer, the Gluttonous, Cerberus, Ciacco, a creative hub, immersed in culture, of eternal, cursed rain, cold and heavy; huge hail, foul water and snow pour down through the gloomy air, and the ground that receives it stinks; fitted with fine mist sprays during dust generating works, new souls in torment erect solid screens or barriers to ensure fumes do not escape site, and share Heaven's sweetness or the bitterness of Hell.

8.1 City Procurement is responsible for an eloquent articulation of contemporary city luxury, underfloor heating, finishes, light, colour, texture and tone blend harmoniously to create an atmosphere that both uplifts and calms, carpet to wall, the baseless fabric, solemn temples, the great globe it-self, yea, all which it inherit, shall dissolve, fine mist sprays in accordance with Local Government Transparency Code 2015, Bribery Act 2010 and Fraud Awareness Policy 2012.

7.1 Any personal conflict of interest arising out of a procure-ment exercise must be the damning fault of gluttony, for which I, Ciacco, as thou seest, lie helpless in the rain, and in my misery I am not alone, for all these denizens are un-der the same penalty for the same fault. Failure to adhere to these conditions will result in disciplinary action and in the most serious cases criminal investigation and prosecu-tion. Distances are straight line measurements from centre of postcode. Computer generated image is indicative only: discover the life within.

6.4 My leader spread his hand, took up earth, and with full fists threw it into the ravenous gullets, setting our feet on their emptiness, which seemed real bodies, profane wretches turning themselves to ensure pedestrians are kept away from trucks and lorries. All equipment must comply with the EC Directives set out in BS 5228. The straight way is lost, but concierge services are your ally to help navigate life in the world's most exciting city, carpet to wall, bespoke drawer set, mirrored vanity unit, cinema room, the baseless fabric of this vision are indicative only and are melted into air, into thin air.

PM2.5 Air Quality index, SO2, CO: Concierge services, re-sponsible for managing freedom of information: Tell me, if thou canst, what the denizens of the divided city shall come to, Temp, Pressure and Humidity. And he said to me: PM10, N02, after long strife they shall come to minimise the need for reversing operations with one-way systems, turning points and vehicle signalling. We are such stuff as dreams are made on, by statutory instrument, site boundary, held within it the bright life, death had undone so many, and leave not a rack behind.

DEN OF SIN

LIZ REVER

I am almost invisible, the dark moon night barely outlining the pale hood of my jacket. I sleep shallow, merging with the soggy green undergrowth of trees inside the park. A branch snaps. I freeze. A muddy heavy boot slams into the side of my head.

Blood smears into my eyes and sticks my red hair to my cheeks. I grab my rucksack and put it between him and me as I turn away from his next blow. He grabs my bag and picks me up by my arm. Weightless, I don't feel my bones or my skin anymore. I try to speak; my words start to pour out fast with shock. He is not listening. He pushes me towards the park exit. I start again, "No, no, I am Su... Bi... you need to let me go."

His breath sour, his face round and thick, his eyes disagree. "Look, I am here to help you. You are hungry, right? I can fix that. You are making me late now, Sue, or ditch bitch, whatever your name is. I have people waiting."

My shrift means nothing. I am just what he's looking for. Cold lost meat. He headlocks me now, if there were others around we would pass as if in a drunken hug. We cross the empty street towards the side entrance of brightly lit new flats; a brass plaque states Clarendon Court, 43 Golden Lane.

Inside a goods lift he takes my bag and shoves the filthy sleeves of my jacket inside my mouth to silence me, before unzipping the side pocket, taking my passport and a folded five-pound note. The lift opens to the sixth floor, the walls oak veneer, the floor an off-white marble. He knocks once at the last flat at the end of the hall. A tall bald man in a tailored grey suit opens the door and quickly hurries us in.

He rants as he locks the door. "Where the fuck have you been? And where did you find this one? Skinnier and uglier than the last? Perfect. We can sell her off with the others after we finish." The other five men in the room agree, putting their drinks down. The idiot who jumped me hands me over for the grand sum of £300. With another blast of nauseating breath, I get introduced. "Hey boys, this is Sue B or Sue for short. Call her what you want, it's just cash on delivery."

The tall bald guy wastes no time. "Welcome to the den of sin, Sue…", as he tears my tracksuit and pushes me face first into a new plush grey corner sofa. The other men gather around, taking off their city suits, spitting into their hands and fumbling with their spongy cocks like some strange brotherhood ritual. His first touch insults my entire being. I lose blood beat and all remaining heat from my body surges into the centre of my brain. My temperature drops, my skin ice cold. The room spins with sudden vertigo. My chest tightens, I feel unable to breathe. I am pure rage. At that moment, my metamorphosis begins. Within seconds a deep blue indigo light implodes through my entire nervous system. A glass chandelier across the room buzzes, dims, and breaks. My entire electromagnetic biofield increases exponentially as I wilfully expand a continuous series of silvery electric threads into each male's etheric field. Blasting them across the room, their bodies now lay naked, supine, unable to move, their dicks poised upright, stuffed with blood. I fuck them all at once as I tone a precise 852 Hz frequency which harvests their sacral seed from their helpless climax, insuring their life force is transmuted and entirely mine. None of them expected a cosmic electrocuted fuck. They smolder from the current. I in turn, transform, in full morph and bloom, into a glistening rare beauty from time immemorial. My hair is golden brown, then flax, now deep copper, and then blue black. My lips, my skin, luminous. My eyes shine kaleidoscopic; a radiant blue to soft green to a piercing hazel, then to a blue of cold oceans. My muscles are curved, strong. My teeth, fanged.

I am Succubi.

I tried to warn you. But you never listened. You easily fell into my trap. My nothingness to you mirrors back your ignorance and repression. I am the catalyst of your demise inherent in your privilege, power and patriarchy. I am the crystalline bringer of new worlds.

Fast-forward hyper-decay dehydrates and moults each man's body to a lumpen geography, the dull grey paper shells of wasp hives. Their souls incarcerate into carpets, curtains, seeping into every wall of the flat.

To this day, an undercurrent of accumulated menace, like some unfinished form of death process, haunts the entirety of Clarendon Court; several flats in the building still remain absent, unsold, a bane. My cycle of beauty, destruction and creation continues however, occupying that liminal space and potency of each dark moon.

And will do so, until all are free.

THE CURSE OF CLARENDON COURT

RICHARD MARSH

I'd seen Chiang Tao cheat with the Tarot pack. As I lay awake in bed I realised I'd been taken for a ride. We'd dined together at the Modern Pantry, then we'd gone to Browns at the top of Hackney Road. The strip club was packed with sweaty gweilos and the heat was insufferable.

"Let's get outta here," Tao suggested almost as soon as we were through the door. "The crush is too much." I agreed and we left.

We both owned ghost flats in Clarendon Court, a set of luxury apartments on Golden Lane designed by the architectural practice Allford Hall Monaghan Morris. Tao had a business in Shanghai and I had one in Shenzhen. We'd both made a number of property investments in London and used these as an excuse to get away from our wives and have a bit of fun. My flat was beneath and one along from Tao's third floor apartment. I followed him into the communal games room.

"What about a game of Tarot?" he asked. "It will be better than going to bed at this early hour."

I agreed. At first we gambled for small stakes. I'd already drunk a lot. At Tao's invitation I quaffed more booze, which he got the concierge to fetch. The Aberlour single malt was wasted on me because I was drunk, a blend would have done just as well in the circumstances. We increased the stakes. I lost and kept on losing. Tao recorded in his notebook the extent of my indebtedness. When he announced the final sum, I was amazed to learn that it was very much more than I imagined, nearly one million US dollars.

"Nine hundred and ninety thousand dollars, Tao! It can't be as much as that!"

"My dear chap, here are the figures, look for yourself."

Tao handed me the notebook. His manner of arranging the amounts I found obtuse, but as I hadn't kept count myself I wasn't in a position to dispute their accuracy. Added up the figures came to the sum he stated. Still I was certain there was a mistake somewhere, although what it was I didn't know.

"Look here," Tao said. "Be a sportsman for once in your life! I'll give you a chance, double or quits!"

I didn't wanna do that. I'd be gambling for almost as much as I'd spent on my ghost flat. But Tao urged me on and I yielded. I must have been very much more under the influence of drink than I imagined. I cut first and drew the queen of coins. As the highest card would win I would have seen it as a good pick had the royal not come out reversed. In an occult Tarot deck this was the queen of pentacles and upside down as I'd drawn it she indicated fear of failure. It was a bad omen.

I watched Tao as he cut, and saw he dropped at least one card from the lot he picked up, and that gave him an opportunity to see its value. He did the same thing a second time. The card he ultimately held against mine was Death, one of the trumps.

"That wins!"

"But that was not the card you first cut, you dropped one."

"What do you mean? I didn't! If I did it must have been by the sheerest accident. What are you looking at me like that for? Don't lose your rag because you lost."

The insinuation was gratuitous and uncalled for. The card might have been dropped by accident, and he might not have noticed what had happened. I got up from my chair, conceding the point.

"That makes one million and eight hundred thousand bucks you owe me, Feng. Better luck next time."

I mentally resolved I would not play Tarot with Chiang Tao again, or at any rate not when we were alone.

I was in a curious state of mind when I returned to my apartment. The events of the evening buzzed in my head. I am very far from being a multi-billionaire, and two million dollars, less twenty thousand, is not a sum to be lightly thrown away. Was the man who I'd regarded as a friend actually a financial and psychic vampire? Was it possible that he had manipulated those figures to his own advantage and deliberately dropped that card? The more closely I reviewed the events of the evening, the less I liked the conclusion I reached.

When I went to bed my thoughts went with me. I could not shake them off. I tossed and tumbled in pursuit of sleep. And when slumber did come, my sleeping experiences were even more disturbing than my waking ones had been.

My repose is generally untroubled. I am seldom visited by dreams. But that night I had a most extraordinary nightmare. So extraordinary that I am still haunted by it. In appearance of reality it was little less than supernatural. Indeed, I do not mind admitting that I have been, and still am, at a loss to determine whether I was not an actual, sentient spectator, and not merely the subject of a vision of the night.

I had only just closed my eyes when something caused me to get out of bed. I have no recollection of putting anything on in the shape of clothes. I did not switch on the light. I had an uncontrollable impulse to go to Tao. I left the room bollock naked. Reaching Tao's door on the floor above mine, I tapped. There was no answer. I hesitated before knocking again and as I considered my next move I heard a strange noise coming from the apartment.

It was as if some furious wild beast was inside the flat. Yelling, snarling, screeching. Then there was a horrid, gasping noise. These sounds followed hard upon each other. Mingled with them were faint cries of someone in the extremities of pain and terror. At that sound I pushed the door. It opened. I stepped inside.

Tao was frantically struggling with a creature whose shape I couldn't make out. It was a mass of whirling movement and hideous sounds. Every part of it seemed to be in motion at once, and with its whole force it was assailing Tao. He was staggering about like a dying man. Presently he fell headlong to the floor. The creature, stooping, rained blows on to his motionless body.

There was something semi-human about the witch-like assailant. He or she appeared to be covered with a flowing robe of some shining, silken stuff, whose voluminous skirts whirled hither and thither as it writhed and twisted. Then using a blade the ghoul slit Tao's throat and wrote the following in his blood on the wall of the apartment:

Shake in your shoes, bureaucrats, the international power of the workers councils will soon wipe you out! Humanity won't be happy until the last bureaucrat is hung by the guts of the last capitalist! Long live the factory occupations! Long live the great Chinese proletarian revolution of 1927 betrayed by the Stalinist bureaucrats! Long live the proletarians of Canton and Xinjiang who have taken up arms against the so-called People's Army! Long live the Chinese workers and students who have attacked the so-called cultural revolution and the bureaucratic Maoist order! Long live the Wiccan revolution! Down with the state!

I am neither a nervous subject nor a coward. But at the sight of those words I turned and fled. And not the least strange part of the whole business was that immediately after, I woke up. I had certainly been asleep for I was sitting up in bed covered with sweat and trembling in every limb.

I looked about me. The blind was up. The moon was shining through. All at once a sound caught my anxious ear. I started forward to learn from whence it came. From the window! I was wide-awake now. In the moonlight I could see someone was standing on the other side of the pane, a faint, mysterious figure. The latch raised itself, the balcony door was pushed open. Out of the moonbeams, like some spectral visitant, a woman stepped into the room.

I held my breath. The figure was real. How could a woman have walked through my second floor balcony window from outside? Where had she come from at that hour of the night? What did she want? Would she kill me?

Unable to move I wondered whether she was intending to seduce and murder me. She left the balcony door open. I could feel the cool night air. She stood a few feet from me apparently listening to find out if her entrance had been discovered. If she'd looked straight ahead she'd have seen me sitting bolt upright up in bed. I was as visible as she was. She remained motionless looking neither to her right nor left. Presently she sighed and a baby's pacifier fell from her mouth. Toys and dummies were often deployed by those possessed by the dragon slaying god Nezha to keep this childlike immortal happy. When Nezha cut his flesh from his bones, his secret father Taiyi descended from the sky and gave him a new body of lotus flowers and the Golden Elixir. With this second skin Nezha became invincible. I silently prayed that this mysterious woman was indeed possessed by Nezha. The sound of her sustained respiration was so seductive I felt she might fulfil my darkest and most masochistic lustmord fantasies by arousing me to orgasm and then spilling my blood.

She moved uncertainly and stumbled against a chair, startled by this contact she put her hand to her head, as if trying to collect her thoughts.

"Where am I?"

The voice was sweet, soft, clear and sexy. It thrilled me. Was the lady a somnambulist who had woken to find herself in a stranger's bedroom? If that was the case what was I to do?

The question was answered for me. I must have fidgeted. She turned towards me.

"Who are you and why are you naked?"

"Do not be alarmed," I replied, "I am Hu Feng and I always sleep in the nude."

"If you're the writer who criticised Mao for overly politicising the notion of literary realism and losing touch with the everyday life of the proletariat, you must be a ghost because you died more than thirty years ago!"

"That was my father, I was conceived very shortly before his death. You see Hu Senior had an affair with the nurse who saw him through his final illness and I am the result of that liaison. My mother named me after him. If you will allow me I will turn on the light so that we may see each other better!"

What a flick of the switch revealed amazed me. At the foot of my bed stood the most beautiful woman I had ever seen. She was tall with a face like Lu Xun and the brow of a banana tree ghost. She had the sweetest pair of eyes I'd ever seen. But there was something in them I didn't understand. It wasn't just bewilderment, it was as if she looked out at the world from inside a dream. The woman regarded me with a curious sort of wonderment and my manhood stood to attention beneath her delirious gaze.

"Where am I? Have we met before?"

"I don't think so. But don't be alarmed. You are quite safe. You must have been sleepwalking."

"But where did I drift in here from?"

"That is a question you will have to answer. Do you live in Clarendon Court?"

"Clarendon Court?"

"We're in Clarendon Court!" I cried. "This is a luxury apartment block in the beating heart of the ancient ward of Cripplegate, just outside the original walls of the City of London, an area historically notorious for its coney-catchers, bawdy houses and molly houses."

"What?" she asked.

"Thieves, conmen, brothels and gay joints." I explained "This area was filled to the brim with them prior to its gentrification."

"Are there still molly houses round here!" she asked.

"I wouldn't know! I'm straight" I shot back. "Do you live in Clarendon Court? Is this your home?"

"My home?" She shook her head solemnly. "I have no home."

"You must have a home! Who are you? What's your name?"

"I don't know."

Was she an imbecile? No! Intellect was clearly marked upon her face. But there was something peculiar in her expression. She looked as if she had recently been roused from sleep and had yet to return to full consciousness. My original surmise was correct. She had been sleepwalking and had yet to regain sufficient consciousness to recognise the actualities of existence, or comprehend what it was she was doing.

The woman was covered from head to foot in a voluminous garment, which set off her face and figure to perfection. I took it to be some sort of opera-cloak, though it resembled a domino buttoned down the front. It was made of a bright plum material, which I afterwards learned was alpaca. A hood, which was attached to the garment, was only half on her dainty head. The whole affair, cloak and hood, was lined with green silk. The front of the cloak was decorated with voluminous green ribbons. One of these was a broad sash-ribbon, some eight-inches wide, reaching from her neck almost to her toes.

Half of this big ribbon was obscured by what looked like wet blood. But it was not just this item that was stained. I perceived here and there that the bright hues of the knots of narrower ribbon were also dimmed. There were even splashes on the cloak itself. She'd raised one arm. There were stains on both her palms. All the perfumes of Arabia would not have sweetened those little hands.

I recalled the extraordinary vision I'd had of Tao's murder. The frenzied figure clad in the woman's cloak with whirling skirts. Here in front of me was the very robe I'd seen. And here too, now sufficiently quiescent, were the whirling skirts. I put my hand up to my eyes and luxuriated in the wonderful thoughts that seemed to rush at me.

"Tell me who you are and where you are from!"

There was silence. I repeated my inquiry. She answered with a question.

"Why do you speak to me like this? And why do you put your hand before your eyes?"

The sound of her words utterly seduced me. It was delightful to imagine a voice that rang so convincingly with the accents of truth belonged to someone false and evil. Removing my hands from my face I looked at her again.

When she ran her fingers over her face she left behind a crimson stain.

"Look what you've done!" I cried.

"What?"

"What's on your hands?"

She held them in front of her contemplating them with an innocent air.

"It's blood." I spat.

"Blood? Where did it come from?"

With her blood-stained face and a ring of innocence to her voice, the sheer emptiness of her eyes went to my heart.

"Try to remember who you are and what you've been doing!"

"I don't know."

"But you must! Don't you see you're covered in blood?"

She gave a little cry. She swayed to and fro. Before I could reach her she had fallen to the ground in a swoon.

I'd heard of women fainting but never before had I seen one in such a pitiful predicament. What was I to do? I thought of calling Clarendon Court's 24-hour concierge. But then I'd have had to explain why I was naked and there was an unconscious woman covered in blood in my apartment.

As I looked at the lovely creature lying so still her utter helplessness filled me with a curious sense of excitement. A resolve grew up within me to constitute myself her champion if she would only avail herself of my services. If she had something to conceal by no action of mine should it be trumpeted to the world. And if she had killed Chiang Tao what was that to me? The cancellation of nearly two million dollars worth of debt made her seem like my avenging angel!

As I considered undressing her and cleaning her up before putting her into my bed, I noticed something was lying beside her on the floor. Where it came from I could not tell. It was hardly the kind of thing to have fallen from a woman's pocket. I picked it up. It was a photograph of Chiang Tao. It was smeared with blood. I thrust it between the leaves of Cixin Liu's short story collection *Weight of Memories,* which was on my bedside table. She moved. Turning I found that she had raised herself a little and was looking at me with her eyes wide open.

"Have I been asleep?"

Her empty gaze coupled with a strange look of bewilderment filled me with a sense of confusion.

"You have not been well. But you are better now. Let me help you to get up."

I held out my hand. Putting hers into it, she rose to her feet with a little spring. When she took her hand away, there was a ruddy smirch on my palm.

"You should take off your cloak."

She looked at me in amazement. "Why?"

"You'll be more comfortable."

I helped her remove the outer garment and flung it over the back of a chair.

"Go into the bathroom and take a shower."

She eyed me with surprise. "Why?"

"You're covered in blood."

"Will it come off if I wash?'

I assured her it would and she went to her toilet. While the woman was cleaning herself up I dressed. I find situations in which one person is clothed and the other naked erotically charged and I was banking on my angel of vengeance emerging from the bathroom nude. When she did appear she'd abandoned her own clothes but had pulled on one of my dressing gowns.

We sat down in the living room to be more at ease, on either side of my sofa. Her beauty awed me. At the back of my mind I knew I'd seen this enchanting vision before. I was at a loss as to how to address her and when I managed to do so I blustered.

"Is there any reason for you to hide your name?" She shook her head. "Then tell me what it is."

"I don't know who I am. I don't remember anything before I entered your bedroom."

I didn't know what to think. If she was playing a part, which seemed likely, she acted with such plausibility that I couldn't uncover the trick. I thought that perhaps after all I should call the concierge. But before that my visitor needed clothes. I maintain a large wardrobe for both myself and any female friends I might make at strip joints and massage parlours. My own cross-dressing garments were the wrong size, but I did have a very short blue dress bought for a future friend that fitted perfectly.

"The concierge on duty tonight knows all about superior ladies of the night. She's called Cynthia Payne. She may be of more assistance to you than me. Will you allow me to call her?"

"Why not?"

This was said with such an air of innocence that I was half-ashamed of the thoughts that filled my mind. But I couldn't help it, I knew I'd like nothing better than to see this woman and Mrs Payne naked and rubbing their pussies together.

Before checking in with the concierge to see if she was up for some fun, I inspected the bathroom to make sure it was clean. I wiped up a few remaining traces of blood with bog-roll and flushed this down the toilet. I bundled up the woman's clothes and bagged them in a bin liner that I hid in the bottom of a wardrobe. Then I changed my mind about ringing, I decided to go downstairs and see Cynthia in person at her desk.

Cynthia was far from the first flush of youth but she was still a very attractive woman with a magnetic personality.

"Has a lady come up lately?"

"Up where?"

"Up to the second floor or anywhere?" Madam Cyn shook her head. "You're sure?" I asked.

"Certain. No lady's been beyond my desk for a good two hours. The last was Mary Frith, she's on the fourth floor. She'd been to the BFI IMAX with the man she brought home. She was the last woman to come in and that was just after eleven. You may not know her as Mary, everyone calls her Moll."

"No one else came in?"

"Well I had to chase off a junkie who took a huge shit on our front steps, but she didn't get through the door. Be careful if you go out coz I haven't had a chance to clean it up. It's the biggest turd I've ever seen in my life! It's absolutely massive! All those drugs the junkies take stop their bowels working properly, then when they do manage to defecate it's such a strain and a monster comes out! It's utterly disgusting!"

"There are drug addicts around here?"

"A lot of them I'm afraid. It became a problem a little bit before Clarendon Court was built. There used to be a police section house where your luxury apartment now stands and when that had coppers living in it, the junkies stayed away. But as soon as the Old Bill went the junkies took over. They use the telephone box just outside Clarendon Court as a shooting gallery. We've been trying to get the phone box removed."

"But aside from this junkie, no other women came to the door?"

"Just a Vietnamese human trafficking victim who'd escaped from one of the local nail bars."

"I didn't know you spoke Vietnamese!"

"I don't."

"Then how do you know she'd been trafficked? Did she speak English?"

"Of course she couldn't speak English. A trafficked Vietnamese broad from one of the local nail bars stumbles in here every few weeks. I don't need to understand their lingo to know about that."

"What do you do with them?"

"I call their boss Mr. Nguyen. He's a lovely fellah. You've probably seen him walking around the neighbourhood with a battery-operated power drill in his hand. When he gets agitated he switches his power tool on and waves it at whoever is annoying him. Some think he's intimidating and unfriendly but I get on very well with him. He gives me a pony for every girl I return."

"What do you do with so many horses?"

"Not horses, silly! A pony! Twenty-five quid!"

"Oh I see." I said. "But no one else came into Clarendon Court? No Chinese women?"

"No."

If my visitor had not come in from the ground floor, how had she gained access to my balcony, which is on the second? I'd told myself she'd probably climbed down from the one above and slightly to the side, which belonged to Tao's apartment. Then Cynthia volunteered a statement on her own account.

"And the last man who went out was Chiang Tao's brother."

I pricked up my ears at this. "Tao's brother?"

"Well his half-brother, same mother, different father. The brother goes by the name of Chan Wai-Man. He came down not three minutes before you, just after Charles Hitchen came in. Chan was in a right hurry. I said good night as he went past, but he blanked me. He had a big parcel in his arms and was struggling to carry it."

"Are you sure it was Tao's brother?"

"It was him right enough. You can't mistake him. It's said he was once a cop in Hong Kong but he has Triad tattoos, a really lovely bit of inking. Of course I couldn't see them tonight as he was wearing a coat, but once when he had a bit of time he let me see them all. He even took down his pants so I could view the tats on his backside. The inking is gorgeous and he's got very good muscle definition too! He looks a lot like his brother but has a much bigger donger. I sneaked a picture of it onto my phone while with Chan's permission I was grabbing images of his tattoos. Chan owns a ghost home in Dance Square and comes to London two or three times a year to meet girls and go shopping. He's impossibly wealthy. I'm pretty sure he bought Tao's flat in Clarendon Court for him."

"He came down three minutes ago?"

"Yes."

This meant he must have been with his brother some time after my visitor had come to me, so perhaps she wasn't Tao's killer. The knowledge left me a little disappointed. Still she'd been covered in blood so it seemed likely she was some kind of murderess. If she ever killed me I wanted her to do it when she was naked. It would be easier to wash down after the crime that way and much sexier too.

"When did Chan arrive?" I asked.

"He went up about an hour ago. He'd got no parcel then. When I saw how he was struggling with the package when he came down, I thought I should call him a cab. I know he only had to walk up Golden Lane and cross Old Street to get to Central Street, but even so he looked like he needed a ride. I was speaking to Charles Hitchen and Chan was off before I managed to get a word out of him."

"I have a lady visitor." I said. I was still wondering if Cynthia would do a lesbian sex show with her for me.

"Very good sir," Madam Cyn replied. "I hope she's a nice professional lady. There's no fun to be had with a drunk amateur who lies back and does nothing for a man."

"The fact is something very remarkable has taken place. I've come down to tell you about it and ask your help."

"Oh, come now, sir, I know you're married but it isn't as if I hadn't seen you taking a variety of young ladies up to your apartment. If you try to tell me you've just lost your virginity then I'll laugh like a loon."

"A young lady has just entered my bedroom through the balcony door."

"From the balcony! Mr. Feng! At this hour!"

"I'm afraid she's not quite right in the head."

"I should think not! Are you?"

"She is quite a lady."

"Looks can be deceptive. I've met thousands of crooks and psychopaths in my time and many of them were extraordinarily beautiful."

"I thought at first she was a sleepwalker. Something strange has happened to her. She doesn't know her name and can't remember anything about herself."

"Is she on crack?"

"Come and speak to her and you'll see she's not on drugs, she's suffering from amnesia."

"Very good, Mr. Feng. I worry sometimes that you're too soft-hearted. Where is this young lady?"

"She is in my apartment."

"Alone?"

"Yes."

"Then she's probably gone back through the balcony door, taking something valuable with her. If we hope to find her we'd better hurry."

Urged by Mrs. Payne we hastened to my apartment. My visitor had not gone. She was asleep on the sofa. The spectacle she presented touched the concierge's heart.

"Now that's a sight that makes me want to go back into the brothel keeping business. With a girl like that I could make a fortune!" Madam Cyn exclaimed. "Why I'd keep her in a back room and tell dozens of clients they were the first to have her so I could claim a virginity premium from them all!"

"Possession is nine-tenths of the law, so she's mine!"

"How pale and beautiful she is!" Payne said changing the subject. "She came through the balcony door you say? How did she get there? Who is she? Where did she come from?"

"I've asked her all those things already and she says she doesn't know the answers."

"Let's try and wake her."

Our efforts were to no avail. Cynthia was convinced I'd slipped her a date-rape drug despite my protestations of innocence. Anyway she helped me get my dressing gown off the woman and carry her naked from the sofa to my bed. When Madam Cyn left I felt like I was walking on air. It was ridiculous. Why should I be affected by the whims and fancies of an apparently half-witted woman who had forced her way into my room at dead of night in a cloak soaked with blood? It wasn't as if I couldn't afford to hire an overnight companion. But the illicit thrill of stripping the woman and placing her naked and unconscious into my bed left me feeling horny and hamster-like. I wanted to hibernate for the next six months with this mysterious serial killer.

The next morning when I woke up my mystery woman was still fast asleep beside me. It really was as if I'd slipped her a date rape drug. I left her naked under the bed sheets and headed down to the front desk. Cynthia Payne had finished her night work and Johnny Edgecombe had replaced her as our daytime concierge.

"Do you know if Chiang Tao slept in his apartment last night?" Johnny asked before I had a chance to speak.

"Why?"

"Because a three-girl stripogram team turned up to surprise him this morning but I could get no answer to calls to his room and knocks on his door. Such a shame as one of the strippers was really cute."

"Tao was here last night. I was with him in the games room and after he went up to his apartment I'm told he had a visitor."

"He must have gone out somewhere then."

"He could be ill," I suggested. "We both drank a lot last night. I could climb up from my balcony to his to find out. I'll do that and tell you what I find."

"Don't be silly!" Johnny told me. "I'll give you a master key and you can let yourself in through the front door."

I don't know what propelled me to this action beyond a sense of adventure and foreboding. Somehow I knew that

Tao was dead. I let myself into my friend's apartment and I saw what I'd seen in my dream. I sprang back into the hall and rushed down to the desk.

"Quick! Come up, there's something wrong!" I shouted at Edgecombe.

Johnny followed me to the dead man's flat. Chiang lay face down on his living room floor. The carpet was stained with blood. His clothes were soaked with the claret too. Had it not been for his clothes I wouldn't have known it was Tao. When we turned him over we saw his face and neck had been hacked to pieces. It was as if some savage thing had torn him apart with its teeth and claws. His flesh had been ripped and rent so that not one recognisable feature was left.

Edgecombe called the police from Tao's apartment, then sped off to fetch Dr. Crippen, an American medic who lived in the building. I cleared the scene of evidence that suggested a woman had committed the crime. On a chair was a pair of white kid gloves. I picked them up and put them in my pocket. Among the portraits on display was the face of the avenging angel who at that very moment was asleep in my bed. I took that photograph too.

The room was in some disarray, but not in such disorder as to suggest a desperate struggle had taken place. Two chairs and a table had been knocked over. There were gouts of blood on the woodwork of a bookcase. I spotted a blotch on the back of one of the books, *The Art Of War* by Sun Tzu. The strange anti-Maoist message I'd seen in my dream was written in blood on the wall. Something lay on the carpet a short distance from the dead man's feet. It was a man's collar, twisted and stiff with coagulated blood. As I stared at it a wild wonder began to take shape and to grow in my brain.

"Feng, what's the matter? What's this murder Edgecombe's told me about? Good grief! What's that anti-Maoist rant written in Tao's blood on the wall? Shake in you shoes bureaucrats! Stalinists denounced by the ultra-left indeed! No wonder Lenin branded left-wing communism an infantile disorder! My God this whole building has such terrible feng shui! I wish I'd never bought an over-priced so-called luxury apartment in Clarendon Court."

It was Dr. Crippen who spoke. He'd come into the room while I was staring at the collar.

Hawley Harvey Crippen is a man who has taken high medical honours but, having private means, he doesn't have a regular practice. His hobby is madness. He's a student of what he calls obscure diseases of the brain and insists everyone has a screw loose somewhere. That out of every happy smile insanity peeps even if it is only the shadow of a shade.

Some strange stories are told of Crippen. His office is in Harley Street and while there is a plate on his door, his patients are few and far between. They aren't always welcome even when they do appear. Still it's useful to have a doctor in Clarendon Court and when push comes to shove he'll take a look at any neighbour who needs his assistance. Tao used to speak of him as "The Clarendon Court Doctor."

Crippen was still in the prime of life, perhaps forty, of medium height, sparely built, clean-shaven, with a high forehead like Shakespeare and coal-black hair. I always felt that he regarded everyone he knew as a possible subject for experimentation. I felt no dislike for him but I suspected he despised me.

"Yes." I replied. "I too wish I'd never bought into the Clarendon Court development, the feng shui is awful! Look at the mad butchery the warped alignments of the building have led to here!"

"To put things in perspective, this bad craziness is no worse than the Manson family being inspired by The Beatles to write things like *Helter Skelter* in their victim's blood on the walls of their California cult crime scenes back in the 1960s!"

"Did you know that The Beatles took their name from a now forgotten horror novel by a fellow called Richard Marsh."

"So it's alleged, but *The Beetle* and The Beatles aren't quite the same thing. Besides Marsh was a pen name. The author was a notorious criminal called Richard Bernard Heldmann."

To underline his sense of superiority, Crippen looked away from me and began to whistle the tune "I Was Kaiser Bill's Batman". He knelt by the dead man on the floor, his usually impassive face alert and eager.

"What happened?" Crippen asked as he broke off from his rendition of the 1967 novelty hit composed by British song-writers Roger Cook and Roger Greenaway, which credited the non-existent Whistling Jack Smith as its performer.

"We don't know."

"Who found him?"

"Me, then I called Edgecombe."

"Was the body lying like this?"

"No, he was face down. We turned him over."

"The man's been cut to pieces."

"It looks to me like he's been scratched to pieces." I observed.

"These wounds are too deep to be scratches. It looks like several narrow blades were used, set in some kind of frame, or a row of spikes. The flesh has been torn open in regular layers. He's been dead some time; he's quite cold. Very curious indeed."

As Crippen spoke he unfastened the dead man's clothes, laying bare the neck and chest. When I looked I saw that the body too was covered in gaping wounds.

"Enough violence was used to kill Tao a dozen times." I laughed. It served the bastard right for cheating at cards.

"Is that all you see?" Crippen said impatiently. "Can't you tell a sharp-pointed instrument has been thrust right through his body? But how was this done without his clothes being shredded? It is extraordinary that with the exception of bloodstains, there is not a mark upon Tao's attire. His clothes are intact. Are we to infer the murder weapon did not pass through them? Was Tao naked when he was attacked and then dressed after being ritually killed?"

"But those are the clothes Tao was wearing them when I saw him last night."

"At what time?"

"About half-past eleven, perhaps a little after."

"That's within an hour of when he was murdered. Perhaps even less. That's very odd."

"Why is it odd?"

"Was he alone when you left him?"

"Yes."

"Did you part on friendly terms?"

"May I ask why you inquire?"

"Feng, it is a question which will be repeatedly put to you. You should have an answer. It seems rather unfortunate that you quarrelled with him just before he was killed."

"I did not quarrel with him."

"No? Your unwillingness to answer my question indicates you didn't part on the best of terms."

"I'll give the information to any one entitled to ask for it."

"So you think I'm not entitled to ask?" Who would you answer? A cop? Do you know if anyone saw him after you left him?"

"I believe his brother saw him."

"Why do you think that?"

"I was told so by the night concierge."

"When?"

"Last night or rather early this morning. Cynthia told me she'd seen Tao's half-brother go up, and that he had just come down again."

"What time was that?"

"Between two and three."

"Tao was dead before the clock struck two and probably before one."

"I found this on the floor just before you came in." I handed Crippen the blood-grimed collar.

"What is it? A collar?" As he turned it over he saw what I'd seen. "Here's a name, Chan Wai-Man."

"I believe Wai-Man is his brother's name, they have the same mother but different fathers."

Crippen gave me a dirty look.

"What do you infer from that?"

"Nothing."

"You're suggesting that when Chan came to see his brother he took off his collar and left it behind him on the floor? Why?"

"It was soaked with blood."

Crippen stood up. "What else have you found?"

I fenced the question. I was not going to speak of the gloves or the photograph. "I haven't looked. The collar was on the floor, I couldn't help seeing it."

"Let's look together. Here's a waste-paper basket, let's see what's in it. This appears to be a letter. Let's see what we can make of it." He read from the scrap of paper he was holding: "'Men like you shouldn't be allowed to live.' That's a strong assertion. And written by a woman in a bold hand. I would recognise that calligraphy if I saw it again. If the person who tore up the letter wanted to conceal its contents they did so with little skill. Here's another fragment. 'Tonight I will give you a last chance.' I wonder if tonight means yesterday? If so he had his very last chance. Here on another piece is part of a signature. 'Woo.' I know a Woo."

I wondered if Woo was the woman in my bed, it seemed likely.

"Are you saying a woman did this?" I cried. "How could a woman be this violent?"

"I scent a woman in this murder. There are women who are as violent as men. But in this instance there is nothing to show that much strength was required. It is a question of what murder weapon was used. Let me be frank, Feng. You are making a serious mistake trying to frame Chan Wai-Man. I know him well. He is a high ranking Triad and if he wanted to kill his brother he'd get someone else to commit the murder for him!"

"I wasn't trying to finger Wai-Man."

"Are you sure there aren't nasty thoughts lurking at the back of your mind?"

"Can you remember your name?"

"No."

"That's an awkward position to be in, not knowing your name or where you are from."

"I remember people shouting. They were screaming at me and clapping their hands."

"Where were you?"

"I remember coming through your balcony door but that's all."

I took the white kid gloves out of my coat pocket. "Are these yours?"

"I don't know? Where did you find them?"

"I want to know if they are yours."

"I'll try them on to see if they fit."

I knew they belonged my avenging angel. They covered her murderous hands perfectly. I wondered if she would kill me. Was Tao naked when he was slaughtered? Was this woman straddling him waiting for him to reach orgasm before she struck? Why did I find the thought of the same thing happening to me so exciting?

"Do you know a guy called Tao?" I asked.

"Tao? I can't remember?"

"Chiang Tao."

"Do you know him?" she asked.

"I do and so do you."

"How do you know I know him?"

"Because last night you climbed down from his balcony to mine." I said.

"What was I doing in his apartment?"

"Try to remember what happened in Tao's flat that led you to make the risky descent from his balcony to mine, so that you could seek refuge here."

"Tao lives in this luxury apartment block! Take me to see him right now!"

Was she mentally deficient? Did she not know she was a sexy fury, a nude assassin? That she was way more beautiful than Chingmy Yau as she stabbed men in *Naked Killer*?

Surely this woman's destiny was to realise my ultimate erotic fantasy. Intelligence was written on every line of her face. What then was the meaning of the cloud that had temporarily paralysed the active forces of her brain? Where was the key to the puzzle?

Just then my iPhone rang. I answered it. "Mr. Feng, can I speak to you for a minute?" It was Cynthia Payne. "Have you heard the news of Chiang Tao's death?"

"I have."

"From what I'm told it seems the killer must have struck just before the young lady turned up on your balcony."

"That's correct."

"'What shall we do?"

"What can we do?"

"Do you think she knows?"

"She's suffering from amnesia, she knows nothing."

"Do you think she did it?"

"I sincerely hope so! I want her to kill me next! I am certain the woman who turned up so unexpectedly in my bedroom made a consensual sex-murder pact with Tao. She has killed but she has not sinned. I need to get her to recall her mission in life, which is to enable men to realise their erotic death wishes. Please say nothing to the police, if my avenging angel is arrested she'll never be able to induct me into the slaughterhouse of love."

"Your wish is my command. I'll do whatever you want. I've never judged men on their kinks, I've just exploited those warped desires for money."

"I'll make a new will later today and leave my vast fortunes to you. Just don't tell anyone I had a young female visitor."

"I never speak about men and their peccadilloes. I would not have made a success of my life had I done such things. Rest assured I'll say nothing to the cops, I'd much rather inherit your money than see the young lady arrested."

Next there was a knock on my door. It was a workman who'd come to remove the fallen plaster from my bathroom.

Shortly after this I received a message from my downstairs neighbour saying cracks had appeared in her ceiling. She was worried that if I showered carelessly then excess water hitting my floor would cause it to cave in and wreck her luxury apartment. She suggested that I visit a Turkish bath, or in an emergency use her bathroom to do my ablutions. Clarendon Court was falling apart because it had never been properly finished. The block was jerry-built, it reeked of drains and swarmed with vermin. Fortunately I had plenty to take my mind off the creepy crawlies that were swarming between floors and behind walls.

I was wondering whether my avenging angel had murdered Tao of her own free will? If so why was she suffering from amnesia? Had some outside force been exerted on her? Were zombie powders or even hypnotism involved? Had she been animated by a malevolent force? Would it take control of her again and provide me with the ecstasy of oblivion? I knew nothing else could equal dying at the height of an orgasm.

It seemed that the deed of murder had acted on the girl like a bolt from the blue. The shock of it had robbed her of her senses. She was undergoing some sort of neurosis, involving complete memory loss. If she could only remember and relish what she'd done in the name of erotic love, her fitness to butcher me would be fully established.

Time pressed and danger threatened. If the true facts became known my angel of death would be arrested and I would never experience the ultimate apotheosis of a love murder. Currently my saviour was in too piteous a condition to stand trial. My angel must be proud and defiant in the dock. She needed to leave a string of dead men behind her, not just one. And when she was found guilty she would take her own life rather than serve time in prison. She had to live fast, die young and leave a good-looking corpse!

In my vision I'd seen my angel lovingly murder Tao. I'd seen the political slogans written in blood on the wall. I'd heard the woman's laughter and although I had a clear recollection of looking around me, I had seen no one else. Yet all the evidence pointed to the dead man's brother being present. Was there lurking deep inside my subconscious a love that dare not speak its name? Ultimately would I find it more erotic to have my life snuffed out by a man? Was this why I bought and hung on the walls of my London apartment Xiyadie's paper cuttings depicting tormented gay desire. Pictures I didn't dare hang on the walls of my properties back home!

The girl was sleeping again. The murder must have tired her out, poor thing. I took her clothes from their hiding place and examined them. Turning over the cloak I came upon a pocket in the green silk lining. There was something in it which I took out. It was an envelope. The writing I instantly recognised, I had seen it on the scraps of paper that Crippen had taken from Tao's waste-paper basket. The envelope bore the name "Hwang Jang Lee" on the front. Without hesitation I tore it open. The contents I give verbatim.

> Dear John, the Silver Fox knows that in the so-called People's Democracies, the opportunists have set up national systems in which all social classes are represented, with the pretence that in this way their opposing interests can be harmonised. In China where the four-class block is in power, the proletariat, far from having assumed political power, is subjected to the incessant pressure of industrial capitalism and had to bear the cost of "National Reconstruction" just like the proletariats of the other countries. I am going to see that recuperator tonight. He'd better take care or something bad will happen to him. I'll write you at length tomorrow. W.

Several points struck me about this odd epistle. It seemed to be written by a far-left fanatic. It contained neither a date nor an address. While Hwang Jang Lee was on the envelope, the letter itself began "Dear John," the inference being that Hwang Jang Lee was an assumed name. The "W" of the signature was no doubt the "Woo" on the scraps of paper Crippen found in Tao's bin.

The letter reassured me that this young girl had gone to Tao with the intention of killing him in an ultra-left love ritual, and that this communist sex witch would do the same for me. Nonetheless its extremist political content was rather disturbing. I did not want my erotic desires channelled so that they furthered the machinations of an occult criminal machine bent on overthrowing the Communist Party of China. But at the same time I so wanted to be sacrificed that it seemed worth risking a proletarian uprising to realise my sexual dreams. While providing a clue to the lady's identity, the letter did not answer all my questions about her.

I tried doing an internet search for Woo but had little luck. The top results were all about trying to gain the love of a woman, usually with an eye to marriage. Nothing was said about gaining the love of a killer who'd indulge her man with a sado-masochistic death ritual, and so I concluded it was not necessary for me to be wooing Woo. An image search did bring up a few women, but none of them were as beautiful as the one I sought. At least I had a photograph of Woo, the portrait I'd taken from Tao's pad, and I figured I could use it to get the lady's full name. I turned the portrait over. There was a stamp for Flash Photography! I resolved to visit the place to find out whose picture I held. As I attempted to depart for the Flash offices, I was accosted by Dr. Crippen.

"I want to speak to you."

We went to the residents' lounge. That Crippen intended to be disagreeable was obvious. I resolved that his intention should be persistently ignored.

"No wonder, Feng, you resented my inquiry as to the terms on which you parted with Tao.

"The death of Tao seems to have affected you more than it has me, which is odd."

"How much did you owe him?"

"You ask some very odd questions."

"When a murder is committed the first thing to look for is a motive. How much did you owe him?"

"Nothing."

"Liar! Feng, I am a pathologist and a student of mental instability. As such I have watched you with growing interest. You appear to suffer from mnemonic intervals."

"I don't know what you mean."

"If you were to kill me now you'd forget your murderous acts as soon as I was dead. Quite possibly consciousness of your action might never visit you again. That is what I mean."

"Crippen!"

"I will explain why I believe you killed Tao. I found in his room a notebook. Let me read you the last entry, dated to last night: 'Played cards with Feng. Have long been aware that as a victim of psychic driving by the Chinese intelligence services he is dangerous. If he could have killed me then and there without being detected, he would have done so. A bad loser. He even accused me of cheating. He owes me nearly two million dollars. I suspect getting it will be like drawing eye-teeth, but I'll have it. The money will be useful.' Do you still claim you owed him nothing?"

"Psychic driving and the Chinese intelligence services. Those are the ravings of a nutjob!"

"It is well known that various intelligence agencies run mind control programmes. Psychic driving was a technique developed by Dr. Donald Ewen Cameron for the CIA as part of its MKUltra programme. While the Americans may have pioneered the use of mind controlled zombie assassins, it didn't take long for the Chinese to pick up on it. Let me put you under hypnotic regression and I'll uncover the whole story for you. I can free your mind from the thought control you're under and you could win a bundle of compensation if you sue for justice here in London."

"But I wouldn't be able to go back to China."

"That's true but why would you want to go back once you know the full truth about what your country's done to you?"

"China made me the man I am today, which is nothing bad, so it is as guiltless as I am over Tao's death."

"I know you were in Tao's room when he died. A girl just told me that in the early hours of this morning she saw you streaking along the corridor, as naked as the day you were born, racing from Tao's apartment towards your own."

"Who saw me in the buff?"

"The witness will be produced in due course. She says that perspiration was pouring down your cheeks."

"My face or my arse cheeks?"

Both and that is odd considering you weren't wearing a stitch of clothing."

Was it possible that my precognitive dream was not a case of extra sensory perception but that I had actually witnessed the murder? As I was endeavouring to juggle Crippen's words in my mind, the door opened and a man came in.

"Are you Feng?" he asked turning towards me.

"I am."

"Then you're Tao's friend. I believe my master murdered him!"

Our visitor was in a state of considerable agitation. Crippen knew him. The doctor jigged towards the man from across the lounge.

"Cheung Lik you'd better come with me. You should speak to me and ignore the guttersnipe I'm with."

I interposed. "He asked for Feng. Therefore he wants me."

Lik looked at Crippen with half dazed eyes. "Dr. Crippen, I know you very well."

"Lik," Crippen barked, "you have no right to speak of your master's private affairs to strangers. I am Chan's friend. I will safeguard his interests. I warn you to keep a strict watch on your tongue, or...."

The doctor was unable to complete the sentence. Even before Lik entered the room he'd been doing the dance of inadequate bladder control. I knew Crippen had problems on the other side too and it looked like he'd just accidentally evacuated his bowels. The doctor departed from the residents' lounge using a strange series of twisted steps that looked like they'd come straight from the Ministry of Funny Walks. He was desperately holding in his transverse abdominis while simultaneously clenching his pelvic floor and glutes. The vile odour emanating from his clothing indicated that a considerable quantity of runny poo had seeped into his pants. Clearly Crippen didn't want any more of the brown stuff falling out of his bottom before he reached a toilet. Given that the plumbing in Clarendon Court had never been properly laid in, the doctor reaching a bathroom was not necessarily going to solve all his problems.

I turned to my visitor. "Pay no attention to my excitable friend, he has a bit of a drug problem and has gone soft in the head, and as you can tell he's also incontinent. I am Feng, Tao's friend. I assume you work for Chiang's half-brother Chan Wai-Man. Tell me what happened."

"I think perhaps Crippen is right and I shouldn't talk about my master."

"But you have accused him of murdering Chiang Tao!"

"No, sir, not that! I didn't mean it! I was confused!"

"Between thought and expression lies a minefield of misunderstanding," I observed. "I'm convinced Chan played no role in his brother's death. Very soon you'll hear from Chan himself an explanation that will blow your mind and send all your doubts away. He will clear the whole thing up once you take me to him."

"But that's just it. I don't know where he is. Isn't he here at Clarendon Court?"

"Are you telling me Chan stayed out all night?"

"Yes and he told me to wait at his flat as there was something important he needed help with in the early hours."

"His London ghost home is in Dance Square off Central Street, is that right?"

"Yes."

"When did he go out?"

"After midnight and in an absolute rage with Tao. You see Chan is very good with money and has US dollar bills falling out of his arsehole. But Tao seemed unable to make money, he was only able to spend it. Chan gave Tao millions and millions of dollars. What he did with it was a mystery but it got to the point where they had violent quarrels over money. Now Chan is hot-tempered but Tao was in the wrong. Once I saw Chan attack Tao with a baseball bat and beat him so badly I had to call an ambulance. And recently the arguing between them has got worse. There's been some trouble over blockchain and cryptocurrencies. Tao has a hacker friend and got him to break into one of his brother's computers. They took all the Fiatcoin reserves Chan and his business associates had built up by using them to buy non-existent drugs on fake dark web marketplace accounts they'd set up themselves."

"Are you certain of your facts?"

"Absolutely certain. Chan has been ranting about it to anyone who'd listen. He's been apoplectic since he found out. Sometimes I think he's gone quite mad. Yesterday afternoon Tao came to Dance Square and there was an awful scene. Chan started shouting: "My brother's a thief! That's not news, you've heard it before but he's been robbing me again. And he'll keep on robbing me until he's buried in his grave. If he's found dead after being flayed alive you'll know who did it, Lik.' And then he went on and on about how his Triad friends were mad as hell because they'd lost everything they'd made from their dark web trading ventures."

Lik paused to wipe his brow with a white handkerchief, then went on: "Last night a man came to see Chan. He wouldn't give his name, and when I told him Chan wasn't in, he said he'd call again. He came again about eleven. Chan hadn't returned so he gave me a letter. It was the witching hour when Chan came in. I gave him the missive and as soon as he looked at it he started acting like a nutjob. 'My brother,' he screamed, 'is a slithering piece of shit. I'm gonna cut him to pieces and make a cannibal feast of his flesh when I get hold of him.' Then Chan tore out of his Dance Square ghost home and headed south towards Clarendon Court. This morning when there was still no sign of him, I came around here to see if Tao knew where he was. That's when I learned Chan's brother had been murdered."

I paced up and down, pondering the tale as Lik told it. I saw how from his point-of-view it looked like Chan must be the murderer. I remained convinced Woo was the killer and ultimately she would butcher me too in an erotic rite of eldritch significance. Still there was something in the whole business that was currently beyond my comprehension, which would show that the deductions Lik drew were erroneous. And while I knew it was Woo who'd killed Tao, Chan's mad as hell triad associates could just as easily be put in the frame.

"Lik," I thundered "you had no right to tell me what you did. Fortunately I will not make any use of it. Take my advice don't breathe a word of this to anyone. Go home and keep your own counsel. If the cops get wind of this they'll make Chan their chief suspect."

"But where is Chan?"

"It doesn't matter. He's your boss and he can do what he likes. Go home and keep mum."

In the end the only way I could get Lik to leave was by stepping out into Golden Lane with him.

I walked all the way from Clarendon Court to Dance Square with Cheung Lik. Once he'd disappeared into the latter development I hailed a cab. Not long after I passed through the portal of Flash Photography in the Dalston district of Hackney. An assistant greeted me.

"I want you to identify the sitter in one of your portraits."

"We don't give out names here. Our discretion is never knowingly undersold."

"It's the exception that proves the rule."

When I handed over the photograph I'd found in Tao's flat, a fistful of what locals quaintly call "Bobby Moores" went with it. As soon as the assistant saw the twenty-pound notes he smiled and there was a twinkle in his eye.

"As you say, the exception proves the rule. This lady is rather famous, or at least notorious, it's Woo Gam."

"Woo who?"

"Woo Gam. She's a pornographic actress whose biggest hit on the dark web is *Chinese Communism Is A Load Of Pork Balls*. It's quite a movie because it features Woo giving blow jobs to a number of high-ranking Chinese Communist Party officials, all of whom were caught on camera without their knowledge. What's more she gets them all excited and then refuses to bring them to orgasm unless they repeat various ultra-leftist critiques of the Chinese state she mouths first. Some people believe Woo is a communist sex witch using high magick to overthrow Maoist state capitalism. She's rumoured to belong to a secret society called the International Communist Coven or ICC. Of course there are those who insist Woo is really working for Chinese intelligence, that the officials she targets are either corrupt or the victims of party feuds and these sex and heresy tapes are just a convenient device to throw people out of office and into jail!"

Either my expression or something else about me afforded the assistant considerable amusement.

"In that case why didn't my online attempts to search for Woo throw up any results?"

"Those who are notorious in the shadows of the dark web generally remain unknown in the light of Google or Yahoo results."

"What is Woo Gam's address?" I asked.

"It's info@communistsexmutant.com."

"I require her private address."

"That, I'm afraid, I don't have."

I pulled out another fistful of Bobby Moores and was furnished with the information I required.

"Woo Gam lives with another porn star called Mary Millington at 666 Royal College Street in Camden."

As I sped towards Camden in a cab, I tried to assimilate the information I'd gleaned. I could hardly believe my luck, my avenging angel was a blue movie sex siren!

Royal College Street proved to be a nice old-fashioned sort of place, and 666 a small block of flats. It was not plush but the impression its exterior made upon me was a pleasant one.

I tried various bells and eventually got hold of Mary Millington. "Can I come up? I have news of Woo Gam."

I was buzzed in and on the second floor I was greeted by a tiny blonde sex bomb. Mary was dressed in studs and leather. She used a judo throw to get me into her flat, where I landed flat on my back.

"Take your clothes off and don't look at me." Mary instructed. "Once you're naked I want you to take all the high-denomination notes out of your wallet and hold them in your mouth. Then you're to crawl on all fours across the room and give the money to me."

I did as I was told. Afterwards Mary made me lie with my chest and stomach on a bolster. She made me stretch my arms out in front of me and shackled my wrists together. My legs were bent at the knees and my backside was resting on my ankles, and Mary also chained my feet together. She put a blindfold over my eyes, put a gag in my mouth and took a switch to my backside. She beat my bottom hard with dozens of strokes. What happened next was even more peculiar.

"You need to relax." Mary told me. "You have a very tight arsehole and you need to stop contracting the muscles if I'm to get even a small buttplug up it. You need some serious anal training."

When Mary had inserted the buttplug she told me she was going out for a few hours and that her anal stimulator had better still be in place when she came back or I'd be in real trouble. Then she put on a looped recording and jacked up the volume before she left. There was a mixture of white noise and rock and roll, and repeated through all this was a woman reading aloud from *The SCUM Manifesto* by Valerie Solanas:

> The male is completely egocentric, trapped inside himself, incapable of empathising or identifying with others, or love, friendship, affection of tenderness. He is a completely isolated unit, incapable of rapport with anyone. His

responses are entirely visceral, not cerebral; his intelligence is a mere tool in the services of his drives and needs; he is incapable of mental passion, mental interaction; he can't relate to anything other than his own physical sensations. He is a half-dead, unresponsive lump, incapable of giving or receiving pleasure or happiness; consequently, he is at best an utter bore, an inoffensive blob, since only those capable of absorption in others can be charming. He is trapped in a twilight zone halfway between humans and apes, and is far worse off than the apes because, unlike the apes, he is capable of a large array of negative feelings—hate, jealousy, contempt, disgust, guilt, shame, doubt—and moreover, he is aware of what he is and what he isn't. [etc. etc.]

While this soundtrack was blasted into my ears, I could feel the buttplug shifting around between my arse cheeks. I struggled to keep it in for a long time, but it eventually fell out with a soft plop. When Mary eventually came back, I don't know how many hours later, this was the first thing she noticed.

"Oh you naughty boy, you're let your buttplug fall out. Now I'm going to flog you and peg you as punishment." she screamed.

The porn star lifted my blindfold briefly and showed me an enormous strap-on that she said would make me bleed when she screwed me with it. I found out later that she substituted it for a smaller one once my blindfold was secure again, since I was an anal virgin and not ready for the "big boy". After I was flogged and banged, Mary put a dog collar around my neck and after untying me led me by a lead into her bathroom. She threw my clothes in with me and told me to clean myself up.

Once I'd showered and was back in my clothes, I found Millington sitting in the living room and acting as if nothing had happened between us.

"So what's up with Woo?" Mary asked.

"It's complicated..." I replied.

"Where is my flatmate?" Millington demanded after a long silence. Given what had happened between us I'd found myself tongue-tied and unable to speak. Eventually I managed to say: "She's at Clarendon Court, a luxury apartment block just over the border from Islington in The City of London."

"What's she doing there?"

"Woo is not herself. She's suffering from memory loss. She entered my bedroom from the balcony early this morning in a curious condition."

"That's a new kink to me. How much did she charge for that?"

"A man was murdered in Clarendon Court around the time she appeared in my bedroom. His apartment is above mine. You can climb down from his balcony to the one outside my window. That's how Woo got into my flat."

"Sounds like a dangerous stunt, she could have slipped. I hope you paid her a lot to do it."

"I didn't pay her anything."

"You're kidding me! She'd want at least two grand I'm sure!"

"When she entered my bedroom her clothes and hands were covered in blood."

"I didn't know she did assassinations. I bet that pays more than sexual services!"

"The horror of what took place in the apartment above mine has temporarily unhinged Woo's brain."

"She's gone off her rocker?"

"No but she's completely lost her memory. She can't even remember her own name."

"Who got knocked off?"

"Chiang Tao."

"Never heard of him. He wasn't one of her johns, I know them all. She's high class like me and doesn't have many."

"She said nothing about having an appointment with Tao last night? Or with anyone else?"

"She said she had an appointment. I assumed it was with a john, but I didn't ask who because she was in a foul mood."

"Mary, you must come to Clarendon Court with me. Your presence may help restore Woo's memory. But regardless you should bring her home. Familiar surroundings would be good for her and I can't have her asleep all day in my apartment. Every time I look at her I want to wake her up and shag her."

"Your views are naïve, money...." But before Millington could finish the sentence her bell rang and she answered it. I couldn't hear the caller's words.

"She's not here," Mary replied.

"Who was that?" I asked.

"Hwang Jang Lee wanting to see Woo."

I rushed down the stairs and into the street. Millington's mention of the caller's name brought to mind the peculiar letter I'd found in the pocket of Woo's cloak addressed to Hwang Jang Lee.

A young man was heading down the street. I ran after him shouting: "Stop! Hwang Jang Lee."

The man turned around and stared at me before swinging on his heels and tearing off. I went after him. Fortunately, I can run fast when I need to. I soon had Hwang by the collar. He was panting like a rabbit. I frogmarched him back to Millington's pad. He didn't try to resist. She was waiting for us at the street door.

"This is Hwang Jang Lee. I bet he can tell us a few things we need to know."

Once we were in Mary's flat, I handed Hwang the missive I'd taken from Woo's pocket. "I believe, Mr. Lee, that this letter is for you."

He eyed it doubtfully, saw his name on it, observed that the envelope had been opened. He turned on me with a snarl. "Who are you? How dare you open a letter that's addressed to me!"

"Read the letter, Mr. Lee. Talk to me afterwards."

He scanned the brief epistle, then snapped at me: "You must have stolen it!"

"Is the person alluded to as 'that recuperator' Mr. Chiang Tao of Clarendon Court?"

"Why do you want to know?"

"Because Chiang Tao is dead."

"Dead?"

"Yes dead, murdered and somebody is responsible!"

"You sound like you're straight out of a b-movie, in fact as if you're playing the detective who discovers Inspector Clay's body in *Plan 9 From Outer Space*. And why is your female friend stripping?"

"Mary is a famous porn star and I assume she's doing a webcam session for a private client."

Lee staggered back against a chair. "A real live cybersex session! And I'm in the room with the camera! Do I get to screw this gorgeous blonde while somebody pays top dollar to watch it?"

"Ask Mary."

Millington agreed Hwang could have sex with her if he'd tell me whatever it was I wanted to know afterwards. So while they went at it I checked emails on my smartphone. Voyeurism has never really interested me and frankly I view the amount of money some people spend on webcam sex services as utterly ridiculous. After what seemed like hours the sex session stopped and Lee began to tell his side of the story.

"I told Woo if she meddled in my affairs she'd make a hash of things. She wouldn't know what she was doing and it would be dangerous because she'd be messing with triads. She's as obstinate as a mule and never takes anyone's advice!"

"You can say that again!" Mary chipped in.

"She's an obstinate as a mule and never takes anyone's advice!"

"Strange sense of déjà vu!" Mary observed.

"Toot toot!" I added. "Mr. Lee, what's your connection to Woo Gam?"

"She's my sister."

"If you're Gam's brother then you're John Woo, her vaga-bond sibling who's robbed her of a fortune. Your face is like a bad copy of Woo's, with half the beauty taken out."

"I'm John Woo no longer, I didn't care for my father or my mother, so I changed my name by deed-poll. I'm Hwang Jang Lee now!"

"Lee, why did your sister go to Clarendon Court last night?"

"It was to do with blockchain."

"Did you do coding for Tao?"

"I just set up some fake drug selling accounts on the dark web and broke into a computer."

"I see. And the laptop you broke into belonged to Tao's brother Chan Wai-Man?"

"Who told you? How do you know?"

"Never mind who told me. Tell me more!"

"Tao's stupid! You don't fuck with the triads even if you're part of the family. They don't mess about. They'd rather kill you than talk about you making it up to them. If it hadn't been for Tao I'd have never half-inched his brother's cryp-tocurrency. I owed Tao a few quid, quite a few quid, and he said if I could rip-off some Fiatcoin from his brother, he'd write off the debt."

"And so you agreed to reassign the currency between you."

"No. It was never his plan to rip everything off. But I fig-ured in for a penny, in for a pound. So I punted the amount he wanted to him and stole the rest for myself. I didn't know at that point it was triad loot. Since I'd taken everything, Chan and his triad friends noticed immediately. Tao realised what had happened and he came to me and said he was gonna tell his brother I was the culprit. And he assured me Chan and his triad gang would kill me very slowly, perhaps adminis-tering opium to ensure I remained conscious for days as they gradually cut me to pieces."

"Did you beg your sister to save you?"

"I mentioned it to her and she was very angry. She told me a lot of things I didn't know about Tao and Chan and the many investors who have bought ghost homes in Clarendon Court and elsewhere in EC1. Woo said she was using sex magick to bring about the downfall of Chinese state capitalism, and that eventually there would be a world-wide proletarian revolution in which money was abolished. Woo said the process of disalienation that would lead to real communism would make everyone cosmic. Nothing made her angrier than the capitalists of Chinese state pretending to be communists. She said it was the lies of the so-called Communist Party of China that had impelled her to join the International Communist Coven and work for the return at a higher level of not just of the modes of social organisation found in primitive communist societies, but also the shamanic magical consciousness that characterised them."

"Wow!" Mary observed. "That's a super-phat and groovy anti-political programme! But then I ought to know, I had a hand in designing it! Communism is cosmic!"

Millington decided that the best thing to do with Hwang was to leave him naked and hog-tied in her flat while we went to Clarendon Court. Mary made sure Lee was secure with a blindfold over his eyes and a gag in his mouth before she wilted his erection by casually saying: "I don't know how long I'll be but when I come back I'll have your sister Woo with me."

We called a cab and once inside the car I asked Mary about communist witchcraft.

"The first shamans, or healer priests, in nature societies were women." Millington explained. "The first male shamans imitated women by taking on their roles and wearing female clothing. Wherever patriarchy has overthrown matriarchy, even in nature societies, the previous religious power of women is feared as something diabolical; and it was only ever overthrown through the cross-dressing of those who pretended they were man enough to be a woman but weren't! Once these new emperors were sufficiently emboldened to throw away their lipstick and skirts, the priestess was transformed into the figure of the witch. There is, of course, a link between the original she-male cross-dressing shamans and homosexuality. The gay male shaman and chicks with dicks who didn't want to get down with male power were turned into heretics."

"So are you saying I have to gear up in stockings and suspenders to be a communist?" I asked.

"Of course not, stupid! Witchcraft is best done in the buff, what is known in the technical vocabulary of our Wiccan revolution skyclad." Mary replied. "Many cave paintings show pictures of nude men with erections dancing together in groups without women, while sisters were doing it among and for themselves too. Among nature people a man's cum and a woman's menstrual blood is often thought to embody ancestral religious power. Animals, especially horned ones, play a large part in stone-age art, and human figures appear wearing animal skins. These figures are probably shamans, since nature societies often identify themselves collectively with the animals they eat and imitate their behaviour — including their sex life — in religious rites. And since homosexuality is rife in the animal kingdom, ancient wo/man realised it was an utter groove too!"

"What's the communist position on blow jobs?"

"We're totally in favour of them! But we don't want all that spunk wasted. You should get your partner to come in your mouth and swallow down all that protein and goodness in his white stuff. It's quite a hit, a good spurt of semen is better than a glass of champagne!"

"But I like girls!" I protested.

"That's just your social conditioning, once you're in a coven we'll soon help you get over it!"

"But I wanna die in a sex-love-murder ritual!"

"Who said you couldn't?"

"Well it wouldn't turn me on if it was a guy doing it?"

"You can only find out by trying it!"

"But once I'm dead I won't have the option of trying it again with someone who's a different gender!"

"Of course you will but you'll have to wait until you reincarnate again!"

"But that might take forever!"

"Learn patience."

"How do I learn that?"

"Patience comes to those who wait!"

It took us 30 minutes to reach Golden Lane. As we approached my apartment we clocked Woo disappearing down the corridor.

"Where is she going?" Millington asked.

"She's going to Tao's room." I explained.

We hurried in pursuit but hadn't caught up with Woo when Crippen grabbed my arm.

"Feng!" he cried. "Miss Millington! What is Woo Gam doing here?"

"Do you know Mary and Woo?" I asked in disbelief.

"I have the pleasure of knowing her Biblically,' he sneered. "But a court of law might not see it that way because our sado-masochistic sessions have never involved penetrative sex."

"How often has she slapped you around and how much did you pay?" The green monster of jealousy was welling up in my head.

"None of your business. I spoke to my mistress but she passed without a sign of recognition. What's the matter with her? She looks ill. Where's she going?"

"She's going to Tao's apartment."

"Feng, why is she going there?"

"I was following her so that I could ask her that question."

I broke from him. Crippen's intervention meant my avenging angel was now well ahead of me. Woo Gam had arrived at Tao's pad as I reached the third floor. A cop stood outside the dead man's front door.

"Is this the flat in which Chiang Tao was murdered in a sex magick ritual?

"Yes. But you can't go in. My orders are to admit no one except the forensic team."

Putting out her arm, touching the cop on the chest, she pushed him aside with a light touch. I saw instantly Woo was a mistress of the vibrating palm and other secret and deadly dim mak techniques. Moments later she was through the door. I reached the rozzer as Woo disappeared from my sight.

"Why did you let her go in?" I asked the cop for want of anything better to say.

The man seemed bewildered and was labouring to breathe. "Let her? She's half killed me. I've a burning pain in my chest and a humdinger of a throbbing erection!"

He saw I intended to follow her and was in no condition to stop me. I grabbed him by the shoulders and sent him spinning down the passage until the wall brought him to a standstill.

"You can't trust a London copper," I shouted at the stricken man as I simultaneously shook my fist. "I bet bribing you would have cost next to nothing, but we're not bothering with that when you're so easily beaten up!"

Then I went after Woo Gam. Mary Millington and Crippen were hard upon my heels. If I'd been wearing a long skirt I suspect those behind me would have trodden on it and caused me to trip over, since the distance between them and me had been reduced to a few millimetres.

I lingered for a moment behind the curtains which veiled the entrance into Tao's living room. Glancing between the voluminous folds, I saw Woo standing in the centre of the room. Something in her expression caused me to hesitate. I checked the advance of Millington and Crippen, who pressed on me behind.

"Wait!" I whispered. "I want to see what she is going to do."

Woo looked around as if the room struck a chord in her memory. She was glancing about her with bewildered eyes, seeking for some familiar object that would serve as a clue towards the solution of the puzzle. At last something arrested her attention. It was the tell-tale stain upon the carpet. She was standing close to the spot on which I had discovered Tao's corpse. His body was gone, but his blood remained behind, a lurid disfigurement on the expensive fabric. She started at it and then got down on her knees and began licking at the blood.

Woo moved from one place to another, as if endeavouring to recall a scene in which she had taken part. It seemed to come back to her in fragments. And she was speaking to herself.

"I failed to complete the ritual to make all the criminal dead of Cripplegate come back from the next dimension and possess the ghost home investors who visited Clarendon Court. I had eaten a little of Tao's flesh and had collected enough of his body to make the special Wiccan cannibal stew when Zhong Kui appeared.

"Who is Zhong Kui?" Crippen and Millington demanded to know.

"He's The King of the Ghosts." I explained. "Now shut up."

"So Zhong Kui said to me: 'Your communist sex magick is pretty good but it can't beat my high Taoist occultism!' Then we battled, trading spells and energy currents. Zhong won because as if from a deep sleep I woke in purgatory. The King of the Underworld, his queens and various flunkies were all around the coffin I woke in, speculating about whether I'd be as much of a sex kitten now I was dead as when I'd been alive."

"She must be on drugs." Crippen whispered.

"Shut up!" Millington and I said that in unison.

"The King demonstrated to me how he could create earthquakes in The Underworld by shaking a pillar. I then headed off to the Cool Inn to eat. There I had a confrontation with Zatoichi, The Blind Swordsman. I got the better of that Japanese fighter, so he left and returned with James Bond, Clint Eastwood and some of Dracula's zombie skeletons. I was surprised to find myself disorientated and defeated by my foes. I was nursed back to health by Wa To and his grand-daughter. They restored my powers so that I could fight successfully in the underworld."

"She's gone absolutely gaga." Crippen muttered under his breath.

"Wa To warned me: 'Young lady I think you've been over-doing it. I cannot say I blame you. But you should just look at yourself. You're wasting away from too much sex.' His granddaughter interjected: 'Grandpa, don't be so unfair. When a girl is a communist sex witch she's got to have her fun!' Then I went gambling but I decided to close down the casino because it was patronised by those who lost all their money in games of chance on earth and then committed suicide. I shared all the money I'd won with everyone present except the one-armed swordsman, I gave cash to his sister instead because he'd lost the money he'd borrowed from her at the casino and couldn't be trusted to repay it."

"This isn't a description of the underworld, it's the symptoms of a mental breakdown." Crippen interjected.

"I set up a gym to teach my new friends who included Popeye and Kwai Chang Caine dim mak, the kung fu death touch. I figured it was safe to teach anyone this deadly martial art in the underworld because they'd only be using it against those who were already dead. I wanted my friends to be able to defend themselves against the gang run by The Godfather and his enforcers including Clint Eastwood, James Bond, Emmanuelle, Dracula with his army of zombies. Later I discovered The Exorcist, who was in charge of The King's bodyguard, was secretly a member of the gang."

"Madness!" Crippen sighed.

"Before long I was battling the blind swordsman again. I proved that dim mak is superior to the blade, so the defeated Zatoichi became an exile and had to leave for elsewhere. James Bond thought he could seduce me and then shag me to death. Just as he was about to go down on me, I spotted The Godfather, Clint Eastwood and James Bond, watching so I pushed my grinding partner aside and got up. The God-father then made me an offer only a communist sex witch could refuse, joining his gang.

My dim mak gym was smashed up by The Godfather's gang, so I went to the quarry where I'd previously fought the blind swordsman to take on Dracula and his army of zombies. Not only did I beat the living dead, I recovered a secret document and interrupted Emmanuelle attempting to bonk The King of the Underworld to death. I explained to The King with regard to Emmanuelle: 'Her pussy's in on this plot too. She was using it to murder you!' The King dismissed the Exorcist as the captain of his bodyguard and replaced him with me."

"Insanity!" Crippen clearly suffered from a compulsion to speak.

"I beat up James Bond after I discovered him with a suit-case full of stolen money. Then Clint Eastwood decided to challenge me, so it was back to the stone quarry for the show-down. I dodged the bullets from Clint's pistol and killed him. The ordinary residents of the underworld started celebrating the fact I'd killed The Godfather's three main enforcers. While everyone was distracted, The Exorcist and The God-father set out to kill The King. The King's only means of defence was to shake his column and cause an earthquake. The monarch saved his own skin but killed many of his subjects. So it was back to the quarry where I took out The Exorcist and The Godfather.

"You couldn't make it up unless you were Woo Gam!" Crippen exclaimed.

"Zhong Kui who'd been brought in as a mercenary by The King could see the heavies of the underworld wouldn't contain me, so he called up some demons and told them to kick my arse. I thought I was going to lose but then Popeye, Kwai Chang Caine and the one-armed swordsman appeared to back me up. I was free to deal with Zhong and having learned his tricks from our previous encounter, this time I beat him. The King of the Underworld had no choice but to agree to my demands. These were for me to be sent back to earth and for The King to abdicate and let the dead run the underworld with a representational system based on workers' councils and instantly revocable delegates. Before he sent me back to earth, The King of the Underworld warned me that the strange vortex of forces involved would put a strain on my lungs. Kwai Chang Caine stuck a baby pacifier in my mouth telling me it would help if I sucked on it during my journey back to the world of the living, and with that I was on my way."

"Stop her! Don't let her go on!" Crippen shouted.

"I shan't stop her. I shall let her say all that she has to say." I replied.

"When I died I was on Tao's balcony but when I was sent back to earth and came alive again I was on Feng's. That accounts for my sense of confusion and loss of memory. Now my acts of communist witchcraft must be completed, so that the ghosts of Cripplegate's dead possess the bodies of Clarendon Court's ghost home investors, and this cursed building and it occupants are finally destroyed!"

Millington moved forward. "Woo!" she cried.

"Mary!" Woo exclaimed.

Gam's sense of herself as a communist sex witch engaged in community activism against the blight of ghost homes in central London had returned. Now I wouldn't have to wait long before she killed me in an act of highly erotic love murder!

"Mistress I love you!" Crippen cried as he threw himself at Woo's feet.

She dealt him a series of blows and the doctor whimpered in ecstasy.

"I want you to strip!" Woo barked at Crippen. "And then masturbate here on the floor. Make yourself come."

The doctor did as he was told. Gam made strange incantations and gestures with her hands as he did this. The tempo of Crippen's hand strokes increased and his body levitated up towards the ceiling. As the doctor reached orgasm his skull smashed against the roof and his neck broke as he crashed back down to the ground.

"No that's what I call communist sexual witchcraft!" Woo cackled.

"What about the cop?" I asked.

"Oh don't worry about him!" Gam assured me. "I gave him the twenty paces touch of death. He couldn't even walk out of this building without killing himself."

"There's one question I want to ask you. Besides you and Tao was there anyone else in the room last night when you engaged in ritual murder?"

"Yes, you were there."

"Moi?"

"Don't you remember coming into the room?"

"No, I seem to suffer from the malady you've just overcome."

"So you don't remember the other man?"

"Chan, Tao's half-brother?"

"You do remember!"

"I don't! I'm guessing!"

"Mary and I have communist witchcraft to perform, so we're going to take you to your apartment and tie you up there. We're gonna leave you for hours, maybe for days."

I was blindfolded and bound on my bed. I was drifting in and out of consciousness when Crippen's ghost appeared to me. My bedroom door was open and his spectral form stood on the threshold, looking in.

"What are you doing here? You're supposed to be dead!" I screamed.

"I came here to tell you that Woo Gam is the only woman I ever loved. And I want you to know that dying for her at the moment of orgasm is an ecstasy you can only dream of, whereas I've experienced it!"

"But she came through my window last night. I will surely die for her too, and the last shall be first!"

"You're only half in love with easeful death, whereas I've passed on. You don't know what you're talking about!"

My conversation with Crippen's ghost rambled on in this way for quite some time. Until my shoulders were shaken.

"Rise from the dead ye little head!" I couldn't see her because I was blindfolded but it was Woo's voice. My avenging angel had come back for me!

"Kill me, I'm rotten." I said

"Here's some news," Woo replied ignoring my request, "Tao's brother Chan turned up at Clarendon Court shortly before I arrived. The concierge offered him condolences over his brother's death and Chan beat him black and blue. I called an ambulance and the management of the block are sending someone to take his place."

"They had some differences over blockchain."

"I didn't come here to chat about cryptocurrencies. I'm going to give you some food and drink, then I'll tie you up again.

That's what happened and after I'd been blindfolded I began to hallucinate. I was in the City Road with a lady when we saw Chan. My companion spotted him first. I glanced in the direction she was pointing. His outline was a little obscured by the mist but I could still recognise him. I quickened my steps and shouted after the man. His back was turned to me but he seemed to have seen us. He darted into the road and sprang into a passing cab. To pursue and leave the lady was out of the question. I was puzzled not only by Chan's flight but by the rapidity with which it had been performed. I saw that my companion had suddenly grown white. The hand she placed on my arm was trembling. Through the fog on the City Road there came the sound of a woman's laughter. It was the same curious laughter I had heard in Chiang Tao's Clarendon Court apartment — soft, low, musical, yet within it a quality that was pregnant with horrible suggestion. At the sound my heart stood still.

In my visions boys were shouting out the biggest news story of the day. The news was flashed across digital display screens. *Clarendon Court Murder. Incredible Claims of Communist Witchcraft and Cannibalism.* This was lucid dreaming and

I could see that Tao had come back from the gates of hell. He was naked when I confronted him and had demons emerging from his mouth and anus. He told me that Woo had taken possession of his soul before killing his brother. She'd dressed Chan's corpse in Tao's clothes and given the mutilated state of the body no one could tell the difference between them. Tao's role was to play his half-brother. He was to infect Dance Square with the demonic curse that was playing out at Clarendon Court. The blight of ghost flats bought by investors in the City fringe was to be cured one development at a time by selected members of the damned being moved through them. Before long every rich scumbag who'd bought into these schemes would be burning in hell for their sins.

I was in the service of more than one lady. I was bound to them and bound hand and foot. Woo was standing before me in a passage but at the end of it behind a door was a greater power, the force she served. A Druid idol that had been buried thousands of years ago at the site of a rotted woodhenge. Everyone knew the ancient Britons constructed stone circles and that the most famous of these was Stonehenge. But equally important were the woodhenges and at all such sites rituals were conducted to ensure that esoteric primitive communism would return with a vengeance when class societies became utterly decadent. A workman from Hounslow had uncovered the idol that lay beyond the door while working on the construction of Heathrow Airport. Coming as he did on his maternal side from a long line of cunning women and witches, Bill Mason, recognised the significance of the fetish as soon as he found it in 1945. He kept it for himself and before long the International Communist coven coalesced around this ancient artefact.

Eventually I found myself in a large barn-like room, the walls an uncertain shade of grey. The floor was bare. At one end was a wooden dais. This and a large skylight overhead suggested the space had once been an artist's studio. A tall screen covered with crimson silk stood upon the dais. This screen was the first object that caught my eye. I wondered if an artist's model were concealed behind it. There were two small tables, one at the side against the wall, the other in the centre of the room.

I did not know what to expect. I had a vague anticipation of incredible horrors. What I saw caused a shock of surprise. The removal of the screen revealed an idol, an ancient British goddess. It was mounted on what looked like a bronze pedestal, a metre and a half from the floor. The figure was more than four metres high. It showed a woman squatting on her haunches. Her arms were crossed upon her breast, her fingers interlaced. It was a brilliant scarlet and its maker had managed to impart to it a curious suggestion of life. But the mystery of the murders was to be found beneath the Goddess, she only inspired them. Various power tools sat beside her. They had been adapted with blades added so that they were perfect weapons for killing ghost home owners.

"I am so glad that the drugs I gave you," Woo said as she removed my blindfold, "combined with the recordings you've been hearing have begun to open up your mind. Do you now understand why the highest forms of proletarian magic entail eating the rich? To fully liberate your brain I must perform a trepanation. A small hole will be drilled into your forehead to open the third eye and enhance your powers of clairvoyance."

Woo was wielding a battery-operated power drill. The instrument penetrated the bone at the top of my forehead. Once the hole was made a very hard, clean sliver of wood that had been treated by fire and herbs was slid down so that it just entered the cavity. I felt a stinging, tickling sensation in the bridge of my nose. It subsided and I became aware of subtle scents that I couldn't identify. Suddenly there was a blinding flash. For a moment the pain was intense. It diminished, died and was replaced by spirals of colour. The projecting splinter was being bound into place so that it could not move.

"You are now one of us, Feng. Or at least part of the Men's Auxiliary, since until you are man enough to become a woman you cannot serve the Goddess as a full member of the International Communist Coven. I must test you to determine whether you now see capitalist social relations as they really are! I want you to say out loud the first words that come into your head."

"The whole discussion now underway on revolutionary forms in China boils down to the judgement to be made of the historical phenomenon of the 'appearance' of industrialism and mechanisation in huge areas of the world previously dominated by landed and pre-capitalist forms of production. Constructing industrialism and mechanising things is supposedly the same as building socialism whenever central and 'national' plans are made. This is a mistaken thesis."

"Having finally understood the capitalist world and how class society functions, it's time to get your groove on." Woo informed me.

I knew now that my fate was the same as Chan's or Tao's. Whichever of the brothers had actually survived would be left to watch the death of Dance Square, just as I would see out the demise of Clarendon Court. The zombified and decaying proletarian bodies of all the prostitutes and criminals of Jacobean Cripplegate were already shuffling through my building. When property investors visited their residential assets they'd be attacked and have their brains sucked out through their arseholes. As the building emptied and fell into disrepair, Hwang Jang Lee organised the Occupy Central Street movement. The slogan "Hong Kong & City of London, one struggle for democracy" proliferated as graffiti on walls throughout the area.

PERMUTATION FOR TAYLOR WIMPEY & THEIR CLARENDON COURT PROPERTY DEVELOPMENT

KATRINA PALMER

Land Grabbing Sucking Shunts. Land Grabbing Shunts Sucking. Land Sucking Grabbing Shunts. Land Sucking Shunts Grabbing. Land Shunts Grabbing Sucking. Land Shunts Sucking Grabbing. Grabbing Land Sucking Shunts. Grabbing Land Shunts Sucking. Grabbing Sucking Land Shunts. Grabbing Sucking Shunts Land. Grabbing Shunts Land Sucking. Grabbing Shunts Sucking Land. Sucking Land Grabbing Shunts. Sucking Land Shunts Grabbing. Sucking Grabbing Land Shunts. Sucking Grabbing Shunts Land. Sucking Shunts Land Grabbing. Sucking Shunts Grabbing Land. Shunts Land Grabbing Sucking. Shunts Land Sucking Grabbing. Shunts Grabbing Land Sucking. Shunts Grabbing Sucking Land. Shunts Sucking Land Grabbing. Shunts Sucking Grabbing Land.

A CURSE UPON ALL THOSE WHO BUY AN APARTMENT IN CLARENDON COURT

THE CRIPPLEGATE COVEN

May all your investments fail!

May whispering sounds keep you from sleep!

May unease dog your every step!

May ominous darkness envelope you!

May ghastly shadows menace you!

May dreadful loneliness befall you!

May spine-tingling shrieks terrify you!

May the living dead pursue you!

May your skin crawl for no reason at all!

May eerie silences unnerve you!

Cower in fear, speculator, as the curses
of the Cripplegate Coven come true!

"DISCOVER THE LIFE WITHIN"

MICHAEL HAMPTON

New building will be as high as the school opposite and use pretty much entire site. Old building was much smaller and left more green space... Although old had 110 social housing units and new will only have 99 ghost home apartments with no one living in them...

Stewart Home, email 23 July 2018

I was on a scouting mission in the Barbican, to get a look-see at the site of the building project quaintly known in corporate-speak as Clarendon Court, and more graphically The Turd. Even as I exited from Bunhill Fields burial ground and spotted the outline of a crane away to the west, it seemed like a good bet that this would be the building site. Cutting though Dufferin Street with the heavy asylum architecture of Peabody Trust Flats on one side, and bisecting the former redlight district of Whitecross Street, then along Fortune Street with its pocket park, I soon reached the gaping corner void where Bernard Morgan House once sat, and The Denizen AKA Clarendon Court will soon come into being. Sandwiched between what was once Cripplegate Free Library (a Grade II listed, red brick Victorian building — which now houses UBS offices — with a classical pediment depicting the figures of Science leaning on a globe as Art looks over her shoulder holding a palette, as Education gazes off into space) and a Welsh Presbyterian Church, this is without doubt a plum location at 43 Golden Lane EC1 by the very back door of the Barbican Centre itself.

The posh name alone is telling as it shouts out designer living space for the casual, well-heeled, uncommitted individual (i.e. the polar opposite of Citizen), someone without any civic involvement, stake in or responsibility for their immediate social environment whatsoever; cookie-cutter nowhere men and women. As it so happens Taylor Wimpey plc's marketing department have turned part-time lexicographers, providing a helpful dictionary definition for free, clearly aimed at not just the well off, but someone who enjoys the flattery which comes from a veneer of doubtful sophistication too.

Denizen (noun) A person who frequents or regularly frequents a particular place.

The notion of a frequenter evokes the kind of pop-up, drop-in and grab lifestyle so beloved of today's capitalist business machinery, sales techniques and product placement honed to seduce the retail customer. The even more desirable concept of regular frequenting also smacks of an absolute complicity, pathological smartphone addiction backed up by spending power: the money shot. Moreover the word "frequents" could be seen as suggesting a ghostly disquieting presence, someone who haunts an anonymous space, returning to it time and time again in search of, well in search of what exactly? Perhaps the lifestyle intimated by Taylor Wimpey's display boards, which carry slick computer-generated images of The Denizen's living quarters. These spotless simulations hive off the groundwork, smart wraps which entreat us pseudo-hippy style to "Discover the life within", which if the stage-dressed décor is anything to go by will be vacuous; the result of horrifying vacuity heaped upon vacuity in fact.

Strangely some of the images look as if they've been lifted straight from a lifestyle magazine, but oddly enough one that is badly out of date, almost reminiscent of the post-war American décor in Richard Hamilton's famous collage *Just what is it that makes today's homes so different, so appealing?*

used on the promotional poster for the groundbreaking Whitechapel Gallery show *This is Tomorrow,* 1956, an exhibition meant to have ushered in the age of pop art. Throughout there are hardwood floors, downlighting and a Siemens oven in bespoke kitchens. In the bedroom meanwhile the obligatory Ansell Adam's sublime landscape photograph hangs over the bed, together with a long goose necked lamp that looks vaguely Terence Conran in style. A coffee-table book about Coco Chanel has been tidied away, and there are all the choice gewgaws, exotic throws and knick-knackery no self-respecting boutique flat can afford to be without. The communal games room is a bit weird, as the concept seems middle-aged, i.e. offering chess, darts and pool which are hardly the Xbox virtual type of gaming the young favour nowadays. The ensemble looks as if it belongs in a Sapper, Dornford Yates or Dennis Wheatley novel, snobbish, dated and dull, the only thing missing a colonial tiger rug on the floor. But a games room is just another symbol of the future tenant's upmarket snooty independence, as with all that clubbish amusement to hand there will be no actual need to socialise in the local boozer. Couldn't these buffered representations of utopian living have been spiced up a bit by a props department severed silicon head with a hatchet buried in it left hanging in the shower?!

Sure enough stock estate-agent images of the block do reveal its mottled mid-brown brickwork, as if it has been deposited, lingering there not unlike those little black bags of canine poo that get left behind in the street by lazy couldn't-care-less dog owners (in my postcode some wag has printed out notices that are pinned to trees advertising Yoga Classes, and how to do the Downward Dog, ie scooping up your pooches smelly gift, the one that just keeps on giving). Lovely. The unrelenting shittiness of modern urban life becomes less obvious the smarter the postcode though, meaning The Denizen AKA Clarendon Court will not so much be a "rent slab" as poet John Betjeman used to condemn 1960s tower blocks, than a way for sundry Chinese or Middle-Eastern buy-to-let investors and shady Russian oligarchs to disguise their ill-gotten gains; so it's actually that London architectural speciality, a residential launderette, for with prices starting at £695,000 unless you have rich parents living in the shires with very deep pockets, who else can even begin to think of living there? And yet Knight Frank's webpage describes it as "an ideal base for students". Maybe they were bored and just having a laugh?*

But as is well known, you just can't polish a turd.

Michael Hampton
August 2018

---

* For a gloomy ground floor, north facing, one bed. The pitch is probably to Chinese investors who want their children to study at London universities.

CLARENDON COURT & THE CITY OF LONDON CORPORATION

PIPPA HENSLOWE

It's about time democracy based on the principle of every adult resident having an equal say in who represents them on the local council was introduced to the City of London. The undemocratic business vote system that is unique to this rotten borough must be abolished. Businesses (mostly banks and legal practices) are given votes to distribute as they chose among their employees, despite the fact this highly paid chosen few already get to vote where they live. Aside from business voters having two votes, many councillors commute into the City and often demonstrate complete contempt for residents' interests because 80% of them are elected by people who don't live locally. Had there been a democratic system of local government in the City of London it seems unlikely we'd have witnessed the council selling the 110 social housing units in Bernard Morgan House, so that Taylor Wimpey could demolish the building and replace it with 99 luxury flats.

This new luxury development is aimed at ghost home investors who will neither live in their apartments nor rent them out, but rather bet on reaping a profit from London's overheated property market. Taylor Wimpey's ghost block overshadows a park, social housing and schools, since it is much bigger than the building it is replacing. With an enormous amount of effort, community activists managed to get the national media to cover some of the more disturbing aspects of this story. For example, *The Guardian* reported on the contentious granting of planning permission for Taylor Wimpey's Clarendon Court development on the site of Bernard Morgan House:

> The story follows a by-now-familiar plot. In May 2017 planning approval was given to Taylor Wimpey, despite strong opposition from local residents and businesses. During this process it emerged that the chair of the City's planning and transportation committee, Chris Hayward, is a director of Indigo Planning, whose clients include Taylor Wimpey. Deputy chair James Thomson was formerly deputy chief financial officer and chief operations officer of Cushman and Wakefield, commercial property and real estate consultants, which marketed and sold Bernard Morgan House to Taylor Wimpey. The committee member and former lord mayor of London Sir Michael Bear was appointed chair of the planning consultancy Turley Associates — which also acts for Taylor Wimpey — a few weeks after planning approval was granted.

> *Developers are using culture as a Trojan horse in their planning battles* by Anna Minton, *The Guardian*, 10 October 2017

City of London residents have found themselves consistently stonewalled by the council when they've raised potential conflict of interest issues on a variety of subjects. In the case of planning permission being granted for Clarendon Court, the blown City of London Police budget and the fact Chris Hayward and James Thomson were on the committee overseeing this is also a potential conflict of interest issue the council has failed to address. In light of *The Guardian* story above (also run by the *Daily Mail)*, it has become apparent that even when concerns are picked up by the national press and amplified in the media, the City of London is not going to listen to its residents — let alone act on what they have to say — because isn't answerable to them. 80% of City of London councillors are elected on undemocratic business votes and this local authority clearly sees its purpose as being global lobbying on behalf of the finance industry and tax havens; it spends millions of pounds on this every year to further the interests of the super-rich and corporations. Not only is this lobbying activity detrimental to most City of London residents, it impacts negatively on billions of people around the world.

The City of London council doesn't care about its residents — and has been particularly neglectful of those who live on the two council estates (social housing projects) within its boundaries — and never will until the business vote has been abolished. Business votes don't exist in any other UK local authority area and they shouldn't in the City of London. As campaigning on local issues is largely pointless for City of London residents because the council is utterly undemocratic, it's best to shift the focus onto what's wrong with this local authority. Say: "No to business votes, yes to local democracy!" Please bring up the issue of undemocratic business votes anywhere you can and especially with your local MP.

Adapted from the About
page of the blog *Reclaim EC1*:
https://reclaimec1.wordpress.com/

THANKS

Special thanks to all the contributors to this book but especially Siu Lan Ko, Katrina Palmer and Tom McCarthy who also participated in *Spectres of Modernism* (alongside the editor). Extra special thanks to contributors Iphgenia Baal and Steve Finbow for giving me support beyond the call of duty. This book is a continuation of earlier protests against both Taylor Wimpey's Clarendon Court & other instances of overdevelopment including *Spectres of Modernism* and *Hex In The Park*. Thanks also to the artists in *Spectres of Modernism* who don't have pieces here: Mark Aerial Waller, Fiona Banner, Deborah Curtis, Adam Dant, Jeremy Deller, Arnaud Desjardin, Margarita Gluzberg, Patrick Goddard, Fraser Muggeridge, Cornelia Parker, Esther Planas, Elizabeth Price, Anjalika Sagar — The Otolith Group, Iain Sinclair, Gavin Turk & Eleanor Vonne Brown. Omnicolour played a vital role in the production of *Spectres* and Fraser Muggeridge Studio (at the time Fraser Muggeridge, Luke Hall, Jules Estèves, Rachel Treliving, Joe Nava and Elena Papassissa) in its design. While some of those who participated in *Hex In The Park* including Liz Rever have contributed to this book, I also wish to thank those who were involved in that event who aren't represented here.

I also need to give a call out to those who played a key behind-the-scenes role in organising *Spectres of Modernism* and related events including Claire Louise Staunton, Mark Lemanski, Immo Klink, Alex Sainsbury and its curator Clare Carolin. It should be stressed that *Spectres of Modernism* was a collective project and would not have been possible without the input of nearly all of those who lived in Bowater House on the Golden Lane Estate in 2017 but especially Emma Matthews and Claudia Marciante who ran the legal campaign against Clarendon Court as Save Golden Lane.

They took advice from Bill Parry Davies. Fred Rogers also played a big role in Save Golden Lane and Anna Minton was the first to get the story of the potential conflicts of interest Fred flagged up into the national press. Saskia Lewis and Mark Lewis did early research into architectural issues around Clarendon Court and the negative impact it would have on Golden Lane. Others who contributed in various ways in anti-Clarendon Court & other protests include Nina Wakeford, Lloyd Corporation, Zoe Brown, Owen Oppenheimer Bioni Samp, Maxim Gertler-Jaffe, Chloe Hur, Mai Omer Teplitzky, Anthony Auerbach, Justin Coombes, Sarah Dobai, Chris Dorley-Brown, Katherine Fawssett, Rut Blees Luxemburg, Eva Stenram & Charles Humphries. Thanks also to Sue Pearson and Graeme Harrower who took their responsibilities as councillors representing local people very seriously.

A sister campaign was run by St. Luke's Community Collective on the other side of Old Street against the redevelopment of Finsbury Leisure Centre and this was inspirational too. Simon Strong published a recent book of mine and in doing so inadvertently showed me how to get this one out. Thanks to everyone named and unnamed, they may or may not have intended to provide inspiration for what's in here, but without that inspiration this anthology of horror stories set in Taylor Wimpey's Clarendon Court wouldn't exist! Nonetheless responsibility for the final shape of this book and any faults anyone may perceive in this lies entirely with me as the editor.

Stewart Home,
London,
August 2020

ABOUT THE CONTRIBUTORS

Chloe Aridjis's fictions include *Book of Clouds*, *Asunder* and *Sea Monsters*.

Iphgenia Baal's fictions include *The Hardy Tree*, *Gentle Art* and *Merced Es Benz*.

Linda Chu is a hacktivist who only writes stories when she can't get an internet connection.

Cripplegate Coven are a group of witches who hex evil and promote love.

Paul Ewen's fictions include *London Pub Reviews*, *Francis Plug: How To Be A Public Author* and *Francis Plug: Writer in Residence*.

Steve Finbow's fictions include *Balzac of the Badlands*, *Nothing Matters* and *Down Among the Dead*.

Tariq Goddard's fictions include *Dynamo*, *The Picture of Contented New Wealth* and *Nature and Necessity*.

Michael Hampton is an art critic who writes for *Art Monthly* and many other publications.

Pippa Henslowe is an activist who runs the blog *Reclaim EC1*.

Stewart Home's fictions include *69 Things To Do With A Dead Princess*, *Blood Rites of the Bourgeoisie* and *She's My Witch*.

Edith Jones's fictions include *The Reef*, *Twilight Sleep* and *The Gods Arrive*.

John King's fictions include *The Football Factory*, *The Prison House* and *Slaughterhouse Prayer*.

Siu Lan Ko is an artist whose works often incorporate the written word.

Richard Marsh's fictions include *A Second Coming, The Goddess: A Demon* and *The Master Of Deception*.

Tom McCarthy's fictions include *Remainder, C* and *Satin Island*.

Katrina Palmer's fictions include *The Dark Object, The Fabricator's Tale* and *End Matter*.

Bridget Penney's fictions include *Honeymoon With Death, Index* and *Licorice*.

Chris Petit's fictions include *Robinson, The Psalm Killer* and *The Butchers of Berlin*.

Liz Rever is an artist who often works with sound and also writes stories.

Charlotte Riddell's fictions include *The Uninhabited House, The Haunted River* and *The Nun's Curse*.

Abraham Stoker's fictions include *The Jewel of Seven Stars, The Gates of Life* and *The Lady of the Shroud*.

Charlotte Stetson's fictions include *The Crux, Herland* and *Unpunished*.

Adeline Woolf's fictions include *Night and Day, The Waves* and *Between The Acts*.

w.o.n.d.e.r. coven are a group of witches who are very actively conjuring up a better world.